Success to the Brave

ALEXANDER KENT

Success to the Brave

G. P. PUTNAM'S SONS
NEW YORK

First American Edition 1983
Copyright © 1983 by Highseas Authors Ltd
All rights reserved. This book, or parts thereof,
must not be reproduced in any form without permission

Library of Congress Cataloging in Publication Data

Kent, Alexander.
  Success to the brave.

  1. Great Britain—History, Naval—19th century—
Fiction. I. Title.
PR6061.E63S9   1983   823'.914   83-11238
ISBN 0-399-12878-6

Printed in the United States of America

For Winifred with my love.
Until we meet again

Contents

How sleep the brave, who sink to rest,
By all their country's wishes blest!

WILLIAM COLLINS, 1746

I

Flag at the Fore

Richard Bolitho leaned his palms on the sill of an open window and stared across the courtyard to the far wall and the sea beyond.

It should have been a perfect May day, and even the squat silhouette of Pendennis Castle which guarded the Falmouth approaches and the entrance to Carrick Roads seemed less formidable. After nine years of war with France and her allies England was at peace. It was still hard to accept. When a strange sail appeared off the coast the young men of Falmouth no longer stood to arms in case it was an enemy raider, or hurried inland with less enthusiasm if the newcomer proved to be a King's ship. The latter always meant the arrival of the hated press-gangs and men snatched from their homes to serve at sea, perhaps never to return. No wonder it was hard to believe it was all over.

He watched the carriage resting in the shadows near the stables. *It was nearly time.* Soon the horses would be led out and harnessed. It was no longer next week or even tomorrow. It was now.

Bolitho turned and waited for his eyes to grow accustomed to the room after the reflected sunlight. The big grey house which had served the Bolitho family for generations was very still, as if it too was holding its breath, trying to hold back the inevitable.

It had been seven months since he had returned here after the battle which had destroyed the enemy's hopes of an invasion and had equally crippled the French bargaining power at the peace negotiations. Seven months since he had married Belinda and had known a sublime happiness which he had never expected.

He walked to the foot of the great staircase and glanced at the shadowy family portraits. They must all have stood here at such a moment, he thought. Wondering when or if they would ever see the house again. His great, great grandfather, Captain Daniel Bolitho, on the deck of his blazing ship. He had died in the War of the Protestant Alliance. The Bolitho features were very clear in the portrait. Like Bolitho's father and his brother Hugh, also dead, and all the others.

Now he was off to sea again and the past few months seemed to have gone in the turning of an hour-glass. When he had been summoned to the Admiralty in London he had not known what to expect. With the Peace of Amiens signed and apparently holding, it seemed as if all the bitterly won lessons had been thrown aside. Most of the fleet had been laid up and thousands of officers and men discharged to fend as best they could.

Posts for junior flag-officers would be few and handed out as favours by the lords of admiralty. Bolitho had been astonished when he had been told of his orders to sail with a minimum of delay for America and then the Caribbean. Not in command of another squadron, but in a small two-decker with a mere frigate for communications and general escort.

He had been courteously if formally received by Admiral Sir Hayward Sheaffe who had succeeded old Admiral Beauchamp. He had seemed to stamp the difference between war and peace, Bolitho thought. Beauchamp, worn out by illness, had died in harness without knowing his last strategy had succeeded with the French invasion fleet's destruction. Sheaffe was cool, practical, the perfect administrator. It had been hard to imagine his ever being through the mill from midshipman to his present lofty appointment.

In this quiet room Bolitho could recall Sheaffe's words as if they had just been uttered.

'I know this must seem a hard decision, Bolitho. After

your escape from an enemy prison and your subsequent victory over the French admiral, Remond, you will have been expecting, and many would say rightly so, a more stable appointment. However . . . ' His voice had lingered on the word. 'War does not end with the last ball fired. Their lordships require a man of tact as well as action for this task. It is not without reward, I think. You are to be promoted to Vice-Admiral of the Red.' His eyes had studied Bolitho's features to seek his reaction. 'The youngest and most junior on the Navy List.' He had added dryly, 'Apart from Nelson, that is, the nation's darling.'

So that was it. Sheaffe was jealous of those who had become known and admired by friend and enemy alike. In spite of his status and power, Sheaffe still envied them.

Perhaps that was why he had failed to mention that the real reason for Bolitho's concern was that Belinda would be having their first child in just a matter of weeks. Sheaffe knew about it, it had even reached the London newspapers that the church here in Falmouth had been packed to the doors with officers and men of Bolitho's squadron on that special October day in 1801, last year. Perhaps he was jealous of that fact also?

Bolitho had said nothing. If Sheaffe wanted him to explain, to plead for a delay in the sailing date, he had not understood him at all.

He heard her steps on the flagged floor beyond the entrance and straightened his back.

Even with the sunlight behind her, and her face part hidden in shadow, she was beautiful. He never got tired of watching her, of the longing she roused in him. The sunlight touched her chestnut-coloured hair and the soft curve of her throat.

She said, 'It's time.'

Her voice was low and level, and Bolitho knew what the effort was costing her.

As if to mock their emotions he heard the hoofs of the two horses on the cobbles, the untroubled voices of the grooms.

She moved towards him and placed her hands on his shoulders. 'I am so *proud* of you, dearest. My husband, a vice-admiral — ' Her lip quivered and a new brightness in her eyes betrayed her distress.

He held her gently, her once slender body pressing against his as if the child was already with them.

'You must take every care while I am away, Belinda.'

She leaned back in his arms and looked at him searchingly as if she needed to remember every detail.

'You are the one who must take care. You have seen to all my wants. Everyone is so kind, wanting to help, to be near, when all I need is you.' She shook her head as he made to speak. 'Don't worry, I will not break down. In spite of your leaving, I am *happy*, can you understand that? Each day in the past months has been like the first time. When you hold me it seems a new experience. When you enter me and we are one, I am filled with love for you. But I am not a fool and would never wish to stand between you and your other world. I see your eyes as you watch a ship sail into Carrick Roads, your expression when Thomas or Allday mentions some place or experience I can never share. When you return I shall be waiting, but wherever you are, we shall remain as one.'

There was a tap at the door and Allday stood watching them, his homely face grave and uncertain.

'All ready, sir.'

Allday, like an oak, who represented so much of that other world which Belinda had described. Now in his best blue coat and nankeen breeches he looked every inch a sailor, the coxswain of a vice-admiral. He had stayed at Bolitho's side since he had been a junior captain. Together they had seen fine and terrible sights, had suffered and rejoiced in equal proportions.

When he had been told of the unexpected and advanced promotion, Allday had remarked cheerfully, 'Flag at the fore at last, eh, sir? Quite right too, in my opinion. Don't know what took 'em so long.'

'Thank you.'

He saw Allday open the new coat for him to slip his arms into the sleeves. Once the impossible dream when he had paced the deck as a harassed lieutenant, or even when he had taken command of his first ship.

She was watching him, her chin raised, her fingers clasped as if to contain her thoughts and words.

'You look so handsome, Richard.'

'That 'e does, ma'am.' Allday patted the lapels into place and made certain that each bright epaulette with the twin silver stars was exactly right.

At sea it would be different, Allday thought. But here in the big house they had given him a real home. He looked away, unable to watch their faces. He was one of the family. Almost.

She said quietly, 'I could come as far as Hampshire with you.'

Bolitho held her again. 'No. The ride to the Beaulieu River would take a lot out of you. Then there is the return journey. I'd be sick with worry.'

This time she did not argue. Although neither mentioned it, each knew that a wrecked coach had once destroyed his happiness, another such accident had given both of them this new life.

Bolitho was grateful that he had to join his ship where it was too far for her to follow and risk an accident with their first child. It was bad enough to be leaving her when she most needed him, without that. Ferguson, his trusted steward, would be here in the house, and the doctor was within easy call. Bolitho's sister Nancy had been more at the house than in her own palatial residence with her husband the squire, who was known throughout the county as the King of Cornwall.

And next week Thomas Herrick's wife Dulcie would be coming all the way from Kent to keep Belinda company at the time of the birth.

Herrick, almost embarrassed by his promotion to rear-admiral, had been given command of a small squadron and had already sailed to Gibraltar for orders.

There would not be many familiar faces this time, Bolitho thought. Maybe it was just as well. No reminders. The doubts, like the successes, were best left in the past.

She said, 'Take good care of yourself, Richard. I hate your leaving, but at the same time I understand why you must go.'

Bolitho held her against him. Why were there never the right words until it was too late?

Ever since his return from the Admiralty with his secret orders she had somehow contained her disappointment, her dismay. Only once during the night had she exclaimed, 'Why you? *Must* you go?' Then, like part of a bad dream, she had lapsed into an uneasy sleep, her question still unanswered.

He heard Allday's voice beyond the door, supervising the loading of some final piece of luggage aboard the carriage. Poor Allday, he thought. Off again after all he had endured with him as a prisoner of war in France. He was always there when he was needed, the relationship stronger than ever, and when Bolitho needed someone to confide in outside of his officers and the chain of command, Allday would be ready to speak out.

Often Bolitho had felt badly about Allday's loyalty. Beyond his service as his coxswain and friend he had nothing. No wife to keep house for him and await his return from the sea, no home beyond these walls. It did not seem fair to drag him off yet again when he had more than earned the right to put his feet firmly ashore for all time. But Bolitho understood that Allday would be resentful and hurt by the suggestion he should not accompany him.

I must leave now.

They walked together to the big double doors, quietly determined, dreading the actual moment.

The sunlight engulfed them like an enemy, and Bolitho looked at the carriage with something like hatred. He had already said his farewells to his sister, to Ferguson, his one-armed steward, to the many familiar faces who worked in and around the big grey house below Pendennis Castle.

He said, 'I shall send word by the first available courier brig. When I reach America I shall probably be required to return home immediately.'

He felt her arm stiffen against his and despised himself for giving her hope.

Admiral Sheaffe had left him in doubt that the mission was important. To sail for Boston, 'neutral ground', as he had called it, and there meet French and American officials to formalize the handing over of an island as part of the agreement made under the Peace of Amiens.

It all seemed wrong to Bolitho. To hand back an island to the old enemy which had been won with British blood. He had blurted out as much to Admiral Sheaffe. 'We gained a peace, Sir Hayward, we did not lose the war!'

Perhaps in that cool Admiralty room it had sounded childish.

Sheaffe had replied calmly, 'And we do not wish you to *provoke* a war either, sir!'

As if to finalize the moment of departure, one of the horses stamped its hoof on the cobbles.

Bolitho kissed her hard on the mouth and tasted the salt of her tears.

'I shall return, Belinda.'

Very gently they prised themselves apart and Bolitho walked down the worn steps to the waiting carriage.

Allday was standing with a groom, but Bolitho gestured to the open door.

'Ride with me, Allday.'

He turned and glanced back at her. Against the grey stone she looked strangely vulnerable and he wanted to hold her just once more.

The next instant he was in the carriage and the wheels were clattering over the cobbles and through the gates.

It was done.

Allday sat with his fingers clasped and watched Bolitho's grave features and tried to measure the depth of his mood.

Seven months ashore seemed a lifetime to Allday,

although he knew better than to suggest as much to Bolitho. It was probably the longest he had been away from a King's ship since that first time when he had made his living here in Cornwall as a shepherd, when a man-of-war, one commanded by Bolitho, had dropped anchor and landed her press-gang to scavenge for hands. There had been several local men caught that day. Allday had been one, the steward Ferguson another. Poor Ferguson had lost an arm at the Saintes but, like Allday, had stayed with Bolitho ever since.

The warm air, the heavy scent of the countryside were making him drowsy, and he knew that although Bolitho wanted companionship for the long haul to the Beaulieu River in Hampshire where their next ship was lying, he did not want to gossip. There would be time enough for that in the weeks and months ahead.

Another ship. What would she be like? Allday was surprised that he could still be curious. In his strong position as the vice-admiral's personal coxswain he had nothing to fear from anyone. But he was too much of a seaman not to be interested.

Not a great first rate of a hundred guns or more, not even a new seventy-four like *Benbow*, Bolitho's last flagship, but the smallest ship of the line still in commission.

His Britannic Majesty's Ship *Achates* of sixty-four guns was one of a dying breed. More like an oversized frigate than a massive line of battleship which could withstand the pounding and destruction of close action.

She was twenty-one years old, a true veteran, and had seen every kind of combat in her time. She had spent most of her recent years in the Caribbean and had sailed countless leagues from her base in Antigua to the far south along the Spanish Main.

Allday wondered uneasily why she had been allotted to Bolitho as his flagship. To his simple reasoning it seemed like one more slur. He should have been given a knighthood for what he had done and endured for England. But always there seemed to be someone in authority who nursed some dislike

or hatred of the man for whom Allday would willingly die if
need be.

He thought of the parting he had just witnessed. What a
fine pair they made. The lovely lady with the long chestnut
hair and the youthful vice-admiral whose hair was as jet-black
as the day Allday had joined his ship as a pressed hand.

From the opposite seat Bolitho saw Allday's head loll into a
doze and felt the strength of the man, was grateful for his
presence here.

Allday had thickened out and looked as if nothing could
ever break him. *The oak.* He smiled to himself in spite of his
sense of loss at leaving Belinda when she most needed him.

He had known Allday like a raging lion on the reddened
deck of one ship or another. And he had seen him in tears as
he had carried Bolitho below when he had been badly
wounded in battle. It was impossible to imagine any place
without Allday.

Bolitho also thought about his new flagship for this special
commission which would take him to America and the
Caribbean.

There was comfort in knowing that her new captain was
also a good friend. Valentine Keen, who had once been one of
Bolitho's midshipmen, who had shared excitement and sorrow in very different circumstances. *Achates'* previous captain
had died of a fever even as his ship had sailed home from
Antigua to the yard where she had been built to undergo a
much needed overhaul and refit.

It would be good to have Keen as his flag-captain, he
thought. He watched Allday's head fall to his chest and
remembered it had been he who had once saved Keen's life,
had personally cut a jagged splinter from his groin because he
had not trusted the ship's drunken surgeon.

Bolitho watched a group of farm workers by a field gate as
they paused to drink rough cider from great earthenware jugs.

A few glanced at the carriage, one even raised his arm in
salute. The word would soon be around Falmouth. A Bolitho
was leaving again. Would he return?

He thought of Belinda in that big, quiet house. If only . . .

Bolitho looked at the new gold lace on his coat and tried to settle his thoughts on the months ahead. He was not the first sea officer to leave home when a wife or family most needed him.

Nor would he be the last.

The peace could not endure, no matter what the politicians and experts proclaimed. Too many had already died, too many scores were still unsettled.

With sixty of England's one hundred ships of the line laid up and out of commission, and some forty thousand seamen and marines discharged, the French would be stupid to ignore such complacency.

He tried to concentrate on *Achates'* eventual destination, the island of San Felipe which lay across the Windward Passage between Cuba and Haiti like a rugged sentinel. The island's history was as wild and bloody as some others in the Caribbean. Originally Spanish, it had been occupied and held by France until the American Rebellion when it had been seized by Britain after a series of attacks at great cost to both sides.

Now, as part of the agreement with France, the island was to be handed back as a sign of good faith. But when Admiral Rodney's ships had taken the island in 1782, just a year after *Achates'* keel had first slipped into salt water, it had been a barren, hostile place. Now, according to all the information Bolitho had obtained from the Admiralty, it was both prosperous and thriving.

The present governor was a retired vice-admiral, Sir Humphrey Rivers, Knight of the Bath. He had made his life on San Felipe, had even named the port Georgetown to mark the island's permanent place under the British flag.

There was an excellent harbour, and the island's trade thrived on sugar, coffee and molasses, the growing prosperity owing much to a secondary population of slaves which had been brought originally from Africa.

Admiral Sheaffe had explained that whereas in war San Felipe had provided an excellent outpost to command the routes to Jamaica and a strategic base for hunting down enemy privateers, in peace it was a liability, unnecessary to the British Crown.

It had made no sense at the time, and as the carriage gathered speed down a steep incline and the sea reappeared on Bolitho's right, it made even less now.

Surely if the island was worth dying for it was worth keeping?

It seemed like a betrayal, more callous than Bolitho would have believed possible. Why then had he been chosen for the task instead of a skilled politician?

A man of tact as well as a man of action, Sheaffe had said.

Bolitho smiled grimly. He had heard that kind of explanation many times. If you were proved right others received the praise. If you made the wrong move you took all the blame.

He shut his orders from his mind. It was useless to plan beyond the written word. Everything might have changed by the time his ship next dropped anchor.

It would be strange not to have Browne as his flag-lieutenant. Intelligent, skilled with the ways of admiralty and government, Browne had been a tower of strength since he had been appointed as his aide. Now Browne was the lord and master of estates and property Bolitho could only guess at, his father having died in the last few months.

Browne had come to Cornwall to say his farewell. It had been a wrench for both of them. Bolitho had decided then and there he would ask his nephew, Adam Pascoe, to take his place. With so many young officers being put ashore it seemed right to offer him the post, even though it went against Bolitho's instinct to use his authority to grant a favour. But he loved his nephew as if he had been his own son, and they had come through many hazards together. The experience would do him good.

Browne had raised a doubtful eyebrow at the idea. Perhaps he had been trying to warn him against having one so close as an aide, one who is supposed to stand aside and remain impartial when required.

But to be without a ship at the age of twenty-one, when he most needed a chance to further his career, had seemed a more weighty argument.

Bolitho rested his head on the warm leather seat.

Valentine Keen, Adam and Allday. They would sustain each other. There would be no other familiar faces this time, or would there?

Achates had originally commissioned at the Nore, whereas Bolitho was more used to West Country ships or those from Spithead.

Belinda had been so pleased at his sudden and advanced promotion, when all he had wanted was to be with her when their first child was born.

Vice-Admiral of the Red. It barely seemed to matter. Some had even compared him with Nelson! Curiously enough, this made Bolitho uneasy, as if he were merely playing a part. It was indeed odd to realize that *Achates* was almost a twin of Nelson's favourite and his last command before his own promotion to flag-rank. His famous *Agamemnon* had been laid down and built in the same yard, that of Henry Adams of Bucklers Hard on the Beaulieu River.

The dwindling number of sixty-fours had one sure advantage. Bigger than anything faster. Faster than anything bigger. No wonder captains of heavier vessels looked on them with begrudging admiration.

Nelson had once said of his little *Agamemnon* that she was an excellent sailer and even when running close to the wind under storm-staysails could match many a frigate.

Bolitho wondered if Keen was equally agreeable with *Achates*. After his recent command of a powerful seventy-four he might already be regretting his decision to accept the role of Bolitho's flag-captain.

The horses slowed to a gentle trot while some sheep crossed the narrow road and bustled their way into an adjoining field.

A young woman with a child on her hip, her husband's midday meal carried in a red handkerchief, stared at the carriage as it moved past. She bobbed her head to Bolitho and flashed him a white smile.

Bolitho thought of Belinda, how she would manage when their child was born. A son to follow the tradition, to walk the deck of a new generation of King's ships. A daughter perhaps, to grow up and win the heart of a young man in a world he might never know.

Bolitho had confided little of his mission to Belinda. He wanted to keep her free of worry. Also she might resent the reason for his leaving her when she had time to think about it.

He tried to think about San Felipe's governor, the man who would have to hand over his tiny kingdom to their old foe.

He glanced at Allday, now rolling gently to the carriage's motion and fast asleep. He had known all about Sir Humphrey Rivers, Knight of the Bath.

Bolitho smiled. Allday gathered information about the comings and goings in the fleet and hoarded it as a magpie guards its treasure trove of coloured glass and beads.

Rivers had captained a frigate named *Crusader* during the American Revolution at about the same time when Bolitho had been given his first command, the little sloop-of-war *Sparrow*.

He had made quite a name for himself hunting French privateers and taking prizes of every shape and size. One day near the Chesapeake he had misjudged the danger in his eagerness to run down an American brig. His *Crusader* had ploughed into some shallows and had become a total wreck. Rivers had been taken prisoner but had been returned to Britain after the war.

He was said to have made influential friends during his captivity, and afterwards when he had been promoted to command a squadron in the West Indies. He had money in the City of London, property too in Jamaica. He did not sound like the kind of man who would fit easily into the plans of the government in Whitehall.

Bolitho grimaced at his reflection in the dusty glass. Not even if the plan was to be offered by someone of equal rank.

The carriage wheels dipped and shuddered through some deep ruts in the road and Bolitho winced as the pain of his wound dragged at his left thigh like a hot claw.

Belinda had even helped to dispel his self-consciousness about that. Occasionally when the pain was re-awakened he found himself limping and he had felt humiliated because of her.

He stirred on his seat as he recalled her touch in the night, her soft body against his, the secret words which had been lost in their passion for one another. She had kissed the wound where a musket-ball and the surgeon's probe had left an ugly scar and had made the injury more a mark of pride than a cruel reminder.

All this and more he was leaving behind with each turn of the wheels. Tonight it would be worse when the carriage stopped for the first change of horses in Torbay. It was better to join a ship and sail with the first possible tide and leave no room for regrets and longing.

He looked at Allday and wondered what he really thought about quitting the land yet again with his future as uncertain as the next horizon.

Flag at the fore. Allday was genuinely proud of it. That was something which the Admiral Sheaffes of this world could never understand.

2

'Old Katie'

Captain Valentine Keen walked from beneath the poop and crossed to the larboard nettings. Around him and along the upper gun-deck, and high overhead on the yards and rigging, the hands were hard at work.

The officer of the watch touched his hat to Keen and then moved to the opposite side of the deck. Like everyone else, he was careful to appear busy but unconcerned at his captain's presence.

Keen glanced along his new command. He had already been pulled around *Achates* in his gig to study her lines and her trim as she rocked gently above her black and buff reflection.

Ready for sea. It was every captain's personal decision as to when that possibility was a fact. There was no room for second thoughts once the anchor was catted and the ship standing out from the land.

It was warm and humid even for May, and the protective folds of the land were misty with haze. He hoped that some kind of wind would soon get up nonetheless. Bolitho would be impatient to get away, to cut his ties with the shore, although Keen knew his reasons were different from his own.

He shaded his eyes and looked up at the foremast truck. *Achates* had never worn an admiral's flag before. It would be interesting to see if it changed her.

He moved into a patch of shade by the poop ladder and watched the activity along the upper deck. The ship had a good feel to her, he thought. Something permanent and hard-won over the years. Several of her lieutenants had once served aboard as midshipmen, and most of her hard core of warrant officers, the backbone of any man-of-war, had been on the books for years.

There was an air of confidence about her, a lively eagerness to get away from the land before she too suffered the fate of so many others. Keen's own ship, *Nicator*, a seventy-four, which had distinguished herself at Copenhagen and later in the Bay of Biscay, was already laid up in ordinary. Unwanted, like her people who had fought so hard when the drums had beaten to quarters.

The previous captain had served in *Achates* for seven years. It was strange that he had commanded the ship for so long a period and had left no trace of his own personality in his quarters. Maybe he had invested it in his ship's company. They certainly seemed contented enough, although there had been the usual desertions during the overhaul here. Wives, sweethearts, children grown out of all recognition; Keen could hardly blame them for giving in to the temptation to run.

Keen ran his finger round his neckcloth and watched one of the ship's boats being swayed up and over the gangway and then lowered on to its tier. Every boat would have to be filled with water if this heat held to stop it from opening up.

Keen examined his feelings. He was glad to be leaving, especially with Bolitho. He had served under him twice before in other ships. First as midshipman, then as third lieutenant. They had shared the pain of losing loved ones, and now that Bolitho had married, Keen was still alone.

His thoughts wandered to his orders which Bolitho had sent to him.

A strange mission. Unique in his experience.

He glanced at the starboard line of black eighteen-pounders, run out as if for battle to allow the sailmaker and his crew maximum space on deck for stitching some canvas.

Peace or war, a King's ship must always be ready. Twice

Keen had served under Bolitho between the wars and had known the folly of over-confidence where a signed peace was concerned.

He heard feet on the companion ladder and saw Lieutenant Adam Pascoe climbing on deck.

It never failed to surprise Keen. Pascoe could have been Bolitho's young brother. The same black hair, although Pascoe's was cut short at the nape of the neck in the new naval fashion, the same restlessness. Grave and withdrawn one moment, full of boyish excitement the other.

Twenty-one years old, Keen thought. Without a war and its demands on lives and ships Pascoe would be lucky to gain advancement or a ship of his own.

'Good-day, Mr Pascoe. Is everything in the admiral's quarters to the flag-lieutenant's liking?'

Pascoe smiled. 'Aye, sir. With four of the after eighteen-pounders removed to the hold and replaced by Quakers, the admiral will have plenty of space.'

Keen looked at the quarterdeck and said, 'I have seen him content with ten paces of a deck. Back and forth, up and down, his daily stroll to arrange his ideas, to exercise his mind as well as his limbs.'

Pascoe said suddenly, 'I see no sense in this mission, sir. We fought the enemy to a standstill so that he *needed* a peace to lick his wounds. And yet our government has seen fit to give up almost all of our possessions which we won from the French. Everything but Ceylon and Trinidad we have let go and cannot even decide definitely to keep Malta. And now San Felipe is to go the same way, and the admiral's lot is to have the dirty task of doing it.'

Keen regarded him gravely. 'A word of advice, Mr Pascoe.'

He saw Pascoe's chin lift stubbornly. That wary glance Keen had grown to know in the past.

He said, 'In the wardroom the lieutenants and others can speak as they please provided their private views do not spread among the people. As captain I stand apart, so too does the flag-lieutenant. Despite your wish to serve your uncle, I suspect you accepted the post more to please him than yourself?'

Keen knew he had guessed correctly and saw the shot go home.

He added, 'Being a sea officer is totally different from being an admiral's aide. You have to be discreet, cautious even, for there will be others who might wish to win a confidence.'

He wondered if he should go further and decided it was too important to avoid.

'Some may want to harm your uncle. So stay clear of the rights and wrongs of something you cannot alter. Otherwise, hurtful or not, it were better for you to go ashore right now and beg a replacement from the port admiral at Spithead.'

Pascoe smiled. 'Thank you, sir. I deserved that. But I'd not leave my uncle. Not now. Not ever. He is everything to me.'

Keen watched the young lieutenant's unusual display of emotion. He knew most of the story anyway. How Pascoe had been born out of wedlock, the son of Bolitho's dead brother. Bolitho's brother had been a renegade, a traitor during the American War, and had commanded an enemy privateer with no less audacity than John Paul Jones. It must have been hard on Bolitho. And on this youthful officer who had been sent to seek out Bolitho by his dying mother as his only hope of a future.

Keen said quietly, 'I understand.' He clapped him on the shoulder. 'Better than you realize.'

The midshipman of the watch hurried across the deck and touched his hat nervously.

Keen looked at him. He was new to the ship as well.

The boy stammered, 'Sir, there is a boat putting off from the yard.'

Keen shaded his eyes again and stared across the nettings. One of the shipyard's own boats was already pulling towards the anchored two-decker. Keen saw the sunlight glint on the gold epaulettes and cocked hat and felt something like panic.

Trust Bolitho not to wait for his barge to be sent across. So he was that eager to get on with the mission, right or wrong.

He kept his face impassive as he said, 'My compliments to the officer of the watch, Mr er . . . er . . .'

'Puxley, sir.'

'Well, Mr Puxley, pipe for the side-party and guard.'

He stopped the boy as he made to run for the ladder. *'Walk*, Mr Puxley!'

Pascoe turned aside to hide a smile. Bolitho had probably said as much to Keen when he had been a grubby midshipman. *He certainly did to me.*

As the boatswain's mates ran between decks and their calls shrilled like trapped birds, the marines stamped to the entry port, their scarlet coats and white cross-belts in stark contrast to the bustling seamen.

Keen beckoned to the officer of the watch and said curtly, *'And* Mr Mountsteven, I would trouble *you* to keep a weather-eye open for your betters in future.'

Pascoe straightened his hat and tucked some of his rebellious hair beneath it. Bolitho had probably said that too.

Keen walked to the entry port and looked towards the boat. He could see Bolitho sitting in the stern-sheets, that old sword clasped firmly between his knees. To see him join any ship without the family sword would be like sacrilege, he thought.

There was Allday too, massive and watchful as he eyed the boat's crew with obvious displeasure. What had Pascoe's predecessor, the Hon. Oliver Browne, called the squadron? *We Happy Few*. There were *very* few of them now. Keen glanced at the big red ensign which flapped only occasionally from the poop. But there were enough.

Achates' first lieutenant, Matthew Quantock, a tall, heavy-jowled Manxman, watched the boat and then said, 'All ready, sir.'

'Thank you, Mr Quantock.'

In his few weeks aboard while the overhaul was completed and he had gone through every list, log and book which

concerned the ship, Keen had felt his way with care. It was
not as if he was new to command. But to this ship's company
he was different. A stranger. Until he had won their respect
he would take nothing and nobody for granted.

The first lieutenant glanced at the signals midshipman by
the foremast and said almost to himself, 'I'll lay odds *Old
Katie* never expected to be a flagship, sir.'

Keen smiled. He had learned something new. *Old Katie*. A
ship with a nickname was usually a happy one.

The boat hooked on to the main chains and Captain Dewar
of the Royal Marines drew his sword. The thin rasp of steel
never failed to touch Keen. Like a memory. A chord of battle.

Keen looked at his command. All the idlers had drawn
away from the entry port, and even the hands working on the
yards high above the deck were motionless as they peered at
the little scene below.

The small marine fifers raised their instruments, the boatswain's mates moistened their silver calls on their tongues.

Keen stepped forward, proud, nervous, apprehensive; it
was all and none of these things.

Bolitho's cocked hat appeared above the scrubbed grating
and as the calls shrilled and twittered Captain Dewar roared,
'Royal Marines! Present *arms!*'

On the last command, as the pipe-clay hovered in a pale
cloud above the slapped musket-slings, the fifers broke into
Heart of Oak.

Bolitho removed his hat to the quarterdeck and then
smiled at Keen.

Together they turned to watch as the Union Flag broke
smartly from the foremast.

Bolitho gripped Keen's hand. 'They do you credit.'

Keen answered, 'And you us, sir.'

Bolitho looked at the stiff faces of the marine guard, the
nervous watchfulness of some midshipmen. In time he would
know most of them, and they him. He was back, and the
green swathe of coastline was only part of a memory.

*

Bolitho tugged his shirt away from his skin and then put his signature to yet another letter which Yovell, his plump clerk, had prepared for him.

He glanced around the spacious stern cabin. It was larger than he had expected in a ship of some thirteen hundred tons.

Ozzard, his little servant, poured some fresh coffee and bustled away to the adjoining pantry. If he was sorry to be leaving the security of the Bolitho house in Falmouth he did not show it. He was an odd bird, who had once been a lawyer's clerk before he had chosen the uncertain life in a King's ship. Some said he had done so to avoid the gallows, but he was worth his weight in gold to Bolitho.

He looked at Keen who was standing by the open stern windows. His good looks and elegant manner revealed nothing of the competent sea officer he really was.

'Well, Val, what do you make of it?'

Keen turned towards him, his face in shadow from the hard sunlight.

'I have studied the chart and appreciate the value of San Felipe in time of war. Whoever commands there is in a strong position.' He shrugged. 'A great lagoon, a fortress on high ground which can control the approaches, the town too if need be. I can see no sense in giving it to the French.'

He thought Pascoe was smiling at his words and added, 'But I assume their lordships know more than I do.'

Bolitho chuckled. 'Do not rely on it, Val.'

The coffee was good. Bolitho felt surprisingly fresh and rested after his first night aboard. The journey had been tiring, the many pauses along the way to take refreshment, to sleep or to change horses had been even more so as he had thought of Belinda and what she had come to mean to him.

But the feel of a ship around him had awakened him also.

The smells of tar and fresh paint, cordage and the packed world of *Achates'* five hundred officers, seamen and marines was something he could not ignore, nor did he wish to.

Achates was a well-found ship, and from what he had already discovered held a record second to none. Perhaps

Admiral Sheaffe's choice had been the right one after all. A small sixty-four instead of a proud squadron which might intimidate the Americans and the French alike.

He said, 'I have already sent word to Captain Duncan at Plymouth. He will sail direct to San Felipe in his *Sparrow-hawk* without delay.'

It was easy to picture Duncan's bluff red face as he read his orders. He too would be glad to get away before his frigate was paid off into oblivion. Duncan had also been with Bolitho's squadron. It was like knowing Keen in some ways, he thought. They were extensions of his own mind and ideas.

That was something which he still found hard to accept. No longer did he have to wait for the written word from his flag-officer. No more did he need to fret over the uncertainty or unfairness of his place in affairs. Now the decision as to when and how to act was his. So too the final responsibility.

He added, 'Duncan's presence at San Felipe may lessen the shock for the inhabitants there. I doubt if the governor will see it in the same way as Parliament.'

Ozzard tiptoed across the cabin and waited for Bolitho to notice his mole-like figure. Even his hands dangled at his waist like paws.

He said, 'Beg pardon, Captain, but the first lieutenant has sent his respects and requires me to tell you that the wind has shifted, though very slight.'

Keen looked at Bolitho and grinned. 'I told him to inform me, sir. It's still not much of a wind, but enough to break out the anchor. With your permission, sir?'

Bolitho nodded. It was infectious. It had not changed after all.

'Yovell, put my despatches in the yard-boat alongside.'

He saw his clerk hold the letter he had written to Belinda with special care. She would be reading it as *Achates* passed the Lizard on her way to the Atlantic rollers, he thought.

He heard Keen's voice through the open skylight, the trill of calls and the slap of bare feet over the dried planks as the seamen ran to their stations.

Bolitho made himself sit in his chair and sip the coffee. Keen would have enough to deal with as he sailed his ship clear of the land for the first time without having him there as well.

How many times had he stood at the quarterdeck rail, his heart bounding with hope and excitement, searching his soul in case he had forgotten something when it was already too late?

Tackles squeaked and cordage squealed through countless blocks, and very faintly, far away it sounded, Bolitho heard the plaintive notes of a violin while the shantyman added his weight to the men on the capstan bars.

Yovell came back breathing hard.

'All despatches ashore, zur.' His round Devonian dialect seemed to match his handwriting on the many copies of signals and despatches he had penned for Bolitho in the past two years.

Keen returned, his hat tucked beneath one arm.

'The anchor is hove short, sir. I wonder if you would care to join me on deck? It would do well for the people to see you are with them.'

Bolitho smiled. 'Thank you, Val.'

Keen hesitated and glanced at Pascoe.

'There is one thing I do not understand, sir. The courier delivered a letter for the flag-lieutenant. He only just reached the ship in time.'

Bolitho looked at his nephew. It was the moment, and it had almost been postponed because of the need to get under way while the feeble wind lasted.

He saw Yovell beaming at him and was suddenly fearful that he had done the wrong thing.

He said, 'I shall come on deck directly, Captain Keen.'

Bolitho took the sealed letter and glanced quickly at it to make certain it was the right one. Then he snatched his hat from Ozzard and walked with Keen to the door.

Keen was saying, 'I expect it was a careless mistake, sir.'

Bolitho pressed the letter into his nephew's hand.

'I shall be on deck if you need me.'

Entirely mystified, Keen accompanied him beneath the shadows of the poop deck and past the great double wheel where the helmsmen and quartermaster waited, tensed, for the anchor to break loose from the ground.

The ship was alive with seamen and marines. The topmen were already high aloft on the upper yards, spread out like monkeys as they handled the loosely brailed sails. The braces were manned, and as the pawls of the capstan clanked round to the tune of the fiddle, petty officers and master's mates watched their divisions like hawks, very aware of the flag at the fore.

Allday was on deck by one of the quarterdeck twelve-pounders when he realized that Ozzard had neglected to clip on Bolitho's sword for him. With a silent curse he darted aft and bustled past the marine sentry into the great cabin.

With a start he saw Pascoe was still there, an open document hanging from one hand.

Like Yovell, who had written most of the letters, Allday knew what the document contained. He had been deeply moved that he was one of the very few who did.

'All right, sir?'

When the youthful lieutenant turned to face him, Allday was shocked to see there were tears on his cheeks.

'Easy, sir! He wanted you to be pleased!'

'Pleased?'

Pascoe took a few paces towards the side and back again. As if he did not understand what was happening.

'And *you* knew about it, Allday?'

'Aye, sir. After a fashion.'

Allday had seen and done many things, and Bolitho had said more than once that with education he might have achieved a lot more than a sailor's life. But he did not need to be able to read what was written on the envelope. No wonder Captain Keen had been all aback, he thought.

The letter was addressed to *Adam Bolitho, Esq., Flag-Lieutenant on board His Britannic Majesty's Ship* Achates.

Adam stared at the writing, his eyes too blurred with emotion to read much further. The lawyer's impressive wax seals, the rights to the Bolitho property in Falmouth. He could not go on.

Allday took his elbow and guided him to the bench seat below the stern windows.

'I'll fetch you a wet, sir. After that we'll take the old sword on deck together.' He saw him nod and added quietly, 'After all, sir, you're a *real* Bolitho now. Like *him*.'

From another world a voice yelled, '*Anchor's aweigh*, sir!'

The stamp of feet and the harsh cries of the petty officers seemed to be held at bay.

Allday poured a glass of brandy and carried it to the lieutenant he had known since he had come aboard Bolitho's *Hyperion* as a fourteen-year-old midshipman.

'Here, sir.'

Adam said quietly, 'You asked me if I was pleased. There are no words for the way I feel. He didn't have to . . . '

Allday wished he could have a drink too. 'It's what he wanted. What he's always wanted.'

The deck tilted as the ship continued to pay off to the wind's thrust in her topsails and jib.

Allday took down the worn old sword from the rack and turned it over in his hands. They had nearly lost it for good last time. He looked at the young lieutenant, the image of the man on deck. It would be his one day.

Lieutenant Adam Bolitho wiped his face with his cuff and said, 'Let's be about it then, eh, Allday?' But the bravado would not hold. He gripped the coxswain's massive arm and exclaimed, 'I'm glad you were here just now.'

Allday grinned as he followed him from the cabin.

Pleased? He was pleased right enough. Otherwise, lieutenant or not, he'd have put the young rascal across his knee and beaten some sense into him.

Adam walked out into the sunlight. He did not see the curious stares, nor did he hear a muttered curse as a hurrying seaman almost fell to the deck as he tripped on the flag-lieutenant's foot. He took the sword from Allday and held it against Bolitho's side as he made to clip it into place.

Bolitho watched him and was glad. 'Thank you, Adam.'

The lieutenant nodded and tried to speak.

Bolitho took his arm and turned him towards the rolling shoreline as it glided abeam, moving away as the ship headed into deeper water.

'Later, Adam. There'll be plenty of time.'

The first lieutenant raised his speaking-trumpet and squinted up through the black rigging.

'Loose t'gan's'ls!'

He glanced at the group by the windward side. The youthful vice-admiral with his flag-lieutenant on deck to see if the ship was good enough, more than likely.

Allday saw the glance and hid a grin.

You've got a lot to learn, matey, an' that's no error.

3

Man of Action

For a full week after weighing anchor *Achates* was the victim of feeble and perverse winds. There was barely an hour when all hands were spared the tasks of trimming the sails in order to avoid losing steerage-way or being forced back over their previous course.

The deadly monotony was having its effect on the ship's company. After all the haste and excitement of getting away from the land, the sudden torpor had resulted in more than one flogging at the gratings because of frayed tempers and bursts of insubordination.

Bolitho had watched Keen's face after one of the floggings. Some captains would have cared nothing for the routine of punishment, but Keen was different. It was typical of Bolitho that it never occurred to him that Keen had gained his experience under his command.

Keen had remarked, 'The worst part of it is I can understand their feelings. Some have not set foot ashore since returning from the Indies. Now they're off again. Grateful to be spared the poverty of being without work, but resentful at what is little better than pressed service.'

The start of the second week brought a freshening wind from the north-east, and with spray bursting beneath her weathered figurehead it had brought life to the ship once more.

The masthead lookouts had sighted only a few sails on the blurred horizon, and these had changed tack and headed away immediately. Home-bound ships, out of touch for many

months with the events in Europe, would take no chances
when sighting a man-of-war. War might have broken out
again for all they knew. Some masters might still not know
that an armistice had even been signed.

It was as if the ship had the ocean to herself. Keen took the
opportunity to get to know his command and for his men to
recognize his standards. Sail and gun drill, musket practice
for the marines, experienced lieutenants and warrant officers
replaced by new and often barely trained counterparts. Keen
may have gained their respect, but was roundly cursed at the
start of each testing exercise.

Bolitho knew from hard experience there was nothing
more likely to breed discontent in a ship's close confines than
too much leisure.

He was having a breakfast of thinly sliced fat pork when
Keen asked to see him.

Bolitho gestured to a chair, 'Coffee, Val?'

Keen sat down and said, 'I believe we are being stalked by
another vessel, sir.'

Bolitho put down his knife. Keen had never been one to
exaggerate or imagine things.

'How so?'

'Two days ago my best lookout sighted a sail. Well up to
wind'rd. I thought little of it at the time. She might have
been a merchantman on the same tack as *Achates*.'

He sensed Bolitho's curiosity and added simply, 'I did not
wish to alarm anyone. But yesterday you will recall I was hove
to while we exercised the starboard twelve-pounders on some
driftwood. That sail was still there, and the moment I came
about the stranger followed suit and stood clear.' He waited
for Bolitho's reaction and said grimly, 'She's there now.'

The door opened and Adam entered the cabin with a chart
beneath his arm.

Bolitho smiled at him. They had said little of his gesture
towards his nephew since the day the ship had weighed
anchor in the Beaulieu River. Yet there was a new closeness
between them. Something which went beyond words.

He remembered Belinda's encouragement and insistence that he acted as he had. She had known from the beginning how Bolitho felt about his nephew, what they had been through.

He could almost hear her saying, 'When our child is born I do not want Adam to feel shut out, excluded. Do it for *me*, as well as for Adam.'

'Have *you* seen the ship, Adam?'

'Aye, sir. I went aloft at first light today. I believe she's a frigate. I took the signals telescope with me. There was a lot of haze, but I judge her rig to be that of a big fifth-rater. She's too agile for an Indiaman or some westbound trader.'

Keen said glumly, 'And if that vessel holds to wind'rd I'll never be able to beat up to him.'

Bolitho shook his head. 'It would lose valuable time too.'

But the news was unsettling all the same. If she was a ship-of-war she represented a menace no matter what his orders dictated. But whose and for what purpose?

His mission was supposed to be secret, but Bolitho knew ships as well as he understood the men who served them. Keen had been surprised at Adam's official change of name, but it had gone through the ship in seconds. A piece of really important information could spread through a shipyard, a town, even across the English Channel in no time at all.

'Keep me informed. If the wind changes in our favour we shall investigate. If not . . . ' He shrugged. 'We'll have to wait for him to show his intentions.'

Later, as Bolitho took his regular stroll up and down the weather-side of the quarterdeck, he found himself wondering about his mission and how the people of San Felipe would accept their new position. He thought too of the ship which was obviously stalking *Achates* with the persistence of a hunter after deer.

French most likely. Ready to support their own viewpoint if required, even at the point of a gun.

Up and down, his feet avoiding ring-bolts and tackles without conscious effort.

Some of the faces among the watchkeepers and the after-guard had become as familiar as those in previous ships. Bolitho hated the invisible wall which cut him off from closer contact. Even Keen as captain was free to talk with his men if the mood took him. More than once Bolitho stared up at his flag and tried to accept the enforced loneliness it had brought him.

He paused by the compass and glanced at it even though it had barely altered for days. He could feel the helmsmen avoiding his eye, and Knocker, the sailing-master, becoming suddenly absorbed in the midshipman of the watch's report.

Hallowes, the fourth lieutenant, had the watch, and even he was bent over the quarterdeck rail with exaggerated attention as he watched the eighteen-pounders at drill.

A boatswain's mate strode along the lee gangway and something about him made Bolitho look at him more closely.

The man hesitated, swallowed hard, and then came towards him.

Bolitho asked, 'Do I know you?' Then the man's name seemed to paint itself in his mind. 'Christy, isn't it?'

The man nodded and beamed hugely. 'Aye, 'tis that, sir. Maintopman in the old *Lysander*, I was. With you at the Nile, sir.'

'I remember. You were nearly lost that day when they shot the t'gallant mast away.' He nodded as the memory closed round them shutting out all else.

The boatswain's mate said, 'Were a sore hard fight, sir. The worst I seen, ever.'

Bolitho smiled and continued with his walk.

The man named Christy hurried away shaking his head. *He remembered him*. Out of all these men.

Quantock, the first lieutenant, who was doing his morning rounds with Rooke, the boatswain, and Grace, the carpenter, paused and beckoned to him.

'Knew your name, did he?'

Christy knuckled his forehead. 'Aye, sir. He did that.'

Quantock snapped, 'Well, don't stand there like a moon-struck farm boy, there's work to be done!'

Christy made his way aft. Why was the first lieutenant in a temper? He thought of that awful day at the Nile, the thunder of the broadsides, and of Bolitho walking amidst the smoke and carnage with that old sword gripped in his hand. And his face as they had cheered him when the enemy had finally struck their colours.

Quantock checked his list, the unending task of every good first lieutenant. The ship had had a refit but the work was always piling up. Sails to be renewed and patched, boats repaired, pumps and tackles overhauled.

He was angry with himself for his sudden hostility towards the boatswain's mate. Christy was a good seaman, and a volunteer as well.

Quantock stole a glance to the weather-side where the vice-admiral was walking up and down. What was so special about him anyway?

The boatswain, a great crag of a man with a lined and battered face, waited patiently for his superior to continue with the morning rounds. He had been irritated by the lieutenant's unwarranted attack on one of *his* assistants.

Rooke, Big Harry as he was respectfully known, guessed the reason for Quantock's temper. He was a good first lieutenant, if you happened to be the captain, that was. But he was hard with the people, unrelenting in matters of discipline.

Captain Glazebrook, who had died after a long bout of fever, had been too ill to see what was happening. Quantock probably thought *he* should be promoted, even be given command of *Old Katie*. Rooke did not like the first lieutenant, and the thought of him being in command of this ship was like blasphemy.

Quantock said sharply, '*Standards*, we must maintain them. I'll not allow anything to interfere with the efficient running of this ship!'

Rooke saw the new captain crossing the deck from the companion. He might have warned another lieutenant but Quantock's outburst was still annoying him.

'And further – '

'Mr Quantock.' Keen waited for the lieutenant to join him where he could not be heard by the men on watch. 'I admire your high standards. I would, however, prefer that you voiced your views to me in future, not the ship's company en masse.'

Bolitho had seen most of it and guessed the rest.

Did his flag at the masthead really make that much difference? Even Keen seemed on edge, regretting perhaps this appointment which was leading nowhere.

No, it was not that. It was uncertainty. An emptiness which the coming of peace had brought. They were used to action, expected it even.

'Deck there! Sail on th' weather-bow!'

Keen looked up and then turned questioningly to Bolitho. Their companion was still there, lurking just below the horizon like an assassin.

Perhaps they would get all the action they wanted even though the ink was barely dry on the peace agreement.

Bolitho continued his pacing with renewed energy, as if he wanted to tire himself out.

He was imagining things, he decided angrily. *He* was the one who craved excitement, if only to take his mind off the relentless passing of time.

Achates would still be making for Boston when Belinda gave birth. It was like being trapped. Helpless.

Bolitho saw Adam at the forward end of the gun-deck talking with Hawtayne, the young marine lieutenant.

I am as bad as Admiral Sheaffe.

I am envious. Not of success but of youth.

He was so lucky to have Belinda. He was after all ten years older than she. And now that she needed him he was marooned out here like a castaway on a rock.

Why you? He could still hear her voice when she had spoken out in the darkness. Why him indeed?

He stopped and allowed his body to sway with the ship as she rode contemptuously across a long Atlantic trough.

Perhaps it was a kind of madness which had never left him. Being taken prisoner by the French, the escape, the lives it had cost in that final battle with Remond's Flying Squadron had been too much and too soon after being badly wounded.

The pain stabbed through his wound again as if to taunt him. He tried to remember her soft touch in the night, when she had soothed the pain of the scar with her love.

But the picture would not form.

He called, 'Captain Keen, we shall douse all lights and change tack tonight. As soon as it is dark alter course to the nor'-west. By dawn I want to see that strange sail where we can run down on it.'

Keen opened his mouth as if to protest but instead touched his hat. Then he said, 'I'll get every stitch on her, sir.'

Bolitho strode into the poop's shadow and made his way aft to his quarters.

He had acted hastily, even childishly, some would say.

Achates was a solitary ship, and yet his responsibility was as great as if he commanded a squadron or even a fleet.

Those around him had not asked to be here. Keen, Quantock, the embittered first lieutenant, even the boatswain's mate named Christy who had been so grateful that he had remembered him, they all deserved better from the man who commanded them.

But there was a difference. To Keen the ship and her company came before all else, and the mission was secondary.

To Bolitho *Achates* had to remain a symbol and, if necessary, a weapon to enforce his wishes.

It was probably the first time he had considered what his new responsibility entailed, and the realization steadied him.

Allday padded into the cabin and replaced the old sword on its rack. Cleaning it made little difference but it gave him an excuse to come and go as he pleased.

He glanced at Bolitho as he sat on the bench seat by the stern windows, his black hair ruffling in the wind across the quarter.

Bolitho looked calm enough. The sudden squall had passed.

'I was wondering, sir . . . '

Bolitho turned, only half aware he was no longer alone.

'What about?'

'Well, I mean, sir, if *you* was the governor of this island we're about to toss away to the mounseers, what would you do?'

Bolitho got to his feet and strode to the wine cabinet where he poured two glasses of brandy.

He handed one to the astonished Allday and replied, 'Thank you. You have put your finger on it.' The brandy burned his lips. *'Do*, Allday? I'd stand and fight. And so probably will he.'

Allday breathed out slowly. He did not quite understand what he had done, but it was good to see the frown gone from Bolitho's features.

Bolitho eyed him warmly, 'You should have been in Parliament, Allday.'

Allday put down his empty glass. He had never seen him in quite this mood before.

'I'm too honest, sir.'

Bolitho laughed and turned to watch the patterns and colours twisting in the ship's wake.

There would be no easy solution for San Felipe.

Maybe that was why Sheaffe needed his 'man of action'.

And it had taken Allday to discover it.

'Hands at quarters, sir, ship cleared for action.'

Keen's voice came out of the gloom and Bolitho could barely distinguish him from the other dark figures at the quarterdeck rail.

The *Achates*' previous captain and Keen's regular drills had made their mark, he thought. All hands had been roused early and had a hot meal before the galley fire had been doused and the ship prepared for battle.

There was little impression of danger or anxiety, however. It was peacetime, so why should they worry?

Bolitho said, 'That was quietly done.'

He shivered as the cold, damp wind whipped over the

deck. In an hour or so the sunlight would raise steam from the planks and melt the tarred seams like toffee.

'Steady on west by north, sir.'

Bolitho nodded. That was Knocker's voice, the sailing-master. At the helm and compass he was king. He was a man who rarely smiled. Thin and gaunt with a priest's face, Bolitho thought. But his chartwork and his grip over the ship's daily progress was as good as any master he had ever known.

Some of the gun crews around the quarterdeck were whispering and nudging each other. Anything which broke the regular routine was welcome. What did it matter if their admiral was mad enough to clear for action because of some stupid stranger?

Another voice said, 'Dawn coming up, sir.'

The lieutenant who had spoken sounded awed by the occasion.

Bolitho turned to look astern and saw the horizon begin to betray the division between sea and sky. How many hundreds of dawns must he have watched, he wondered? And how many had he thought might be his last?

Someone remarked, 'The bugger might have slipped us during the night.'

The sergeant of marines tapped his hand-pike on the damp planking and muttered, 'Easy, lads. Stow the chat!'

The cross-belts of the marines who lined the poop nettings were already brighter, and when Bolitho looked up to the mainmast truck he saw it was touched with pale gold, like the tip of a lance.

The lookouts in the cross-trees or crouched in the swaying tops would see the other ship first. If she was still there.

All night long Keen had worked his ship upwind, a slow, wearying task with the yards so often close-hauled that they seemed to reach above the deck in a single barrier of spars and canvas.

All they had said of *Achates* was true. She handled well, and responded to sail and rudder like a thoroughbred.

Bolitho listened to the sluice of water below the lee side, the occasional creak of gun tackles as they took the strain.

The light seemed to spill down from the horizon like a separate layer, as if it was in pursuit of the ship which lay over to the wind just out of reach.

'*There she is!* Fine on the lee bow!'

Everyone was talking at once, and Bolitho saw Keen's teeth, very white in a grin, as he nodded to the sailing-master.

They had done even better than expected. Had taken, and could now hold the wind-gage if it came to a chase.

Bolitho stared at the distant shadow as the other vessel took on shape and substance against the dark water.

Keen closed his telescope with a snap. 'Bigger than a fifth-rate, Mr Pas—, er Bolitho.'

Several of those nearby chuckled, and Bolitho was glad Adam was here with him.

He heard his nephew say, 'I agree, sir. A cut down two-decker seems more likely.'

Keen crossed to Bolitho's side. 'What orders, sir?'

'Wait a while longer. He has not sighted us yet. But when he does, tell him to identify himself.'

It seemed incredible that *Achates* had got so near and yet remained unseen. The other ship lay less than a cable now across the larboard bow, and they could see the white tail of her wash beneath the counter. Even the din of *Achates'* canvas and drumming stays and shrouds seemed loud enough to wake the dead, but Bolitho knew from experience it was an illusion.

Suddenly above the noise of sea and wind Bolitho heard a shrill whistle. He could picture it exactly. A sleepy lookout, who had most likely been ordered to seek out *Achates* as soon as it was daylight, the watch on deck thinking of little but being relieved and getting something warm to eat and drink. It was all normal enough.

Quantock said sharply, 'She's setting her t'gan's'ls!'

Keen said, 'They're making a run for it, sir. So they *are* up to something.'

Bolitho felt a chill run through his body as if it was the first time. Elation, excitement or madness, who could say?

'As soon as it is light enough, make your signal. Until then hold him on the larboard bow.'

Keen nodded. The excitement was infectious. With him it had always been the same even as a midshipman a million years ago in another ocean.

'Hands aloft, Mr Quantock, if you please. We must make more sail.'

Calls trilled and the seamen swarmed up the ratlines on either side, their bodies and limbs glowing suddenly as they climbed higher and the pale sunlight discovered them.

'Bring her up a point. Hands to the braces there!'

Spray burst over the beak-head and bowsprit and spattered across the forecastle like tropical rain.

The other ship had also set more canvas and appeared to be drawing away.

Bolitho felt the deck quiver as *Achates* lifted and smashed down into a shallow trough. He could sense the rising power of the extra sails, and watched the huge main-course spread and thunder out to the wind as the seamen freed it from its yard.

Bolitho climbed on to a gun-truck and steadied his glass on the leading ship. The light was strengthening rapidly and already he could see the gilded gingerbread around the other vessel's poop and quarter gallery, the pale sunlight reflecting in her stern windows as if she had taken fire.

Keen said, 'Not a Frenchie.'

Someone else suggested, 'Dutch maybe.'

They were all wrong. Bolitho had seen ships very similar to this one and could be pretty certain which yard had laid down her keel.

He said, 'Spanish. I've crossed swords with her like before.'

Nobody spoke and Bolitho hid a smile. Right or wrong, you never argued with an admiral, no matter how junior.

Keen nodded. 'I agree with the flag-lieutenant, sir. She's

too large for a frigate. She's well armed by the look of her, fifty guns at least, by my reckoning.'

'Signal her to shorten sail.'

Bolitho sensed the sudden indifference of the men near him. The game was over before it had begun.

Flags soared up the yards and broke to the wind. Above the other ship's deck nothing appeared, not even an acknowledgement.

'She's falling off a mite, sir.'

Bolitho trained his glass again. He thought he saw the sun glint on a telescope near one of her poop lanterns. *Achates'* change of station during the night must have surprised them if nothing else.

Keen called, 'Follow her round. Alter course to west by south.' He glanced at Bolitho's impassive features.

Bolitho said, 'Keep the signal hoisted.'

Both vessels were in line now, as if the other one was towing *Achates* on an invisible cable.

Keen strode this way and that as he tried to estimate the stranger's next move. If he fell off to leeward *Achates* would hold the advantage. If she tried to claw upwind with so close a chase she would lose ground and precious time and *Achates* could drive alongside if so ordered.

The lieutenant of the after-guard lowered his glass. .

'She does not acknowledge, sir. Even the Dons should know our signals by now!'

Quantock shouted, 'Take those men's names, Master-at-Arms!' He gestured angrily with his speaking-trumpet towards an eighteen-pounder's crew who had left their positions to peer at the other ship. 'God damn it, what are they thinking of!'

Keen was saying, 'If the wind holds I'll get the stuns'ls on her . . . '

Bolitho wiped his eye and raised the glass yet again. *Achates* was keeping pace with the other ship, even though the stranger had set her royals in an effort to draw away. But. the wind might drop or go altogether. If they could not catch up before nightfall they might never know what she was doing.

It was very strange. He concentrated on the small, silent world within the telescope's lens. She was well painted, as if freshly out of a dockyard like *Achates*. But the broad red band across her counter had no name upon it. She had either put to sea with great haste or wished her identity to remain a secret.

He heard *Achates'* wheel begin to creak as the other ship's rudder moved further to leeward.

He blinked and peered through the glass again. For an instant he thought the light or his eye was playing tricks. On either side of the ship's rudder a gun-port had opened, and even as he watched he saw the daylight play across a pair of long stern-chasers.

Quantock exploded, 'Hell's teeth, he'd never dare fire on a King's ship!'

The air cringed from a double crash of cannon fire, and as the smoke rolled downwind in a thick cloud Bolitho felt iron smash hard into *Achates'* bows like a giant's fist.

Voices yelled to restore the sudden pandemonium, and faces peered aft to the quarterdeck as if each man was too astonished to move.

Bolitho snapped, 'Load and run out, Captain Keen.'

It was sheer stupidity for the other captain to try and mark down a sixty-four. In a moment Keen would stand away and loose off a full broadside. Men would be killed, and for what purpose?

Along *Achates'* side the port lids opened as one, and to the blast of a whistle the eighteen-pounders rolled squeaking down the tilting deck until they showed their muzzles to the sea and sky. On the deck below the main armament of twenty-four-pounders would be just a few feet above the water as it curled along the rounded hull. *Achates* was carrying such a pyramid of sails it was a wonder the sea was not already lapping through the lower ports.

'Bow-chasers!'

Keen had his hands clasped behind his back, and Bolitho could see the force of his grip betrayed by the pale knuckles. What did he see? An unexpected prize, or his own ruin?

Bolitho could hear Allday's heavy breathing behind his shoulder and sensed Adam on his other side. Extensions of himself. Each needing the other in a different way.

The other ship fired again, and Bolitho tried not to flinch as a ball ripped through the main-course and the wind tore it into a great flapping slash.

Achates' gunner had been caught napping. The bow-chasers would probably not even bear on the enemy, Bolitho thought.

Every gun-captain along the upper deck had his hand in the air.

Keen said tersely, 'Be ready to come about, Mr Knocker! We'll cross his stern and rake him. That'll give him something to ponder on.'

He sounded angry. Hurt that this should happen.

'Lee braces there! Stand by on the quarterdeck!' Quantock's magnified voice seemed to be everywhere.

At that moment the other ship fired again. Bolitho thought he saw the blur of falling shot before one heavy ball crashed through the forward gangway and the other hissed above the forecastle at extreme elevation.

A last desperate attempt to break off the chase, and it worked.

There was a single, terrible crack, and seconds later the whole of the fore-topgallant mast, the spars and wildly thrashing canvas plunged down to the deck. With torn canvas and rigging trailing after it like serpents, the broken mast thundered across the lee gangway and into the water with a tremendous splash.

Bolitho heard one of the midshipmen stifle a cry of terror as some seamen were plucked bodily over the side with the broken rigging, their voices lost in the din.

Like a great sea-anchor the trailing spars and cordage were already having effect as they pulled the ship's head round, further and further, until all the sails, so carefully set for the chase, were in wild confusion.

Rooke, the boatswain, was already among the chaos with his men, axes flashing as they hacked the debris clear.

The gun crews were working feverishly with tackles and handspikes, but as the ship was dragged still further down wind their muzzles pointed blindly at the sea, their target already standing well away.

Bolitho tried to relax his limbs but his whole body felt like a taut lashing which was about to snap.

In the blink of an eye, *Achates* had been rendered helpless.

Had this been a fight in earnest, their attacker would already be tacking about to rake them from stem to stern.

High above the deck the topmen yelled to one another as they tried to shorten sail before the ship was completely dismasted.

Keen exclaimed despairingly, 'I'll never forget this. *Never!*' He looked at Bolitho as if for an answer. 'They fired on us without cause.'

Bolitho saw order being restored, the motion becoming easier as *Achates* responded to the helm, her shorn topgallant mast poking above the confusion like a broken tusk.

He said, 'They had a cause right enough, and I intend to discover what it was. When that happens we shall be ready.'

Keen saw some of his lieutenants hurrying aft for orders. The older hands would be comparing him with the previous captain. Whatever they thought, it was not a good beginning.

Bolitho said, 'Stand down the people and get the ship under way.'

It was all he could do to keep his voice level. They had been hit, and men had been lost, unless the quarter-boat had found any survivors among the flotsam astern.

But for some instinct, a sense of warning, he might never have ordered Keen to close with the stranger.

It was pointless to pursue the chase, the other ship was already drawing away under every sail she could carry.

He felt sorry for Keen. After all his work to obey his admiral's wishes, his success at surprising the other captain, when the trap had been sprung the enemy had been ready, Keen had not.

Tuson, the ship's surgeon, his white hair ruffling in the wind, was gesturing towards the piles of tangled rigging. Some other men must have been caught there too.

Keen listened to his lieutenants, his face pale and grim.

It was a lesson he would not forget, Bolitho thought.

He saw Adam watching him anxiously. Thinking perhaps of his father. When he had flown false colours and fired on Bolitho's ship.

Bolitho walked to the poop and ducked his head as he strode into the shadows between decks.

I too had forgotten the lesson. It could have been the last dawn after all.

4

A Place to Meet

'Nor'-west by north, sir. Steady as she goes!' Even the helmsman sounded hushed as under topsails and jib *Achates* glided very slowly towards her anchorage.

It was noon, with the sun high overhead and burning the bare-shouldered seamen who waited at the braces or were spread out on the topsail yards for the last cable or so of their journey.

Bolitho stood apart from Keen and his officers as he watched the shoreline spread and strengthen through a shimmering haze.

They had passed abeam of Cape Cod at dawn, but with the wind dropping to a mere breath of a breeze it had taken them this long to close with the land.

Bolitho raised a glass to his eye and studied the foreshore, the mass of masts and furled sails, the living evidence of a port's prosperity. Ships and flags of every nation, with lighters alongside and harbour craft plying back and forth to the jetties like water-beetles.

There were several men-of-war, he noticed. Two American frigates, and three Frenchmen, one a big third-rate with a rear-admiral's flag flapping listlessly at the mizzen.

Bolitho shifted his glass to the spit of land which was reaching out slowly towards the larboard bow. There was a tell-tale line of grey fortifications with a flag high overhead.

He examined his feelings, aware of the sudden dryness in his throat. It was about nineteen years since he had sailed along and landed on these shores. Another war, and different ships. He wondered how it might have changed, how he would react.

He heard Keen say sharply, 'Begin the salute, Mr Braxton!'

The crash of the first gun echoed and re-echoed across Massachusetts Bay like a thunder-clap while the smoke billowed over the quiet water as if unable to rise. Gulls and other sea-birds rose screaming from their perches and from the sea itself, as gun by gun the ship and the shore battery exchanged salutes.

Bolitho thought of the days which had followed their mauling by the unknown ship. The anger and humiliation had given way to a feverish determination to 'put the score right', as Allday had described it. There had been more damage to rigging than to the hull, and everyone from Keen to the ship's boys had seemed unflagging in their efforts to complete the repairs before the ship anchored at Boston.

A new topgallant mast had been set up, fresh rigging and sails hauled aloft even in the teeth of a strong north-easterly wind. Paint, tar and sweat had achieved wonders.

The mood had been infectious, and Bolitho had even ordered the four wooden Quakers to be removed from his quarters and replaced by the eighteen-pounders. It might mean less room, but it marked a new determination that he would never lower his guard again.

He saw an American guard-boat riding above her own reflection, the oars motionless as she waited to guide the British man-of-war to the allotted place.

Bolitho shaded his eyes to watch the shore. White houses, several churches, the glitter of sunlight on carriages and windows along the waterfront. Perhaps there were many there who were watching the slow-moving ship and remembering the bitter times of revolution and war, brother against brother, hate against hate.

'Ready, sir!'

Keen replied, 'Hands wear ship!'

Quantock responded like a pistol-spring. 'Lee braces there! Wear ship!'

Bolitho glanced at the main-topsail. It had barely enough air to move its belly. Another minute or so and they would have lost the wind altogether.

'Tops'l sheets!' Quantock was leaning over the quarterdeck rail, his speaking-trumpet weaving from side to side as he watched his men high above. 'Tops'l clew-lines!'

Keen said, 'Helm alee.'

Achates turned gently into the dying breeze, the white ripple beneath her stem almost gone as the way went off her.

'*Let go!*'

Keen crossed to the opposite side of the deck before the great anchor had hit the sea-bed.

'Awnings and winds'ls, Mr Quantock. Lively now. There are a thousand glasses on us today.'

Bolitho bit his lip. Keen was on edge. He more than anyone aboard was still brooding over the short encounter with the mystery ship.

Two men had died that day. One drowned, the other crushed under an avalanche of broken rigging and canvas. But it went deeper than that with Keen. A sailor's life was full of hazards. More men died of falls from rigging and yards, or were permanently injured in their fight against sea and wind, than under an enemy's broadside.

Keen felt it badly. In spite of his experience and un-doubted skill in battle, he felt himself to be lacking in judgement. Or perhaps it was because he was Bolitho's flag-captain which made it seem so much worse.

Bolitho had been a flag-captain more than once himself and could guess what Keen must be enduring. Once he had been grateful when his admiral had left him alone to consider his mistakes and to put them to rights. He would certainly allow Keen the same opportunity.

Achates swung easily to her cable, while on deck and gangways the hands worked like demons to sway out the boats and spread awnings in an attempt to hold the glare at bay.

Bolitho saw Knocker, the master, dismiss the helmsmen

and rub his long chin as he examined some calculations on the midshipman of the watch's slate by the compass.

He should feel pleased with himself, Bolitho thought. In spite of everything *Achates* had sailed from Hampshire to Massachusetts Bay in the record time of sixteen days. For a two-decker, repairing her wounds under way, that was no small achievement. He thought of voicing his congratulations to the unsmiling sailing-master but when he looked again he had vanished into the chart room.

Bolitho walked to the nettings and watched the boats which were already pulling slowly around the new arrival. Tanned faces, bright gowns, curious stares. Boston had seen every kind of vessel drop anchor, but not many King's ships since 'the troubles'.

He heard a step on deck and saw his nephew with a great wad of papers under one arm.

'I see you are taking your duties seriously, Adam.'

The black-haired lieutenant smiled. 'Aye, sir. I would never wish to rise higher than my present station if *this* is the reward!'

Bolitho matched his mood. They had still barely mentioned the one gesture which had drawn them even closer together. But it was there. Like a bond, something unbreakable.

In the evenings, as the ship had continued on her passage to Boston, Adam had made a point of visiting him in his quarters when Bolitho had known that the conviviality of the wardroom would have been far more in keeping for any young officer. But as day followed day Bolitho had thought of Belinda, had wondered how she was faring as her time approached. Adam had sensed his anxiety and had wanted to share it or, better still, dispel it altogether.

Bolitho knew that had he been in Keen's position the work and demands of the ship would have kept him from his private worries, but alone for long periods of time, or with only Allday or his clerk to talk to, he had too much leisure to brood on his concern for Belinda.

Now, with the ship at anchor, her work done for the present, it was at last his turn to act, to repay the confidence Sheaffe had allowed him.

Lieutenant Mountsteven, who was the officer of the watch, touched his hat and said, 'Boat approaching, sir.'

Keen nodded and looked at Bolitho. 'Visitors, sir.'

Bolitho knew it was his polite way of asking him to leave. 'I'll be in my cabin if you require me.'

Bolitho turned aft and heard the marines hurrying to the entry port, the bark of commands as *Achates* prepared to receive a greeting from the land.

Ozzard was tidying up the great cabin, although it always appeared perfect to Bolitho. He glanced at the tethered shape of one of the eighteen-pounders and was glad he had ordered its replacement. It would act as a reminder. The task he had been given was not going to be easy. He tried to stifle the bitterness. If it was a routine task, a more important officer would have been sent in his place. But if anything went wrong, they would, as always, require a scapegoat in the halls of admiralty.

He heard the calls trilling at the entry port and pictured the visitors being received with customary formality.

He walked to the open stern windows and saw a boat idling beneath *Achates'* great shadow, the passengers pointing and peering at the ship's gilded stern and counter.

It was unnerving to realize his brother had once sailed from here, had walked the streets among people like these. He had known nothing of Adam's existence then. Now Adam was here in his place. He felt a twinge of uneasiness. Perhaps he had been wrong after all to bring him, career or not.

The door opened and Adam stood watching him, a heavily sealed envelope in his hand.

He said, 'We are invited to a reception this evening, Uncle.' He held out the envelope. 'I have just been told that the President of the United States has sent one of his own senior advisers to meet you.'

Bolitho smiled wryly. 'In that case the whole world will

know what we are about, Adam. If they were expecting us it was hardly surprising we suffered that encounter just eight days out from England.'

Adam nodded. 'We seemed to have caused quite a stir.' His face broke into a grin. 'Perhaps they want to pay their taxes to King George after all!'

Bolitho shook his head. 'If you talk like that ashore, Adam, we are far more likely to start another war!'

Later, as he lay back in a chair and Allday shaved him with extra care, he tried to measure the extent of his responsibility.

The frigate *Sparrowhawk* would be on her way here shortly. Captain Duncan was less of a diplomat than he was. He would make his report to San Felipe's governor before continuing his way to Boston for orders, but would leave little doubt as to what the eventual outcome would be.

It seemed inhuman and senseless to hand the island back to the French, no matter what Sheaffe had said. It was not a question of strategy or diplomacy, it was a matter of people. The island had defended itself more than once against enemy assaults, and had sent its own vessels to seek out prizes and harass ships and islands alike in the King's name.

In London and Paris it would seem different. Now, as Allday's razor moved steadily around his throat, it took on the complexity of a Chinese puzzle.

The evening air was mercifully cooler after the oven-heat in an anchored ship, and as Bolitho climbed down into the barge he felt strangely excited. Like someone stepping into the unknown.

Allday growled, 'Give way, all.' Then with measured strokes the green-hulled boat pulled away from the main-chains and turned in a shallow arc towards the shore.

The first lieutenant had been left in charge of the ship, a bitter pill in such a pleasant looking town, Bolitho thought. He glanced at Keen who was joining him at the reception and wondered if he was feeling less strained. He had been kept busier than anyone since the anchor had been dropped, for quite apart from the ship's affairs there had been a steady stream of visitors, each of whom had been received as befitted his station. The captains of the American frigates and some of their subordinates, the officer of the guard, and an extremely pleasant young man who was the son of their host this evening.

The barge pulled strongly beneath the tapering jib-boom and Bolitho could not resist the temptation to look for some sign of the damage sustained in their short encounter. He saw nothing, a compliment to the carpenter and his crew.

He glanced at the handsome figurehead. It was pure white, with one arm outstretched, the other holding a short sword. Achates, faithful friend and armour-bearer of Aeneas.

Beneath the paint the carved wood was smooth and well-worn. It had seen more horizons than any of the ship's company and had weathered every kind of storm.

The barge swept past a lordly Indiaman which was busily loading cargo, despite the lateness of the hour. An officer hurried to her taffrail and doffed his hat as the vice-admiral's boat swept past the stern.

It was ironic that it had been a Company dispute over tea which had fanned the fires of revolution, Bolitho thought. Now, whereas men-of-war were restricted to the necessary areas of their respective flags, the powerful traders came and went as they pleased.

Allday rapped out another order and the bowman rose from his thwart, boat-hook ready to snap down on to a mooring chain.

There were plenty of townspeople thronging the jetty, and many of them had seemingly been here all day to watch the anchored *Achates*. The watermen of Boston must be making a fortune from their curious passengers.

Keen, Captain Dewar of the Royal Marines, two lieutenants and Adam Bolitho were to be the guests of an influential Boston merchant named Jonathan Chase, while some of the ship's other officers had been invited elsewhere. Keen had warned them to guard their tongues and to listen for any mention of their encounter with the strange ship which would show that the news had preceded their arrival.

Bolitho glanced at some of the young women on the jetty. A few of the trusted seamen and marines would also be allowed ashore, and from the look of these smiling girls the British sailors would be hard put to hold their tongues.

But everything must appear normal and relaxed, with all the old animosities put aside if not actually forgotten.

The bargemen tossed their oars, and Allday removed his hat and watched to make sure Bolitho did not slip on the stone stairs.

Bolitho smiled at him. 'Good crew, Allday.'

Even Allday had admitted that the new barge was a credit to the ship. In their checkered shirts and tarred hats, each man with a pigtail exactly the same length, they could not have been better chosen.

Their host's son, Timothy, was waiting beside two elegant carriages.

As Bolitho approached and some of the onlookers pressed forward for a glimpse of the newcomers, Timothy Chase extended his hand.

'You are *welcome* here, Admiral. My mother says it is a sign for the future.'

Captain Dewar climbed swiftly from the barge and the sight of his bright tunic brought a cry from the crowd.

'Watch out, boys, the redcoats are comin' back!'

But there was no hostility and more than a few guffaws from the onlookers.

The journey to the Chase residence passed all too quickly for Bolitho, with his host's son pointing out landmarks and fine houses as the carriage rattled along the road from the harbour.

He was obviously very proud of the town where he had been born and brought up. At a guess he was about the same age as Adam, although less reserved as he described each important house and its occupants.

'Boston houses, taken collectively, make a better appearance than those of any other town in New England, sir.'

Most of them were built of wood, Bolitho noticed, but some had façades which had been cut and shaped to represent stone.

Bolitho smiled to himself. His host had done well. But he knew from his secret instructions that Chase had made his original wealth from privateering against the British during the revolution.

Boston had been a privateering lair, as had many smaller harbours as far north as Portland.

The two carriages left the road and rolled up a long driveway towards a beautifully proportioned house of three storeys. Like many of the others it was white with tall green shutters by each window, some of which were already brightly lit and welcoming.

Bolitho said quietly, 'Well, Adam, what d'you think?'

Keeping his features equally composed, his nephew answered, 'I could very easily get used to luxury, sir.'

It was not hard to picture their host as he had once been on the deck of a privateer. He had a loud, thick voice which must have found its edge when shouting orders in a storm or above the crash of cannon fire. Jonathan Chase was square and heavily built, with iron-grey hair and skin like tooled leather.

'Well, Admiral, this is indeed a pleasure.' He grasped Bolitho's hand and eyed him curiously. 'An honour too, to have such a gallant sailor in my home.'

Bolitho warmed to him. 'It was good of you to offer your house for this meeting.'

Chase grinned. 'When Thomas Jefferson *suggests* a thing you don't argue too much, my friend! He may have been president for only a year, but he's learned already that power is heady medicine!' It seemed to amuse him.

Negro footmen whisked away the hats of the guests and Bolitho followed Chase into a great hall filled with people. Chase nodded towards a tray which was loaded with glasses.

'I hope the wine is to your taste, Admiral. It's French.'
Bolitho smiled gravely. 'Is it, indeed.'

Faces swam round him, and as Chase introduced his
friends and associates Bolitho became very aware of the man's
presence and authority.

Keen had been immediately partnered by two very attrac-
tive ladies, and Captain Dewar was being led out on to a
terrace by another who was clinging to his arm as if she
intended to share him with nobody.

Chase lowered his glass and studied Adam for several
seconds.

'Your aide, Admiral, what is he, son, or little brother?'

'Nephew.'

Chase beamed. 'You and I will creep away presently and
split a bottle of excellent brandy.' He tapped the side of his
nose. 'We can have a talk before our government man
arrives.'

He gestured suddenly. 'Nephew, eh. Should have
guessed.' He raised his voice. 'Over here, Robina. Someone
I'd like you to meet.'

The girl named Robina was a beautiful creature. Slim,
graceful, and with a sparkle in her eyes which would turn any
man's head.

Chase boomed, 'My niece, Admiral.'

She slipped her arm through Adam's and said, 'I'll show
you the gardens, Lieutenant.' She tossed her head at her
uncle. *'They'll* want to yarn about old times!'

Bolitho smiled. Adam was obviously entranced and
allowed himself to be led away without a word.

Chase chuckled. 'Look good together, eh?'

Then he glanced around at his chattering guests.

'I think we can go to my study now. They've forgotten we
exist.'

The great study was panelled and like a part of America's
young history. Chase had collected many relics of the sea and
ships, symbols perhaps of his own stormy beginnings.

Whales' teeth and a harpoon were just a small part. 'To

remind me of the old days here.' Paintings of battles, with a British ship on fire in the process of surrendering.

Chase said cheerfully, 'You didn't win all the fights at sea, y'know, Admiral.' He became suddenly serious. 'Samuel Fane, the President's emissary, is a hard bargainer. I like him well enough, for a government man that is, but he hates the British.' He grinned hugely. 'Thought you should know, though from all I've read and heard about you, you're more than able to take care of yourself.'

Bolitho smiled. 'I appreciate your frankness.'

Chase slopped some brandy into two enormous glasses.

'Think nothing of it. I fought against King George and I was good at the trade. But peace, like war, makes strange bedfellows. You accept that or capsize in the world *we* live in.'

In the gardens at the rear of the big house the trees and shrubs were already deep in purple shadow. Adam walked arm in arm with the girl, barely daring to speak in case he said something clumsy and spoiled the moment forever. She was without doubt the most beautiful being he had ever laid eyes on.

She stopped and, seizing his hands in hers, swung him round to face her.

'Now, *come along*, Lieutenant, I have done too much talking. They say I chatter so. I want to know all about you. Your name is Adam and you are the admiral's aide. Tell me more.'

Surprisingly, Adam found it easy to speak with her. As they strolled through the shadows he told her of his life as a sea officer, of his home in Cornwall, and all the while he was very conscious of her hand through his arm.

She said suddenly, 'You are the admiral's nephew, Adam?'

Even the way she spoke his name was like pure music. 'Yes.'

She said, 'I do not live in Boston. My family is in Newburyport, some thirty miles north from here. It's strange, I hadn't thought of it before. My father sometimes speaks of a man who used to live in our town. His name was Bolitho too.'

Adam tried to think clearly. 'In Newburyport?'

'Yes.' She squeezed his arm. 'You sound as if you have remembered something.'

He looked at her and wanted to hold her.

'I think it must have been my father.'

She was about to laugh when she realized the seriousness of his tone, the importance of this discovery.

'My uncle says that your ship will be in Boston for weeks. You shall come to Newburyport and meet my family.' She reached up and touched his cheek with her gloved fingers. 'Do not be sad, Adam. If you have a secret, I can share it with you. But tell me only when you want to.'

'I want to.' He found that he meant it with all his heart.

From the study window Bolitho saw them cross the terrace and was moved.

It was time Adam found some enjoyment, even for a fleeting moment. He had known nothing but war and the hard life in King's ships since he had walked all that way from Penzance to find his place in the Bolitho family. Bolitho could picture him exactly. A thin, frightened boy, and yet with the defiant restlessness of a young colt. He thought he heard the girl named Robina laugh. Yes, he was glad for Adam's sake.

A footman opened the double doors of the library and a tall figure in a bottle-green coat and white stockings strode into the study.

Chase said quickly, 'This here is Samuel Fane from the capital.'

Fane had a narrower face with all the animation contained in a pair of deepset eyes which crowded against a strong, beak-like nose.

'Vice-Admiral Bolitho.' He nodded a greeting. 'Well, let's get down to business.'

Bolitho let his arm fall to his side. Maybe Fane did not like shaking hands with an old enemy. But it was a snub, intended or not.

Curiously, it made him feel calmer in some strange way.

Like fighting a duel. When you accept there is no easy way out after all.

Fane said in the same flat voice, 'San Felipe. Now, could you please explain to me, Admiral, how it is that your government thinks it has the right to take or give away people and territory as if they were of no consequence? By what *right*?'

Chase said uneasily, 'Calm down, Sam. You know it is not like that.'

'Do I?' The deepset eyes had not moved from Bolitho.

Bolitho said, 'It was agreed at the peace conference.' He smiled gently. 'As I am sure you are aware. May I assume that the French government has already spoken to yours about it?'

Chase interrupted angrily. 'Course they did. Tell him, Sam, and get down off your high horse. The war's over, remember?'

Fane regarded him coldly. 'I am constantly reminded of it when I see how some have grown rich on the blood of others.'

Bolitho saw the sparks in Chase's eyes and said, 'I thought the French were still your friends?'

Fane shrugged. 'Once, and in the future mebbee. But on San Felipe, across the southern approaches, that's different.'

Bolitho said, 'The people on San Felipe are British subjects.'

Chase grinned. 'So were most of us. Once.'

Fane did not hear him. 'Some while ago I received a despatch from the governor of San Felipe. He was worried, naturally, at the British government's intransigence. He has no desire to accept the choice given him, that is to leave a prospering island to the French or to remain there under a foreign flag.'

'I can understand that.'

'Can you, Admiral? That encourages me a little. However, the United States government is not prepared to stand by and allow human beings to be used for barter like cattle in an African slave village.'

Bolitho found that he was on his feet, his voice angry as he retorted, 'Then there is no point in my wasting your time, Mr Fane, or mine!'

Chase said quickly, 'Easy, you two! Blazes, Sam, the admiral is my guest. I'll not have you brawling like a pair of hell-cats!'

Fane relented slightly. 'It will have to be a compromise.'

Bolitho sat down again. 'In what fashion?'

'Our government would be prepared to accept San Felipe's request to come under the United States' protection.'

'That's impossible.'

'If the French agree, Admiral, would *you*?'

Bolitho glanced at Chase but he was staring at the whales' teeth.

He knew too. They all did. It was not a compromise at all. It was blackmail.

He tried to keep his voice calm. 'The governor had no authority to make such a request, from you or anyone else. We are caught in the tragedy of history. There is nothing we can do about it.'

Fane regarded him bleakly. 'We shall see.'

He added, 'Your flagship has the extended courtesy of my government. This matter cannot be settled in minutes. We must think on it further.'

Bolitho nodded. Fane had been testing him, goading him, for reasons he could still only guess at.

He could not resist saying, 'Your government has also extended a welcome to another of my ships, Mr Fane. The *Sparrowhawk*. She will be joining me shortly.'

Fane grunted. 'Yes. I know.' He thrust his hands beneath his coat tails and added, 'I must leave now.' He gave a curt nod. 'Admiral.'

Chase left the room with him and Bolitho walked to the window again. But where the young lieutenant and the fair-haired girl had been walking was all in darkness.

Bolitho turned to face the doors as he heard Chase's heavy footsteps returning.

In many ways it was harder than fighting a battle, he thought. And far less rewarding.

5

'There may be thunder . . .'

The weeks which followed the reception at Chase's fine house
taxed Bolitho to the limit. Jonathan Chase and several other
wealthy Bostonians took it upon themselves to make them
welcome, and nightly entertainment of one kind or another
had become a regular feature for *Achates'* wardroom.

And yet Bolitho was plagued by the idea that the lack of
news and assistance by the President's representative, Samuel
Fane, were linked in some way.

Perhaps he should have ignored the outline of his orders
and proceeded first to San Felipe without entrusting the
opening move to Captain Duncan in the *Sparrowhawk*. But
had he done so his action might have been construed as
arrogance or worse.

And where was *Sparrowhawk*? What had Duncan found
so important that he had delayed joining him here at
Boston?

On this particular day Bolitho had been unable to touch
his midday meal at all. The meat and bread were fresh,
brought off shore by one of Chase's own boats, yet he could
not face it.

Around and above him the ship was resting in the swelter-
ing heat, and there was the usual heady smell of rum as each
mess issued its ration for the day.

Maybe Sheaffe had known it would all be a waste of time
which might end in disagreement with the Americans.

He tugged the shirt away from his skin. It felt like a wet
rag. He made himself remain in his chair, knowing he would

only begin to pace about the cabin like a caged lion if he did not.

Belinda. He twisted round in the chair and stared through the stern windows until his eyes watered. It would be over by now. They would have a child, unless . . .

Suppose something had gone wrong? It was her first time. Anything might happen.

He saw the distant houses move into view as *Achates* swung indifferently to her cable. It would be better to get to sea again. To *do* something.

There was a light tap at the screen door and Keen entered, his eyes moving quickly to the untouched plate on Bolitho's table.

'The American frigates are shortening their cables, sir.'

Bolitho nodded. 'Yes. Only the French will be here now.'

Keen said, 'In my opinion, sir, we should have another vessel attached to us for communications.'

'You've been thinking about Duncan's *Sparrowhawk* too?'

Keen shrugged. 'Well, yes, as a matter of fact. Without even a brig in company we are deaf and dumb to everything beyond the harbour limits.'

Yovell, the clerk, hovered in the doorway. 'Beg pardon, zur, there are some papers for yew to sign.'

Bolitho thought suddenly of his nephew. Adam had asked permission to escort Chase's niece to her home in Newburyport. He could envy him his freedom from the endless waiting and the uncertainty. Bolitho knew he had been poor company and he had even exploded over one of Allday's comments. He had immediately relented. It was not Allday's fault. It was not anybody's.

Bolitho read swiftly through Yovell's handwriting and then put his signature at the bottom. No wonder they said the Admiralty was crammed with written reports. Did anyone ever read them? he wondered.

He said abruptly, 'I shall try once more to discuss the matter of San Felipe with the Americans, after that I shall be pleased to sail for the island, *Sparrowhawk* or not. You might

send word privately to Antigua if you can discover a ship's
master for the task. The admiral at English Harbour should
be told what we are about. If I add a line to your despatch we
might even worm a brig out of his command, eh?'

Ozzard entered and removed the tray with nothing but a
reproachful glance to reveal what he thought about it.

Keen said, 'You don't think the Americans would interfere
with our affairs, sir?'

'Those frigates, you mean?' Bolitho shook his head. 'It
would be unwise. They may voice their displeasure, but
they're more likely to remain on the fence as spectators.'

The first lieutenant appeared at the screen door, his head
stooped beneath the deckhead beams.

'Your pardon, sir, but Mr Chase's launch is approaching.
He has the *other* gentleman with him.'

Bolitho and Keen exchanged glances.

Bolitho said quietly, 'Fane, the President's emissary, at
long last. Now perhaps we can settle the matter.'

Keen picked up his hat and grinned. 'Full guard of honour, Mr Quantock. If there is to be a squall, it will not be of
our making!'

Allday padded from the adjoining cabin and glanced at the
sword rack, then with a slight hesitation he took down the
brightly gilded presentation blade which had been given to
Bolitho after the Battle of the Nile.

He gave the old sword a pat and murmured, 'You rest
easy.'

Bolitho allowed him to clip the glittering presentation
sword to his belt.

The old family sword was for fighting. This was a time for
diplomacy.

Some twelve hundred miles south of where Bolitho contained
his impatience and waited to receive Mr Samuel Fane, His
Britannic Majesty's frigate *Sparrowhawk* of twenty-six guns
was becalmed in blinding sunlight. Two of her boats moved

sluggishly on tow-lines ahead of their parent ship, more to
give her steerage-way than with any hope of finding a wind.

It had been like this for three whole days since the frigate
had weighed anchor in San Felipe, her mission there only
partially completed.

In his cabin Captain James Duncan sat at a table, his face
set in a frown, as he added another paragraph to an already
lengthy letter. It was to his wife and, like most married sea
officers, Duncan continued each letter with the same regular-
ity as a personal log. He did not know when the letter would
be completed, even less when he would be able to pass it to
some home-bound vessel so that his wife would eventually
read it in their Dorset home.

Duncan, for all his bluff ways, was very soft where his wife
was concerned. They had been married for only two years,
and he had been with her in that time for less than a month.
He had no regrets, it was part of the sacrifice you had to make
if you intended the Navy as a career. Duncan was a post-
captain and had only just passed his twenty-seventh birth-
day. If he held this command under Bolitho there would be
no stopping him, even in a time of uneasy peace.

Like many of his contemporaries, Duncan had little faith
in a lasting peace. He had distinguished himself in three
major battles and had been extremely successful in other
ship-to-ship engagements where the cut and thrust of every
good frigate captain showed its worth.

He admired Bolitho tremendously, not merely for his
courage and skill—that Duncan could take for granted—but for
his true interest in those who served him. Although he would
never admit it, Duncan tried to model himself on Bolitho.

That was the main reason for his frown. His visit to San
Felipe had not been a success. The governor, Sir Humphrey
Rivers, had treated him more as a stupid subordinate than the
captain of a King's ship and Bolitho's own representative.

Duncan knew all about ships and the sea, but he had no
knowledge at all of men like Rivers.

Rivers had lost his temper at their first meeting. In his

impressive house which nestled comfortably amidst a great plantation, Rivers had shouted, 'There's a graveyard by the harbour, Captain! Full of good men who have fought for this island. I'll not betray their trust by handing over everything to the French. Damn your eyes if I shall!'

Duncan secretly agreed with him, but he was used to obeying orders. In any case, he did not like the man, and thought him an arrogant pig.

Bolitho would not thank him for bringing him such empty news. If Rivers refused to comply with the agreed terms he might find himself charged with treason, or an act of mutiny, or whatever governors were disciplined by. Duncan frowned more deeply and put his pen to paper again.

The deck gave a shudder and a pair of brass dividers clattered from another table.

Duncan lurched to his feet as the ship slowly came to life beneath him.

He hurried on deck and found his first lieutenant and sailing-master staring up at the limp canvas as very gently a breeze pushed against the rigging.

Duncan dashed the sweat from his eyes. It was not much, but . . .

'Mr Palmer! Recall those boats and hoist 'em inboard. Pipe all hands.' He clapped the lieutenant on the shoulder and added, 'God damn it, Mr Palmer, maybe we've seen the last of this place, eh?'

He crossed to the side and grasped the sun-heated rail with his powerful hands. He saw the first boat cast off the tow and pull gratefully towards the ship, its sunburned oarsmen almost too weary to make the effort.

Duncan wondered how the other ship was faring. They had sighted her just before both vessels had been becalmed in the stifling heat.

The first lieutenant returned as the hands swarmed up to man halliards and braces.

He said, 'The masthead reported that our shy companion was still with us at eight bells, sir.'

To confirm it the lookout's voice made several of the seamen look up at his lofty perch.

'Deck thar! Ship on th' weather-bow! She's settin' 'er t'gan's'ls!'

Duncan grunted and turned to watch his own ship lean slightly to the mounting pressure. The second boat was being swayed up and over the gangway. His *Sparrowhawk* was moving again.

The sailing-master said, 'She'll be on a converging tack with us, sir.'

'Put a good man to watch her.'

Duncan pushed the sudden anxiety from his thoughts. For a small moment he had thought it might be *Achates*, Bolitho coming to look for him, to discover the meaning of the delay.

Blocks clattered and lines snaked through the sheaves as slowly, and then more confidently, *Sparrowhawk* responded to the pressure in her sails.

'North by west, sir! Full an' bye!'

Duncan rubbed his reddened face and waited for the sails to fill again. It was not much, but enough to make her thrust through the water. Even the tiny island which had shown itself on the horizon had dipped over the sea's rim before the master had identified it. Probably one of the islets of the Bahama chain, Duncan thought.

There were some little ones off San Felipe too. One even had a strange mission church on it, and he had been told that some monks existed there, entirely cut off from everything.

San Felipe had originally been Spanish, so it seemed likely that the monks were the last survivors of that occupation.

Duncan felt in better spirits. He had, after all, done what he had been ordered to do. Bolitho would know how to interpret what he had seen and heard.

'I'm going below, Mr Palmer. I've a letter to finish. Who knows, I may be able to send it off sooner than I thought!'

Palmer smiled. When the captain was in good humour the ship was always a better place.

As the wind continued to fill the sails, and froth gurgled

around the bows, the other ship grew larger while she continued purposefully on a converging tack.

Too large for a frigate, Palmer thought, as he clung to the weather shrouds and trained his telescope on her. She was shining in the bright glare, her chequered gun-ports almost awash as she found the wind which had not yet reached *Sparrowhawk*.

West Indiaman probably, he decided. They were as smart as paint these days. It was said that a grocery captain could earn as much on one passage as would take ten years in the Navy.

'She's hoisted a signal, sir!'

'I can see that, dammit!' Palmer was tired from standing so long in the heat, praying for a wind. It put an edge to his voice which was unusual for him.

The signals midshipman swallowed hard and levelled his big glass on the other vessel, his face screwed up with concentration as he held the lens on the brightly coloured flags at her yard.

'She wishes to speak with us, sir!'

The first lieutenant swore under his breath. It was probably of no importance at all, and to heave to while they exchanged useless information might mean losing the wind again.

He snapped, 'Acknowledge the signal, Mr Clements.' He beckoned to the midshipman of the watch. 'My respects to the captain, Mr Evans. Tell him we shall have to heave to.'

Palmer swung away. The captain's good mood would vanish now.

Duncan, his shirt open to his waist, strode from the companion-way and eyed the other vessel without comment. She could have important news which had a bearing on their mission. Her master might just as easily be eager to exchange gossip. Two ships meeting far from home were all that was required.

'Shorten sail, Mr Palmer. Stand by to come about.'

He clasped his hands behind him and watched his men scamper to their stations.

'Put the helm down!'

Duncan beckoned to the midshipman. 'Glass, Mr Evans.'

He took the telescope from the boy's hand and glanced at him as he did so. Midshipman Evans was thirteen, the youngest in *Sparrowhawk*'s gun-room. A likeable youth, who had been mastheaded more than once since leaving England for his practical jokes.

Duncan levelled the glass and braced his legs as the ship heeled violently in a trough and the men up forward loosed the head-sail sheets to allow *Sparrowhawk* to swing through the eye of the wind. To a landsman the ship would appear in confusion, with rippling sails and clattering rigging, but in a moment or so she would come round on the opposite tack and reduce sail even more.

Duncan smiled grimly. He liked his ship to be handled firmly, like a strong-willed horse.

He stiffened as the other ship swam hugely into the lens. Her yards were swinging, her sails filling like metal breast-plates as she changed tack, not into the wind, but to starboard, and as her fore-course thundered out from its yard she seemed to lean forward as she swept down across the frigate's stern.

Duncan yelled, '*Belay that order*, Mr Palmer! Bring her about again!'

Men tumbled in confusion and braces and halliards squealed through the blocks and more hands threw themselves among their companions to try and haul the yards round.

Duncan reeled as his ship tried to respond, but she was nearly aback, the sails billowing and cracking against the masts and shrouds.

'*Beat to quarters!*'

Duncan stared wildly at the other ship, his skin like ice despite the sun's heat. *He should have seen it*. Now it was already too late, and even as he stared he saw the other vessel's gun-ports open, the black muzzles poking out into the sunlight, while his own startled marine drummers started the staccato beat which brought more men pouring up from between decks, some still unaware of the danger.

Duncan made himself face the regular flashes along the other vessel's side, the darting orange tongues and rolling bank of smoke. Then in seconds a torrent of iron smashed into the frigate's hull and above the deck, tearing down rigging and spars, punching holes in the flapping canvas, and worse, ploughing through the stern to turn the crowded gun-deck into a bloody shambles.

Duncan clung to the nettings, bellowing like a wounded bull as a ball slammed into one of the quarterdeck guns and flung splinters across the planking, cutting down men and daubing scarlet patterns to mark where they fell.

He felt a blow in his side like the blade of an axe, and when he looked he saw blood pumping down his leg, and when the pain came he could hear himself moaning with agony.

A great shadow swept over him, and with a thundering roar the mizzen-mast and rigging crashed over the side carrying seamen and marines with them.

More violent shocks battered at the hull like iron rams, and Duncan had to hold on to the nettings to prevent himself from falling. Their attacker was following them round, her sails rising above the smoke like the wings of hell itself. She was firing without a break, and still not one of *Sparrowhawk*'s guns had been loaded. Men lay dead and dying everywhere, and when he peered at the helm Duncan saw that the wheel was in fragments, the master and his helmsmen scattered by the fury of the bombardment.

'Mr Palmer!'

His cry was less than a croak. But the first lieutenant was on his knees by the rail, his mouth like a black hole as he screamed silently at his hands which lay before him like torn gloves.

Duncan fell down as more great crashes rocked the hull. He could hear the balls slamming through the deck below and saw smoke rising from an open hatch. *She was on fire*.

He tried to stand, his rage and his despair making him

terrible to see. He had fallen in his own blood, and he could feel the strength running away to match the terrible patterns on the deck around him.

'Let me help, sir!'

Duncan thrust his arm around the boy's shoulders. It was little Evans, and the realization helped to steady him.

He gasped, 'Done for, boy. See to the others.' He felt the midshipman shudder and saw the fear bright in his eyes. He gripped him more tightly with his bloody arm. 'Stand to, boy, you're a King's officer today. Get them – ' Then he fell and this time he did not rise.

A few seamen and marines ran aft and would have flung themselves into the sea astern but for the thirteen-year-old midshipman.

He shouted, 'Quarter-boat! Bosun's mate, take charge there!'

When one tried to knock him aside he snatched a pistol and fired it above their heads. For a moment longer they stared at each other like madmen, then, obedient to their training, they tossed their weapons aside and ran to haul the quarter-boat alongside.

A few shots were still hitting the hull, but *Sparrowhawk* had no fight left in her. She was settling down, the sea exploring the orlop and reaching up further still so that there was a glint of water below the companion.

Evans ran to aid his friend, the signals midshipman, but he was already dead, a hole in his chest big enough for a man's fist.

Evans stood up very carefully, his feet sliding in blood as the stern began to go under.

He thought he heard one of the other boats nearby, the third lieutenant trying to restore order and rally the survivors.

He looked at his dead captain, a man he had feared and admired. Now he was nothing, and Evans felt unnerved by it, cheated.

A burly marine, one of his comrades over his shoulder like

a sack, paused and gasped, 'Come along, sir. Nothin' 'ere now.'

The wounded man groaned and the one who was carrying him peered round, looking for a boat. But something in Evans' face held him there like a shouted command on the square. The marine had been at St Vincent and the Nile, and had seen many of his friends die like this.

He said roughly, 'You've done yer best, so come along er me, eh?'

The hull gave a great shiver. She was going.

The midshipman walked with the marine and did not even blink as the foremast thundered down like a falling cliff.

'I'm ready, thank you.' It seemed little enough comment for such a terrible moment.

As guns tore themselves loose from their lashings and crashed along the deck among the corpses and whimpering wounded, *Sparrowhawk* lifted her bows and dived steeply. The whirlpool of swirling wreckage, men and pieces of men remained for a long time, long enough for their attacker to make more sail and alter course to the westward.

There were two boats and a roughly lashed raft left as evidence of what had happened, with survivors floundering in search of a handhold or a place in one of them.

A week later, the American brig *Baltimore Lady*, on passage from Guadeloupe to New York, sighted one drifting boat and hove to to investigate. The boat was filled with sun-blackened men, some dead, apparently from wounds or burns, others barely able to speak. Deep score marks on the boat's planking showed where sharks had torn others from their handholds alongside. There was an officer of sorts in charge of the boat. The brig's mate later described him as 'less'n a boy'.

Midshipman Evans had obeyed Duncan's order, '*See to the others.*'

It was something he would remember for the rest of his life.

*

Samuel Fane regarded Bolitho without emotion as he said, 'I have spoken with the President and have also discussed the matter of San Felipe with the French admiral.'

Bolitho watched him calmly. There was no point in attacking Fane for going behind his back and speaking with the French flag-officer. He had every right to, if Boston was to be a neutral ground for the discussions.

Also, being aboard his own flagship made more of a difference than he would have expected. Ashore in Chase's fine house he was the stranger. Here in *Achates*, with familiar faces and sounds all around him, he felt assured and confident.

He said, 'No steps can be taken until I receive the report from my frigate captain. A compromise may be worked out, but only under the present conditions. Sir Humphrey Rivers is the British Governor of San Felipe, but nothing more than that.'

Jonathan Chase, who had swallowed two glasses of claret in his anxiety that it should be a better meeting than the previous one, exclaimed, 'No harm in that, eh, Sam?'

Fane's deepset eyes settled on him only briefly.

'Our government will not tolerate a war, large or small, where it might endanger United States' trade and progress. It makes more sense to me that the island should come under *our* protection, if that is the will of the people there.'

He gave a deep sigh. 'But if the admiral wishes to show his authority *first*, then I suppose we must indulge him.'

Chase held out his glass for Ozzard to refill.

'God damn it, Sam, do you never relax?'

Fane smiled wryly. 'Hardly at all.'

Feet moved on the deck overhead, and Bolitho heard a voice calling an order. It was his world. This sort of double-tongue was alien to him.

He stood up and walked to the stern windows. There was a slow, hot wind across Massachusetts Bay and the sky was slashed by thin, pink clouds. How inviting the sea looked.

Fane was saying, 'It might take a few months to settle, but

what of that? The French will not insist on immediate occupation of the island. It will give all of us time.'

Bolitho suddenly saw a naval brig turning into the wind, her anchor splashing down even as her sails were smartly furled at their yards. The ensign which licked out from her gaff was the same as the one at *Achates'* taffrail.

He replied, 'His Majesty's Government has entrusted me with the task of handing over the island, sir. None of us wants an uprising, especially now that the West Indies are recovering from the war.'

A boat had been dropped from the brig and was already speeding across the water towards the flagship.

Bolitho felt a nerve jump in his throat. What was it? News from home already, could it be . . . ?'

He forced himself to face the others, his eyes almost blind in the cabin's shady interior.

'I shall send a letter to your President. I appreciate very much what he is trying to do – ' He broke off and turned sharply as Ozzard murmured, 'It's the captain, sir.'

Keen stood in the doorway, his hat jammed beneath his arm.

'Please forgive this interruption, sir.' He glanced at the others. 'The commander of the brig *Electra* is come aboard. He has news for you, sir.' His eyes were pleading. 'Very serious news.'

Bolitho nodded. 'I'll not be long, gentlemen.'

He followed Keen from the cabin and saw a young officer waiting by the chart room.

Keen said tightly, 'This is Commander Napier, sir.'

Bolitho looked at him impassively. 'Tell me.'

Napier swallowed hard. *Electra* was his first command, and he had never spoken with a vice-admiral before.

'I was on passage to the south'rd when I sighted an American brig. She signalled for assistance, and when I boarded her I found her to be carrying British seamen.' He flinched under Bolitho's gaze. 'They were survivors.'

Bolitho saw Keen's face, he looked pale in spite of the sun.

The commander added quietly, 'From *Sparrowhawk*, sir.'

Bolitho clenched his hands together behind him to control his sense of shock. In his heart he had nursed a dread that something had happened to the little frigate. A storm, a reef, or one of a dozen disasters which can befall a ship sailing alone.

Napier continued, 'She was attacked, sir. A two-decker to all accounts, although — '

Bolitho could see it as if he had been there himself. Just as their attacker had fired on *Achates*. Without warning, except that this time her victim had been hopelessly outgunned even if Duncan had been expecting trouble.

'How many?'

Again the young commander could barely speak above a murmur.

'Twenty-five, sir, and some of those are in a poor way.'

Bolitho felt his skin go cold. Twenty-five, out of a company which had numbered two hundred souls.

'Any officers?' He barely recognized his own voice.

'None, sir. Just a midshipman. First commission too.'

Bolitho eyed him bitterly. Duncan had perished with his ship. He could picture him without effort. Duncan had even been to his wedding at Falmouth. A good man, strong and reliable.

It was impossible. A nightmare.

The commander took his silence for displeasure and hurried on, 'The midshipman said that the third lieutenant was in another boat but was badly wounded in the face and neck by splinters. During the night the boats drifted apart, and then the sharks came.' He looked at the deck.

'Bring the midshipman to me.' He saw his hesitation. 'Is he wounded?'

'No, sir.'

Keen said shortly, 'See to it.'

As the commander hurried away Bolitho said, 'Send word to my flag-lieutenant. He must return at once. Fast horse, anything.'

Keen stared at him. 'It *was* the same ship, wasn't it, sir?'

'I'm certain of it.' He eyed him steadily. 'Ask the surgeon to help with the wounded. The rest of *Sparrowhawk*'s people can be signed on to your books. I want them to be with us when we run that butcher to earth!'

Bolitho strode aft to the cabin. He knew he must look different in some way. Chase had a glass poised in the air, Ozzard was frozen in the act of refilling it. Fane's eyes followed him to the stern windows before he asked, 'Bad news, Admiral?'

Bolitho looked at him and tried to fight the sudden all-consuming anger which coursed through him like fire.

'I am leaving harbour as soon as all my people are aboard.'

Chase shifted in his chair as if to see him better.

'Not waiting for your frigate after all?'

Bolitho shook his head.

'I'm heartily sick of waiting.'

He saw the brig's boat going alongside again. It was cruel to send for the young midshipman after what he had endured. But he had to know everything the boy could tell him.

He said quietly, '*Sparrowhawk*'s been sunk.'

He heard Chase's quick intake of breath.

Bolitho added, 'So you see, gentlemen, there may be thunder before we can settle things to *everyone's* satisfaction.'

6

No Easy Way

Captain Valentine Keen sat with legs crossed on one of Bolitho's chairs and watched his superior as he read through a despatch for the Admiralty. It would be put aboard the brig *Electra* and eventually be transferred to a fleet-courier so that it would be completely out-of-date by the time Admiral Sheaffe was able to examine it.

Keen glanced through the open stern windows and silently cursed the oppressive heat. It seemed to pin the whole ship down so that even the smallest movement was uncomfortable.

Bolitho signed the last page where Yovell had indicated and looked questioningly at his flag-captain.

'Well, Val, are we ready for sea?'

Keen nodded and instantly felt a trickle of sweat run down his spine.

'The water-lighters have cast off, sir. There's just your — '

Bolitho stood up as if pricked by a thorn and strode to the windows.

'My nephew. He should be back on board by now.'

He was thinking aloud. The ship was waiting to weigh anchor. Boats were hoisted, and all hands accounted for. He stared hard at the little brig which had brought the news of *Sparrowhawk*'s loss. Napier, her young commander, would be glad to rid himself of his responsibility to an admiral other than his own. His tiny command would soon be free of Bolitho and hurrying to Antigua to pass the news of the mysterious assassin, the ship which bore no name and showed no colours. Bolitho would have given a lot to hold on to the *Electra*, but the need to spread the word of the unknown attacker was paramount. Other ships might be lost in the same fashion.

Keen watched the emotions as they chased each other across Bolitho's features. They had seen and done so much together in every kind of action. Now, supposedly in peacetime, they were faced with something which was both baffling and terrible.

Feet thudded overhead, and calls trilled as the watch on deck was ordered to some new task under the first lieutenant's eye.

Bolitho did not see Keen's sympathetic scrutiny. His mind kept swinging from tack to tack, as if he was imprisoned by his own thoughts. Wait in Boston or set sail for San Felipe? It was his decision alone, just as his decision had cost Duncan his life. Keen had spoken with the one surviving midshipman, Evans, but had got little out of him. Bolitho had asked Allday to speak with the boy in his own way and the result had been startling. Allday had that casual, effortless way of talking to people, especially youngsters like Evans, and as he had described what Evans had told him Bolitho had been able to relive that brief, savage encounter which had ended with *Sparrowhawk*'s total destruction.

It was a wonder a boy like Evans had not collapsed completely, Bolitho thought. It was not like going to war with the fear of death a constant companion. It was Evans' very first commission, his only voyage in a man-of-war. He did not even come from a naval family but was the son of a tailor in Cardiff.

To see his best friend, a fellow midshipman, smashed down like a slaughtered animal, to be the last one to speak with the mortally wounded Duncan while the ship exploded around him was more than most could have withstood. Perhaps later, months later, the shock would show itself.

Allday had explained how Evans had sensed an explosion even as his boat had pulled away from the sinking frigate.

The gallery fire had not been doused. Flames had probably spread to the magazine or powder-room, so that for many of the ship's company the end had been quick and the horror of the sharks held back for the others.

Another of the survivors, an experienced gunner's mate, had told Allday that the cannon fire had sounded flatter and louder than he would have expected. She was carrying far heavier weapons, he thought, even though the numbers had been reduced.

Bolitho glanced at the eighteen-pounder near his desk. Probably thirty-two-pounders. But *why*?

The door opened cautiously and the clerk, Yovell, peered in at them.

Bolitho said, 'Despatches are ready to go.'

What did they matter anyway? He knew it, and so did Keen. Words, words, words. The facts were plain as they were brutal. He had lost a fine ship with most of her people. And there was Duncan and his pretty widow. He had been a good friend. A brave officer.

Yovell remained hovering in the screen doorway.

'There is a mail-packet coming to anchor, sir.' He hesitated. 'From England.'

Bolitho stared at him and was shocked to see the anxiety on Yovell's round features.

My God, he's afraid of me. The shock hit him like a fist. He's terrified because there may be no word from Belinda.

The realization did more to steady his apprehension and doubts than anything. He recalled how only yesterday, as he had waited for Adam to return on board, Yovell had said something to put him at ease. Bolitho had exploded and had cursed him roundly for his interfering. Yet Bolitho had always hated martinets who used their rank and authority to terrorize their subordinates. And it was all too easy. A captain was like a god, so an admiral could do no wrong at all in his own eyes.

He said, 'Thank you, Yovell. Take the quarter-boat and pass my despatches to the *Electra*. Also any letters from our people.' He watched the man's uncertainty and added, 'Then go over to the mail-packet, will you? There may be something, eh?'

As the clerk made to leave he said quietly, 'I treated you badly. There was no cause for that. Loyalty deserves a whole lot better.'

Keen watched the clerk's wariness change to gratitude, and as the door closed he said, 'That was good of you, sir.'

Bolitho made himself sit down and tugged his shirt free from his moist skin.

'I have been hard on you too, Val. I apologize.'

Keen gauged the moment and said, 'As your flag-captain, I have the freedom to suggest and warn if the occasion arises.'

'You do.' Bolitho smiled grimly. 'Thomas Herrick was quick to use that freedom, so speak your mind.'

Keen shrugged. 'You are beset from every side, sir. The French will not discuss San Felipe with you, nor do they need to as our two governments have signed an agreement on its future. The Americans do not wish to have the French on their doorstep as it could make their own strategy difficult in any future conflict. The governor of the island will fight you all the way, and I suspect that Admiral Sheaffe knew that from the beginning. So why should *we* worry? If the governor refuses to submit we can arrest him and put him in irons.' His tone hardened. 'Too many men have died to make his position count. Better we take command of the island than to leave its future with him. He probably craves independence from the Crown and will play one faction against the other if we allow it.'

Bolitho smiled. 'I have thought of that. But *Sparrowhawk's* loss and the unwarranted attack on this ship do not fit the pattern. That ship was Spanish-built, if I'm any judge, and yet His Most Catholic Majesty has voiced no protest about San Felipe. So we either have an attempted coup in the offing or piracy on the grand scale. Hell's teeth, Val, after all these years of war there would be plenty with the experience and the desperation to play for such high odds.'

Keen placed his fingertips together. 'And I know you are deeply concerned for your wife, sir.' He watched, waiting to see Bolitho's grey eyes give a flash of danger. 'The waiting has been hard on you, especially after your experiences as a prisoner of war.'

A boat pulled below the counter and Bolitho strode to the windows to examine her passengers. But they were only a few sight-seers, a local trader or two still trying to bargain with the sailors on the upper deck.

Adam was not here.

Keen read his thoughts and said, 'He is young, sir. Maybe it was a wrong choice to appoint him flag-lieutenant.'

Bolitho swung on him hotly. 'Did Browne say as much?'

Keen shook his head. 'I formed my own opinion. Your nephew is a fine young man, and I have nothing but affection for him. You have watched over him from the beginning, treated him like a son.'

Bolitho faced him again. He had no fight left. 'Was that wrong too?'

Keen smiled sadly. 'Certainly not, sir.'

Bolitho walked past his chair and rested his hand momentarily on the young captain's shoulder.

'But you are so right. I did not accept it because I did not wish to.' He waved down Keen's protest. 'I never saw Adam's mother, nobody did. The one good thing she ever did was to send him across the country to Falmouth, to me. But you were correct about me. I love him like a son, but he is *not* my son. His father was Hugh, my brother. Maybe there is too much of Hugh in him — '

Keen stood up quickly. 'Let it stop there, sir. You are tiring yourself to no good purpose. We all look to you. I believe we are in for trouble. I do not think we would have been sent otherwise.'

Bolitho poured two glasses of claret and handed one to Keen.

'You are a good flag-captain, Val. It took courage to say that. And it is true. Personal feelings do not come into it.

Later maybe, but now the slightest anxiety may transmit itself through this ship.' He held the glass to the sunlight. 'And *Old Katie* will have enough to contend with. She can manage without an admiral who is so wrapped up in his own troubles he can think of nothing else.'

There was a nervous tap at the door and Yovell entered, his eyes fixed on Bolitho.

Keen looked away, unable to watch as Bolitho took the single letter from his clerk's hand.

He wanted to leave but, like the clerk, was unwilling to snap the spell.

Bolitho read the short letter and then folded it with great care.

'Get the ship under way, if you please. The wind will suffice to clear the harbour.'

He met Keen's even stare.

'The letter is from my sister in Falmouth. My wife . . . ' His lips hesitated on her name as if they were afraid. 'Belinda is not well. The letter was written some time ago for the packet made another landfall before Boston. But she knew that the packet was sailing. And she wanted to let me know she was thinking of me.' He turned away, his eyes suddenly stinging. 'Even though she was too ill to write.'

Keen looked at Yovell's stricken face and gave a quick jerk of the head.

When the clerk had gone he said gently, 'It was what I would expect her to do, sir. And that is how you must see it.'

Bolitho looked at him and then nodded. 'Thank you, Val. Please leave me now. I shall come up directly.'

Keen walked through the adjoining cabin space and past the motionless marine sentry at the outer screen door.

Herrick would have known what to do. He felt helpless and yet deeply moved that Bolitho had shared his despair with him.

He saw Allday beside an eighteen-pounder and gestured to him.

Allday listened to him and then gave a great sigh. It seemed to come from the soles of his shoes, Keen thought.

Then Allday said, 'I'll go aft, sir. He needs a friend just now.' His face tried to grin. 'He'll no doubt take me to task for my impertinence, but what the hell? He'll crack like a faulty musket barrel if we allows it, an' that's no error.'

Keen strode out into the noon sunlight, adjusting his hat as his lieutenants and the master turned to face him.

'Stand by to get under way, Mr Quantock. I want to see your best today with half the port watching us.'

As the officers hurried to their stations and the boatswain's mates sent their shrill calls below decks, Keen ran lightly up a poop ladder and looked briefly at the anchored shipping, at the angle of the masthead pendant.

Then he glanced at the open skylight on the poop deck and thought of the man beneath it.

He cupped his hands. 'Mr Mountsteven, your men are like cripples today.'

He saw the lieutenant touch his hat and bob anxiously.

Keen made himself breathe out very slowly.

That was better. He was the captain again.

The negro groom wiped his hands on a piece of rag and announced, 'Wheel all fixed, sah.'

Adam helped the girl to her feet and together they walked reluctantly from the shade of some trees and down to the dusty road.

The carriage had shed a wheel as it had rounded a bend in the road and had dipped into a deep rut.

There had been momentary confusion, the carriage lurching over and a door opening to reveal the road rising to meet them. Then in the sudden silence Adam had realized his unexpected good fortune. What might have ended in injury and disaster had become a perfect conclusion to the visit.

As the carriage had bounced to a halt Adam had acted instantly and without conscious thought other than to save his companion from hurt. Then as the dust settled, and the coachman and groom had hurried fearfully to look inside, Adam had found the girl held tightly in his arms, her fair hair pressed against his mouth, her heart pounding to match his own.

It had taken longer than expected to repair the damage, but Adam had barely noticed. Together they had walked through the green woodland, had held hands while they had watched a stream and spoken of anything but their true feelings.

The whole visit to Newburyport had been an adventure, and Adam had been taken to visit a small, comfortable house by Robina and her father, and they had watched him, fascinated, while he had walked through every room with the owner, a friend of the family, and had touched the walls, the fireplaces, and one old chair which had always been in the house.

Robina had tried not to weep as he had sat in the big chair, his hands grasping the well-worn arms as if he would never let go.

Then he had said quietly, 'My father once sat here, Robina. *My father.*'

He still could not believe it.

She slipped her hand through his arm and nestled her cheek against his coat.

'You must go, Adam. I have made you late enough as it is.'

Together they moved back to the coach and climbed inside.

As the horses came alive again in their harness, the girl said softly, 'We shall be in Boston very soon.' She turned and looked directly into his eyes. 'You may kiss me now if you wish, Adam.' She tried to make light of it by adding, 'No one can see us here. It would not do for local folk to think that Robina Chase was a fizgig!'

Her mouth was very soft and she had a perfume like fresh flowers.

Then she gently pushed him away and dropped her eyes.

'Well, really, Lieutenant . . . ' But the jest eluded her. She said breathlessly, 'It's love, isn't it?'

Adam smiled, his mind in a daze. 'It must be.'

The coach rolled across cobbles and on to a stretch of old ships' timbers.

Several people paused to glance at the fair-haired girl and the young sea officer who helped her protectively from the coach.

Adam stared in astonishment and then looked at the girl on his arm.

'What shall I do now, Robina?'

It was like a douche of cold water. *Achates* had gone.

'So here you are.' Jonathan Chase nodded to his niece and then said grimly, 'Sailed yesterday. Your admiral was hell-bent for San Felipe.'

He toyed with the idea of telling the young lieutenant about the *Sparrowhawk*'s end, but as he looked from him to his niece he decided against it.

Instead he said, 'You'd better come home with me, young fella. Tomorrow I'll see what I can do about arranging passage for you. You'd not want to miss your ship, eh?'

He saw their hands touch and knew they had not heard a word.

Chase led the way to his own carriage, his face frowning in thought. His niece was the apple of his eye, but you had to face the facts squarely as you did a problem at sea.

They made a striking pair, but the family would never allow it to go further. He could not imagine what he had been thinking of when he had first introduced them.

A young sea officer, an English one at that, with few prospects other than the Navy, was not the right match for Robina Chase. So the sooner he found his ship again the better.

Bolitho left the shadow of the poop and walked forward to the quarterdeck rail. He noticed the curious glances darted in his direction by the bare-backed seamen who were working on the endless tasks of a fighting ship. Even now they were not used to having a flag-officer in their midst, and could not accept that he did not dress in the style suited to his rank. Like the other officers, Bolitho wore only an open-necked shirt and breeches, and would willingly have stripped naked to gain relief from the heat had that not violated every rule in the book.

He looked up at the canvas, sail by sail. Filling tightly for the present, but at any moment they could fall limp and useless as they had for much of the time since leaving Boston.

Bolitho tried not to allow his mind to dwell on it. Why had his sister Nancy written? Was it really as Keen had suggested, or was she trying to prepare him for bad news? Belinda had been ill. It might be something from her earlier life in India when she had nursed her sick husband until he had died.

He paced across the pale planking, worn smooth by a million bare feet in *Old Katie*'s twenty-one years at sea.

He tried to shift his thoughts away from Falmouth but they lingered instead on his nephew.

Bolitho had wanted, *needed* to remain in Boston more than anything in his heart and soul. To wait for one more word from Belinda, and to have his nephew rejoin the ship. He should not have allowed him to go to Newburyport. Maybe Keen, like Browne, had been right about that too. He ought not to have chosen one so close as his aide.

Keen crossed the deck and said, 'Wind's holding steady, sir.'

He watched Bolitho's reaction. For eight of the longest days he could remember Keen had worked his ship to the southward, spreading every stitch of canvas to coax another knot out of her. It had been a poor average all the same, and he guessed that Quantock was comparing him with the last captain. He did not care about his dour first lieutenant, but was more conscious of the fact that Bolitho had never levelled a single criticism or complaint. He knew better than most that in these waters the wind was never reliable, rarely an ally when you most needed it.

Bolitho looked at the flapping masthead pendant.

'Tomorrow then, Val.'

'Aye, sir. Mr Knocker assures me that we shall be off San Felipe by noon, if the wind holds.' He sounded relieved.

Bolitho looked abeam, at the regular swell and occasional feather of spray as a fish broke the surface. Like Keen, he had studied the charts and sketches of San Felipe until he could see them in his sleep. Fifty miles long but less than twenty miles wide at its broadest parts, it was dominated by an extinct volcano and a huge natural harbour on the southern side. The northern approaches were fiercely guarded by reefs, and there was a further barrier of coral adjoining the little islet on the opposite side. It was a formidable place, even without the old fortress which commanded the approaches to Rodney's Harbour, as the anchorage was named. There was fresh water in plenty, while rich crops of sugar and coffee made a tempting prize. Bolitho found himself inwardly agreeing with the island's governor, Sir Humphrey Rivers, that it was a madness to hand the place back to the French.

Keen was saying, 'I shall use the prevailing wind to approach the harbour from the south-east, sir. I'd not care to run in under cover of darkness.'

He was making light of it, but Bolitho could guess at his concern for his ship. The waters around San Felipe were used to brigs and trading-schooners, but a ship of the line, even a small sixty-four, needed room to breathe.

Bolitho said, 'I shall go ashore and meet the governor as soon as possible. We know that Captain Duncan had an audience with him.'

He glanced forward as Midshipman Evans walked past some of the sailmaker's crew who were speaking with Foord, the fifth lieutenant. The midshipman turned and stared at the little group and then hurried, almost ran, to the nearest hatchway.

Keen explained, 'Another of *Sparrowhawk*'s wounded has died, sir.'

Bolitho nodded. One more dead. The sailmaker's mates would sew him up in an old hammock and drop him overboard at sunset.

'Tell Midshipman Evans to report to my clerk for duties in the cabin. Keep his mind off things.'

He strode away and began to pace up and down until his shirt was plastered to his skin.

Keen shook his head. *Take his mind off things*. Bolitho had enough worries and responsibilities for ten men, yet he could still spare a thought for the stricken midshipman.

'Deck there!'

Keen looked up and shaded his eyes against the fierce glare.

The masthead lookout on his perch in the cross-trees yelled, 'Land on th' lee bow!'

Keen looked at the master and grinned. 'Well done, Mr Knocker. We shall remain on the present tack until we can gauge the final approach.'

Knocker grunted. His priest's face gave away neither pleasure nor resentment.

Keen glanced at Bolitho. He had heard the cry but gave no sign either.

'I'll drop the corpse outboard during the last dog watch, sir.' Quantock was tall and ungainly but could move like a cat.

Keen faced him and tried not to feel dislike for his senior lieutenant.

'We shall *bury* him with due honour, Mr Quantock. Have the watch below piped aft at dusk.'

The lieutenant shrugged. 'If you say so, sir. It's just that he was not one of ours – '

Keen saw the little midshipman being led away by Yovell, the clerk, and said sharply, 'He was *somebody's*, Mr Quantock!'

And as shadows crept down from the horizon and enfolded the slow-moving ship, *Achates* paid her respects to the dead.

Bolitho donned his uniform and stood beside Keen as he read a few words from his prayer-book, a boatswain's mate holding a lantern so that he could see the page, although Bolitho suspected he knew the words by heart. He noticed too that the man with the lantern was the one he had spoken to who had served in his *Lysander* at the Nile.

He looked at the darkening horizon but the island had already disappeared. All that day it had risen slowly above the dark blue line, taking shape, spreading out as if growing in size.

Keen said, 'Carry on, Mr Rooke.'

Bolitho heard the slithering sound on a grating, then a splash alongside as the sailor made his journey to the sea-bed.

Bolitho felt himself shiver, and then a sudden stab in his wounded thigh, like a taunt, a reminder.

A Royal Marine was already folding up the burial flag, the hands were moving away to their messes. The officer of the watch was eager to hand over to his successor and join his companions in the wardroom. The ship's routine took over again, as it always did.

But Bolitho pictured the pathetic bundle sinking in *Achates'* wake. He had heard the first lieutenant's comment and Keen's angry retort.

Not one of ours.

Next time, he thought bitterly, it would be.

The sky above Massachusetts Bay looked angrier than it had since *Achates* had first come to her anchor.

As Adam stood with a small group on the quay he noticed that several of the ships in harbour had men working on deck, as if they expected a storm.

Jonathan Chase rubbed his chin and squinted at the fast-moving clouds.

'Sorry to hurry you, Lieutenant, but it's best you use the tide before the weather closes in. Won't last much longer than a few hours.'

Adam turned to the girl whose hair looked like silver in the dying light.

He said, 'It was good of you to find me a vessel, sir.' But his heart and eyes told another story.

She took his arm and they looked at the little brigantine which was already pitching heavily, her loosely brailed sails puffing and drumming in the hot wind. She was named *Vivid*, and Adam guessed it was just luck that Chase had been able to find a master willing to make the passage of some fourteen hundred miles to San Felipe.

The girl said in a fierce whisper, 'Don't go, Adam. There's no need. You can stay with us until . . . ' She looked at him, part pleading, part defiant. 'My uncle will find you employment.' She squeezed his arm more tightly. 'You'll be like your father then.'

Chase said gruffly, 'Here comes a boat. I've had your gear sent over, and a few luxuries to carry back to your ship. Give your uncle my best wishes.' He was speaking quickly as if to hasten the moment of departure.

Adam bent his head and kissed her. He felt moisture on her skin. Spray or tears, he did not know. He knew that he loved her more than any living thing. That he was just as surely going to lose her. He felt as if he was being torn apart. In hell.

The small boat scraped alongside and a voice called roughly, 'Jump in, Lieutenant! No time to dawdle!'

Adam tugged his hat firmly on to his head and did as he was told. The boat was old and scarred, but the oarsmen smart enough.

He peered astern as the boat butted away from the piles and saw her watching him, her face and raised hand very pale against the land.

I shall be back.

He gritted his teeth as spray swept over the gunwale and the boat's coxswain said curtly, 'Here, get ready!'

The brigantine was pitching right above the boat, her two masts spiralling as she tore at her anchor cable.

Adam was almost glad of the sailor's abruptness. He did not want courtesy. They were doing it for Chase's money, not out of respect for a foreign officer.

He clambered up the side and would have fallen headlong but a big man loomed from the shadows and gripped his arm to steady him.

Adam noticed that the man walked with a bad limp, and as he made to thank him saw to his astonishment that he had only one leg. But there was no mistaking his authority as he shouted at his men to work on the capstan.

'Get below, if you please.'

He had a powerful voice with an easy colonial drawl, quite unlike the Bostonians. He was already limping away to supervise his small crew but hesitated and came back again.

'Would you mind takin' off your hat?'

As Adam removed it, and his hair ruffled in the wind, the *Vivid*'s master nodded, well satisfied.

'Thought so. Soon as I laid eyes on you.' He rubbed his hand down his jerkin and thrust it at him. 'My name's Jethro Tyrrell. Welcome aboard my humble command.'

Adam stared at him. 'You knew my father?'

The man called Tyrrell threw back his head and laughed.

'Hell no! But I *knew* Richard Bolitho.' He limped away and added over his shoulder, 'Useter be his first lieutenant, would you believe?'

Adam groped his way aft to a tiny companion-way, completely mystified.

It did not really matter who commanded the *Vivid*'s destiny, he thought. He was taking him away from Robina. The first love of his life.

7

To Start a War

'The entrance to Rodney's Harbour is narrow, sir. A mile wide at the most.' Keen lowered his telescope and pursed his lips. 'A well-sited battery could hold a fleet at bay.'

Bolitho walked to the opposite side of the quarterdeck so that his view of the island would not be obscured by shrouds and rigging.

They had made better progress during the night, and now with the morning sunlight outlining the massive pyramid of the extinct volcano he could gauge its size and the rugged shoreline of the island.

The helmsman called, 'Nor'-west by west, sir.' And Knocker grunted an acknowledgement.

Keen glanced at the masthead pendant. It pointed towards the larboard bow with barely a shiver. The wind was still holding.

Bolitho could feel Keen's mind at work as his ship headed warily towards the pointing spur of headland.

The wind would take them directly into the shelter of the harbour. But they were on a lee shore, so every care was necessary. Keen had sent two good leadsmen forward to the chains at first light and their regular cry of 'No bottom, sir!' warned of the dangers.

The sea-bed shelved very steeply, but once they drew level with the small islet off the southern tip of the headland there would be reefs ready to rip out the keel if the ship lost steerage-way.

'Take in the fore-course, Mr Quantock.' Keen sounded

calm but his eyes were everywhere as he watched the topsails hardening to the wind.

'Deck there!'

Bolitho grasped his hands behind his back as the lookout yelled down, 'There's a boom across the entrance, sir!'

Keen stared at him. 'What the *hell* are they thinking of?'

Bolitho said sharply, 'Send an officer aloft. Then prepare to anchor.'

'But . . . ' Keen's protest stopped with the one word. He knew that Bolitho understood well enough. To anchor on a lee shore in deep water was tempting disaster. If the wind got up *Achates* might drag her anchor and run helplessly on to the hidden coral.

Bolitho took a few paces while he considered it, determined not to watch a lieutenant's frantic scramble to the masthead.

The governor could reasonably do what he liked to protect the island. Maybe he had already been attacked, and would withdraw the boom when *Achates* was identified. He dismissed the idea instantly. The ship had served in these waters for most of her life. She would be easily recognized before any other vessel.

The lieutenant who had climbed up to join the lookout called, 'The boom is a line of moored craft, sir!'

He was one of the junior officers who had recently been promoted from midshipman and had a shrill, almost girlish voice, so that several of the seamen on the quarterdeck grinned and nudged each other until silenced by a roar from Quantock.

Keen shut his telescope with a snap. 'Stand by to come about. Man the braces. Anchor party up forrard at the double!'

The young lieutenant shouted again, 'There's a yawl approaching, sir!'

Keen looked at Bolitho, anxiety in his eyes.

Bolitho said shortly, 'Anchor then.'

'Helm alee! Stand by, Mr Quantock!'

The yards swung noisily when they turned into the wind, the canvas banging and clattering as the way was taken off the ship.

'*Let go!*'

The anchor hit the sea violently and threw spray high over the beak-head, while Rooke, the boatswain, and a lieutenant of the forecastle peered over the side. At the same time the topmen worked above the deck to take in the sails and ease any strain on the cable as it continued to run out into deep water.

'All secure, sir!'

Keen nodded but murmured, 'Bloody bastards!'

The yawl thrust slowly away from the land, tacking this way and that as it clawed towards the anchored two-decker.

The midshipman of the watch said, 'There's an officer of sorts on board, sir.'

Captain Dewar of the marines asked, 'Man the side, sir?'

Keen glared at him. 'After refusing my ship an entrance? I'll see him in hell first!'

The yawl's tanned sails were furled, and as she glided against the *Achates'* tumblehome Bolitho said, 'I'll receive him in the cabin.' He strode aft, unable to watch Keen's anger and humiliation.

It seemed an age before the visitor was brought to the cabin, and Bolitho found himself wondering what Nelson might do under this set of circumstances.

He could not blame the islanders, nor could he condone this behaviour.

The door was opened by Yovell and Bolitho looked at his visitor as he strode to the centre of the cabin. He was certainly dressed in uniform, a blue tunic and white trousers, and wearing both sword and pistol on a highly polished belt. He was aged about thirty, Bolitho thought, and when he spoke he had a faint West Country accent. A Devonian, he decided, like his clerk.

'I bring word from the governor.'

Keen, who had followed him aft, snapped, 'Say *sir* when you speak to the vice-admiral!'

Bolitho said, 'And what is your name, may I ask?'

The man glanced angrily at Keen. 'Captain Masters of the San Felipe Militia.' He swallowed hard. 'Sir.'

'Well, *Captain* Masters, before either of us says something which cannot be retracted, let me explain *my* intentions.'

The man was recovering his confidence and interrupted, 'The governor has instructed me to tell you that the boom will remain in place until all negotiations are completed. After that . . .'

Bolitho said quietly, 'After that, as you put it, you are not concerned. But how am I expected to see the governor if my ship is prevented from entering?'

'I shall take you in the yawl.' He saw Keen take a pace forward and added quickly, 'Sir.'

'I see. Now I will tell *you*, Captain Masters of the San Felipe Militia. I am going ashore in my barge and will pass the written decision of His Majesty's Government to the governor.'

Masters said, 'He will not accept it!'

Bolitho looked at Keen. 'Have my barge dropped alongside.'

He saw a protest forming on Keen's face. Just like Thomas Herrick.

Masters persisted, 'I shall lead the way then.'

'No. You are under arrest. Any act of rebellion will be treated harshly, and you shall hang for it, do I make myself clear?'

Bolitho saw his calm words smash home like pistol shots. Masters was probably used to bullying slaves on the plantations and the sudden change of fortune left him speechless.

Keen snapped, 'Remove those weapons.' He raised his voice, 'Sergeant Saxton, take charge of this man!'

Masters gasped as the Royal Marine removed his sword and pistol, and exclaimed, 'Your threats do not frighten me, Admiral!'

Bolitho stood up and walked to the stern windows. Many eyes would be watching the ship from the fortress, waiting to see what would happen. The governor might fire on his barge, even hold him as hostage until . . .

He stopped his racing thoughts and said coldly, 'Then they should.'

When he turned round Masters had been led away, and he heard shouted commands as armed marines took charge of the yawl.

Keen asked anxiously, 'Let me ram the boom, sir? Then we'll enter harbour as planned and rake the mutinous scum for good measure!'

Bolitho eyed him fondly. 'It would take a full day, maybe much longer. Even if you succeeded it would cost many lives, and if the wind rose unexpectedly you would have to disengage and beat clear of the land, past that battery again.'

Keen seemed resigned. 'Which officer will act as your aide, sir? I think I should come with you.'

Bolitho smiled, suddenly relieved that the waiting was over, no matter what the outcome might be.

'What, leave your command? With both of us at Rivers' mercy there's no saying what might happen!' He relented at Keen's crest-fallen expression. 'A junior lieutenant and, er . . . the midshipman, Mr Evans. They will suffice.'

Ozzard took down the old sword from its rack but Bolitho said, 'No. The other one.'

If anything went wrong today the sword would be here for Adam. He knew from their glances that they had both guessed the reason.

On deck the sun had risen above the volcano and the decks were already as hot as bricks in a kiln. Tinder-dry, with tarred rigging and sails which would flare like torches if the island's battery used heated shot. Even with ordinary balls a well-sited battery was more than a match for a slow-moving vessel within the confines of a harbour.

He saw Allday watching him grimly, the curious stares of the seamen and marines on the gangways.

He hesitated at the entry port and looked at Keen.

'If I am *wrong*.' He saw the captain's jaw tighten. 'Or

should I fall today, promise me you will write to Belinda. Try to explain.'

Keen nodded and blurted out, 'If they lay one hand on you sir . . . '

'You will do as I ordered, Val. Nothing more or less.'

He touched his hat to the quarterdeck and climbed down into the waiting barge.

He found Trevenen, the sixth lieutenant, and Midshipman Evans already seated in the stern-sheets and said, 'A fine day for it, gentlemen.'

Trevenen was beaming at the unexpected honour of being the admiral's temporary aide, but by contrast Evans looked around him, his eyes dark and empty.

Allday murmured, 'This is no good, sir.'

Bolitho settled down and glanced at the waiting bargemen.

'It won't help by talking about it.'

Allday sighed. He recognized all the signs by now.

'Bear off forrard! Give way, all!'

Bolitho glanced quickly astern and saw the ship drawing away, the faces at the entry port merging and losing individuality.

He looked at his companions. The ship's most junior lieutenant and a thirteen-year-old midshipman might hardly be what the governor would be expecting. But, as in leaving the family sword aboard, he was taking no chances. If things went badly wrong, Keen would need every experienced officer and sailor he could lay hands on.

As the barge dipped into the inshore swell Bolitho heard a clink of metal and realized that cutlasses and pistols were stacked beneath each thwart within easy reach.

He looked up at Allday's impassive features and for a moment their eyes met.

It did not need words, he thought. Allday had made plans all of his own.

The lieutenant said nervously, 'There is the other island, sir.'

Bolitho shaded his eyes and studied the humpbacked islet. It was treeless but with plenty of vegetation around the stone-built mission and outhouses. There was a strip of white beach, and he saw some boats pulled up clear of the surf. Monks, priests or whatever they were, they had to fish and cultivate their land as well as pray, he thought.

He turned his attention to the boom. Lighters and old hulks had been moored in the middle of the entrance, the channel which *Achates* and any ship of her size would have to use. He looked up at the fortress. Bigger than he had expected, with a sheer drop on the seaward side, impossible to scale, and impervious to twenty-four-pounders.

He could see pale houses on the far side of the harbour. He smiled wryly. Georgetown, Rivers' little kingdom. There were several craft at anchor, mostly traders and fishing boats.

Allday said between his teeth, 'Armed men on the boom, sir.'

Bolitho nodded. 'Steer for the starboard side of the entrance.'

He turned briefly to look for the ship but she had been shut off by the spur of headland. Only *Achates'* mastheads and topgallant yards showed above the land as if they had been planted there.

Beside him Evans shifted on his thwart and his fingers locked suddenly around his dirk. Like taking a needle to stop a charging bull, Bolitho thought.

He said, 'I brought you with me in case you should remember something.'

The boy looked at him and replied quietly, 'I know, sir.' His gaze shifted beyond the makeshift boom to the centre of the harbour but he said nothing further.

Bolitho guessed that Evans was seeing his ship *Sparrow-hawk* lying there under the guns of the fortress. A King's ship, his home, the start of a career, friends like the other midshipman who had been shot down. But something, anything, might jar his memory. They did not have much else to go on.

Allday tensed at the sharp bang of a musket, and Bolitho saw a ball skip across the water like a fish before dropping abeam.

He said, 'Hold the stroke. Keep pulling.'

His calm tone steadied the bargemen who, with their backs towards the boom, must be expecting the next shot to hit them.

Bolitho squared his shoulders. His cocked hat and bright epaulettes would make a fine marker for any sharpshooter, he thought.

But there were no more shots, and as the barge thrust past the end of the boom he saw groups of men peering at them. All were armed, and one shook his musket threateningly at the grim-faced sailors.

There was no turning back now. No escape.

Bolitho watched a cluster of figures on a jetty below the fortress. It suddenly seemed a long, long way from Sir Hayward Sheaffe's quiet office in the Admiralty where this precise moment had been predicted.

Bolitho was not sure what he had been expecting in San Felipe's governor, but Sir Humphrey Rivers was not it. He was tall, heavily built to a point of grossness, his face very red from both climate and drink, Bolitho thought. But he greeted Bolitho with a jovial, expansive grin and ushered him straight into the cool shadows of the fortress.

As he led the way through a studded door and into a corridor which had been transformed by rugs and several paintings, Rivers said over his shoulder, 'Later I hope you will visit my house. But I guessed you would be eager to settle matters, eh?'

Bolitho saw another door open, a bewigged negro footman giving a bow as they passed him.

Rivers mopped his face with a silk handkerchief and eyed Lieutenant Trevenen and the small midshipman with some amusement.

'By God, Bolitho, do you have a company of boys to do the Admiralty's bidding?'

He snapped his fingers and another footman stepped noiselessly forward with a tray of goblets.

Rivers gave a dry smile. 'Maybe your young companions would care to withdraw?'

'I agree.' There was no point in involving the others. Then Bolitho said, 'You know why I am here, Sir Humphrey?'

Rivers settled his bulk on a chair and examined his goblet critically.

'Of course. Everyone does. Equally, you know what I think about it?' He chuckled and drank deeply. 'I apologize for the inconvenience of the boom but it *is* necessary.' He seemed to remember that Masters had not returned with Bolitho and asked abruptly, 'Where's my captain of militia?'

'On board *Achates*, Sir Humphrey.'

'I see.' He lowered the goblet to be refilled. 'The signs are that the wind is getting up. You will know from your own experience in these waters that it can be savage even at this time of year. It would not do to let your, er, flagship remain so close inshore under such circumstances.'

Bolitho sipped the wine. It was strange he could feel so calm. Rivers had thought of everything. Where a ship would have to stand off if the harbour remained closed.

Rivers was watching him intently. 'Let's face facts. Your ship cannot stay there indefinitely. Soon you will have to weigh. You can ration water until the people are ripe for mutiny, you can even wait for assistance which may never arrive. *Or* you can draw up a fresh agreement here and now. I will remain as governor with total responsibility for the island's betterment and defence.'

And profit, Bolitho thought.

Rivers stood up with some difficulty and walked to a window.

'This place is impregnable. You must know that. The Americans will help me if need be. I'll not have the Frogs

hoisting their colours here. I told your impertinent frigate
captain as much.'

'The *Sparrowhawk* was sunk soon after she left here.'

He watched Rivers' florid face and knew it was a complete
surprise to him.

'*Sunk?* What are you saying?'

'She was attacked by a larger man-of-war, blown to hell
without a challenge or chance to defend herself. So you see,
Sir Humphrey, there are those other than the French who are
interested in the island's future.'

Rivers tossed back the wine and turned away to hide his
confusion.

'I don't believe it. Probably a pirate, the waters are full of
them. With the King's Navy cut to the bone, it's hardly
surprising.'

'I want to show you something.' Rivers almost threw down
the empty goblet and strode panting to another door at the far
end of the chamber. A footman darted ahead of him like a
pilot-fish to open it.

Beyond the door the rugs and comfortable chairs were
gone. A long embrasured stone wall and a line of heavy
artillery looked across the water. Rivers' authority.

Rivers strode to the end cannon and laid one hand on its
rounded cascabel with something like affection.

'Here, take a look, Bolitho.'

He stood aside and Bolitho could feel his sense of power.
He was filled suddenly with loathing for this man who cared
nothing for Duncan or anyone else.

He stooped and peered along the black barrel and saw that
the gun was laid on a line of mooring buoys. Tied to one of
them was his barge. He could even see Allday standing to
shade his eyes and peer at the fortress.

Rivers added smoothly, '*Sparrowhawk* was there. I could
have sunk her just as easily as I can that boat of yours.'

Bolitho stood up and eyed him calmly. 'You were a flag-
officer yourself, Sir Humphrey. You know the Navy would
never rest — '

Rivers snorted. 'There would be no choice. To suffer great losses to aid the French? Even Parliament would not be that stupid!'

Bolitho glanced across the anchorage again. The water was ruffled like beaten pewter. The wind was rising steadily and he could see the flags whipping out from the moored craft. But they were in shelter. *Achates* was not.

He said, 'I shall return to my ship.' He did not hide his contempt. 'Unless you wish to detain me also?'

'No agreement, Bolitho?'

'Do not try to deceive me, Sir Humphrey. You knew I would not condone treason.'

Rivers smiled. 'Not like some in your family, eh?'

Bolitho took his hat from a footman. He did it slowly to give himself time to control his anger. It was just as well Adam was elsewhere. Such a crude slur on his father would have brought out his sword, and Rivers' guards would have ended it here and now.

He said, 'That was cheap, but not totally unexpected.'

Rivers sat down and mopped his face again. He could not hide his excitement, the pleasure which his victory was giving him.

Bolitho walked to the door and saw Midshipman Evans standing alone beside an open window.

Rivers said, 'I have taken the liberty of detaining the young lieutenant until my boat and men are returned.'

Bolitho nodded gravely. 'As you wish.'

Rivers seemed disappointed. 'There is still time for you to reconsider.'

Bolitho gestured to Evans and replied, 'You said yourself, Sir Humphrey, that these waters abound with pirates. I think I have just been speaking to one of them.'

He turned abruptly on his heel and strode through the door, half expecting a shot or a sudden challenge.

Evans almost had to run to keep up with him.

Bolitho snapped, 'Signal the barge.'

He felt the hot wind on his cheek, saw the air of menace in

the sky. It would have to be smartly done, he thought. There was no choice. Not for him anyway.

Allday watched gratefully as Bolitho and the midshipman climbed into the boat and murmured, 'That's that then, sir.'

Bolitho watched the oar blades dig into the water and said, 'An *easy* stroke, if you please.' His mind was reeling with the urgency of what must be done, but under no circumstances must Rivers suspect his intentions.

Once in the great cabin Bolitho tossed his gold-laced coat to Ozzard and watched Keen, Quantock and the two Royal Marine officers as they were ushered in by Yovell.

'I intend to attack, Captain Keen.' Bolitho was surprised that the glass of wine which Ozzard had just given him did not splinter in his grasp.

Keen said, 'Mr Knocker has doubts about our safety here, sir. The wind – '

'Is it steady?'

Quantock said in his hard voice, 'Rising by the hour, sir.'

'That is not what I asked. Is it steady?'

Keen looked anxious. 'Aye, sir.'

'Very well. So make ready for sea.' He saw Keen's sudden relief vanish as he added, 'Then Rivers' lookouts will imagine we are leaving.'

'With respect, sir, no sane man would believe otherwise. We will surely drag our anchor if we remain.'

Bolitho smiled at him. 'Remember Copenhagen, Val?'

Keen nodded, his face pale. 'I do, sir. So you intend to attack in the dark?' He sounded incredulous.

'I do. I know how the battery is laid on the entrance and the main anchorage. Rivers was good enough to show me, although I think he had different reasons.'

What was happening to him? It could and would probably end in complete disaster. *Remember Copenhagen?* he had asked Keen. This was nothing like it. There they had had a whole fleet, and they had had Nelson.

There was a world of difference here. If he lost the ship

there was nothing, a costly failure which if he survived would end in a court martial, and would break Belinda's heart.

Yet, in spite of the terrible risks he was actually elated, a madness coursing through him like ice-water.

Keen cleared his throat and glanced at the other officers. 'Right then, sir.'

Bolitho looked away. Keen had accepted. Right or wrong he would follow his orders to hell.

Bolitho made himself smile but his lips felt stiff and unreal.

'At dusk we shall send Masters and his yawl into harbour to exchange with Mr Trevenen.'

Keen shook his head. 'I had forgotten all about *him*!'

Bolitho looked at the two marines. 'And that will be when you come into things.'

It was a matter of perfect timing, and Lady Luck, as Herrick had always proclaimed. Keen thought it was an act of madness, or vanity to cover his defeat by Sir Humphrey Rivers.

That was their only chance. That Rivers would imagine himself to be safe with such odds.

He was probably on the fortress wall at this very moment. Picturing the argument and despair he had flung in their midst.

He briefly outlined his plan of action and saw their varying expressions, their doubts and their uncertainty. But there was the same excitement too. Even Quantock, who said very little, seemed fascinated.

Bolitho said quietly, 'It is hard to fight a war, gentlemen, as you all know. But it seems a great deal easier to start one.'

They filed out to speak with their subordinates and Bolitho sat at his table, a pen poised above some paper.

There might be no time later on, and he wanted her to know his thoughts, just as she had tried to send him her best wishes.

Feet thudded overhead and tackles creaked as his barge was hoisted on to the tier.

Suppose he was mistaken? That Rivers was right about the island being impregnable.

He tried to force the new uncertainty from his mind and wrote, *My dearest Belinda* . . .

Then he deliberately folded the paper and put it in a drawer. If he was killed she would soon know. There was no point in reopening the wound with a letter which might reach her months later.

Allday entered the cabin and stood watching him, his body angled to the screen door as the ship swayed restlessly in the wind.

Allday said bluntly, 'Attack, sir.'

Bolitho nodded. 'Yes. Did you do as I asked?'

Allday had to grin despite the gravity of the moment.

'Aye, sir, we trailed a boat'd lead an' line all the way to those mooring buoys. It only touched bottom once, and there's room a-plenty for *Old Katie*, once she's snug inside.' He shook his head with admiration. 'With all those other things to bother you, I don't know how you thought of it, and that's no error!'

Bolitho said, 'Pour us each a glass of brandy, Allday.'

He watched the man's powerful fist as he filled two goblets and waited for the deck to settle.

Allday added as an afterthought, 'Mebbee that's how you becomes an admiral, knowing them things, sir?'

The officer of the watch paused in his prowling on the poop deck as their laughter came through the skylight.

It would be his first action as a lieutenant. He had felt the iron fingers of fear dig into his stomach as Quantock had explained what must be done.

But hearing their vice-admiral laugh like that with his coxswain gave him new strength and he continued with his pacing.

8

Faith

Bolitho took a last glance through the stern windows before
Ozzard fastened them tightly and closed the protective shutters. *Achates* was pitching heavily at her cable, and Bolitho
guessed that Keen had doubled the anchor watch for a first
sign of its dragging.

It should still have been daylight, but low, angry clouds
and drifting spume had closed around the ship like an early
dusk.

He could not wait much longer. *He dare not.*

With the cabin sealed Bolitho felt the air tormenting him
like steam and he was running with sweat in seconds.

There was a tap at the outer door and Keen's voice murmuring to someone. He was exactly on time. Had probably
been aching for the moment to arrive.

Bolitho nodded to him. 'Let's be about it then.'

He saw the unwilling hostage in the background flanked
by the ship's corporal and Black Joe Langtry, *Achates'* fearsome master-at-arms. The latter had a pair of grotesque black
brows and, despite years at sea, an ashen countenance. More
like an executioner, Bolitho thought.

'Well, Captain Masters, you will be leaving us directly.'
He watched the gleam return to the man's eyes. He had
strong faith in his master and might be quick to throw
Bolitho's words back in his face. But there was no time to
waste.

'The yawl is waiting to cast off and take you back to
harbour.' Bolitho lifted his arms and saw Masters' eyes shift

to the curved fighting hanger which Allday deftly clipped to his belt. 'I am afraid it will be carrying a different crew this time, but *you* will take us past the boom.'

He watched his words touch a cord in Masters' mind.

'But, but . . .'

'The governor has acted unlawfully. I intend to take control of the island, and to do that with a minimum loss of life you will steer us through the entrance.' He counted seconds before adding quietly, 'What happens to Rivers will depend on others. But if you attempt to raise an alarm you will be killed. If you betray us in any other way I will treat such action as treason against the Crown. You know what that will mean.'

He adjusted the hanger on his belt, sickened by the man's stunned features, by his own brutal remedy.

Then he thought of Duncan and the others and said, 'Put him aboard the yawl. I shall follow.'

He looked at Keen. 'This is the only way. *You* must command the ship.'

They both glanced up as the wind moaned through the shrouds and ratlines like a taunt.

'Your first lieutenant is an excellent seaman, but ashore with men he sometimes abuses too much, who can tell? And we have *no margin at all for error.*'

He looked from Keen to Allday. Friends. Comrades. So few of us left.

'You, Allday, have the most dangerous part. You will lower the barge at the seaward side. It cannot be seen now from the fortress.'

Allday eyed him stubbornly. 'I know what to do, sir. Take the boat past them moorings and light a beacon.'

'It is a hard thing to ask. If we fail you will be cut off.'

Allday grunted. 'I'd rather stay with you, sir. It's my right, my place.'

Bolitho gripped his arm and tried to hide his emotion.

'Without that beacon *Achates* has no chance of entering harbour. No chance to avoid running aground in this wind.

And you *shall* be with me, old friend. Make no mistake about it.'

Keen said, 'I still believe . . . ' Then he shut his mouth and gave a rueful grin. 'But it's done.' He loosened his shirt and touched his sword. 'Rivers may be surprised, but that compares little with my own feelings!'

He nodded to Allday and strode from the cabin, his voice going ahead as he rapped out his orders.

Bolitho took a pistol and thrust it into his belt. Did it really matter if Quantock led the attack? In his heart he knew it did. Men being asked to face death while fighting for a cause they did not understand, or if they did probably had a greater sympathy for the foe, needed to see him there too. To watch him die or share whatever fate he had flung them into.

Allday followed him from the cabin, breathing hard as he ducked beneath the deckhead beams. Around them in the gloom half-naked seamen were already standing to the guns, while on the deck below the hands had cleared for action with barely a sound or an order being shouted by the lieutenants and warrant officers.

On the quarterdeck more figures stood in dark clusters or tottered about in the hot wind. It felt like burning sand, the spray hard enough to blind a man.

Bolitho tilted his head to peer at the thrashing canvas as it rippled and boomed against the spars. Once set free the ship would be like a wild thing. A good sailer, they said. She would need to be all that and more.

Tackles squeaked and he heard the barge being lowered down the side. Even though he was hidden in the menacing gloom he could almost feel Allday's resentment, his anxiety, as once more he was parted from him, from his special place in things.

Keen shouted, 'Good luck, sir!'

They made a quick handclasp, their fingers running with warm spray. Then Bolitho was out and swinging down to the pitching yawl, where hands reached out to help him aboard.

A voice growled, 'Who's this, Ted? Gawd, let's get on with it!'

Another gave a hoarse cheer. "Tis th' admiral, lads!'

They pushed round him as if they did not believe he was joining them. In his sodden, grubby shirt he could have been anyone, but they knew, and from the darkness a voice called, 'Welcome, Equality Dick!'

Bolitho groped his way aft, moved and, as usual, ashamed that he had not even considered that these unknown seamen might trust him.

He heard Mountsteven, the second lieutenant, say cheerfully, 'Smells like a Portland whore-house, sir.' His total lack of respect showed that he too was caught in the madness like the rest.

'It's powerful.'

Bolitho reached the tiller and peered at the men nearest him. He saw Christy, the boatswain's mate who had been in the *Lysander*, and the vague shape of Masters, who was easily recognizable in his militia uniform.

The boat certainly stank. It was crammed with inflammable materials. Old canvas, cordage soaked in grease and pitch, oil and various oddments from the gunner's store. One careless spark and the whole boat would ignite like a grenade.

Once they had seized the boom and cut its moorings, Allday's barge, followed by *Achates'* two cutters with the marines, would spread the attack. He had noticed that the yawl's original crew, like the guards he had seen around the fortress, were mostly of slave stock, left-overs and half-breeds from the island's various occupations.

It was unlikely that officers like Masters would live in quarters within the fortress. It would take time for them to be called from their comfortable homes. He shivered slightly. Unless of course Rivers had already seen through his scheme and every gun was loaded and ready for the first sign of an attack.

He said, 'Cast off, Mr Mountsteven. Show a lantern forrard

as planned.' He glanced at Masters. 'You have your instructions. If you value your life and the chance to rejoin your family, I would advise you to be prudent.'

He heard Christy rattle his cutlass in its scabbard as an unspoken warning.

With the mooring lines released and the sails spreading over the deck like giant wings, the big yawl reeled away from *Achates'* protection.

Rivers' men on the boom would be wary, but they had no cause to expect such a rash course of action. He had a sudden stark picture of *Achates* in the first dawn light, wrecked across the entrance and a ready target for the great guns.

A voice whispered, 'Land ahead, sir!'

Bolitho felt a murmur run through the crowded space between decks where the mass of seamen crouched and waited for the onslaught. Blades scraped each other, and men groped for pistols and muskets in total darkness to make certain they were dry and ready. One foolhardy move, a musket being fired by accident, and all would be lost. Bolitho was grateful that *Achates'* people were mostly experienced hands. Well trained, part of a family.

He clung to a backstay and peered through the spray towards the darker wedge of land on the larboard bow. To starboard the fortress and the fifteen-hundred foot high volcano were a vague blur in this eerie light.

A lantern bobbed across the water, seemingly from the sea itself, and Bolitho thought he heard a shout.

Masters said harshly, 'Dip the forrard lantern!' He sounded as if he could barely breathe. *'Twice!'*

The lantern dipped and rose twice as directed, and Bolitho found that he was holding his breath. It was Masters' chance to betray him, to prove his last loyalty to Rivers. But nothing happened, and the light on the boom remained steady and flickering above the tossing wavecrests.

The tiller-bar creaked as Masters guided the helmsman's hand. He had committed himself and had no intention of drowning because of faulty steering.

Bolitho saw the end of the boom and a few hunched figures around the guide light. Someone was shouting at the yawl, and Masters waved, his lordly gesture made pathetic by his treachery.

'*Now!* Helm hard to starboard! Take in the sails!'

The seamen, used to working in all weathers in daylight or darkness, brought the yawl hard against the moored craft and heavy timbers. As their grapnels soared across the startled guards the first concealed sailor leapt on to the boom, his cutlass silencing a challenge and changing it to a terrible cry.

The boom was suddenly swarming with men, and while some took care of the wretched guards, others dragged out the yawl's dangerous cargo and wedged it into position.

'Light the fuses! Slow-match there! *Lively!*' Mountsteven barked out his orders while the prisoners were flung unceremoniously into the yawl.

Bolitho peered up at the fortress's blurred shape. No sound or sign. Maybe Rivers had really expected him to ignore his honour and his future and sign some illegal document. It would not have been unique in naval history.

'Moorings cut, sir!'

One slow-match sparked briefly like a glow-worm and then another as the last sailor jumped into the tossing boat.

'*Cast off!*'

Barely glancing at the cowering survivors from their swift attack the seamen thrust with long sweeps, boat-hooks and anything else they could find to carry the yawl away from the boom.

Lieutenant Mountsteven in his excitement seized Bolitho's arm and pointed with his hanger.

'There goes your man, sir!'

With only the oar blades visible like trailing white snakes the barge swept through the gap and was into the harbour before the yawl had staggered clear.

'Steer for the shore!'

Bolitho strode to the opposite side where Masters was leaning over the gunwale to peer towards the fortress.

It was like being in a mill-race, with the deck swaying from side to side, sometimes awash as the sweeps fought to hold steerage-way.

'That was well done, Masters.' Bolitho ignored the man's astonished glance and shouted, 'Stand by, lads!'

There was a muffled explosion and suddenly the yawl and their upturned faces were bathed in a vivid orange glare as the drifting boom burst into flames. In seconds it had moved well past the headland and was breaking up into smaller fiery shapes as the lashings parted.

Bolitho tightened the hanger's thong around his wrist and tested his wounded leg. If it failed him now . . .

The yawl hit the land, rebounded with the sea boiling over the gunwale and sweeping men aside like untidy sacks, and then drove ashore yet again. Bolitho heard wood splintering, the inrushing water surging and dragging at his legs as the boat continued to batter its way along a line of rocks.

But grapnels were already finding a grip, and as the first men clambered cursing and spluttering on to firm ground Bolitho heard the far-off blare of a trumpet.

He tried to fix the picture of the hillside in his mind, then turned to watch as another part of the drifting boom exploded in a great plume of sparks and flames.

The whole of Georgetown must surely be on the alert by now.

Crack . . . crack . . . crack . . . Musket shots whined impotently through the spray as some sentries fired from the fortress walls.

'Rally the men, Mr Mountsteven.'

The lieutenant was regarding the remains of the yawl. There was no way out by that method.

Someone gave a hoarse cheer which was instantly silenced by an unseen petty officer.

But Bolitho felt like cheering too. The *Achates'* cutters were pulling like demons as they swept through some last remnants of the boom, the marines' white cross-belts stark and clear despite the gloom.

From the bows of one came the sharp crack of a musket and a yell of command, magnified through a speaking-trumpet to add unreality to the moment.

A cutter was pulling directly for one of Rivers' own boats. Doubtless one which was bringing the unfortunate Lieutenant Trevenen to be exchanged. If they had harmed him . . .

He did not let his mind dwell on it as Mountsteven shouted, 'All accounted for, sir!'

'Carry on! Fast as you can! Across the track from the town. Scatter the men among the rocks, anywhere so that they can slow an attack until the marines support us!'

In spite of his racing thoughts he almost smiled at the absurdity of his orders. More like a general than a naval officer with a boatload of seamen and a company of marines, if they ever managed to reach here.

He ran with the seamen through dark rocks and great bushes which loomed and shook like monsters in the fierce wind as if to frighten them from their purpose.

'Here, sir!'

That was Christy, and Bolitho dropped beside him but gasped as the pain stabbed from his wounded thigh.

Christy was peering at his pistols and had a cutlass bared and lying beside him.

Bolitho saw others running and stooping as they sought out cover, while more musket shots whimpered overhead. Where was Rivers, he wondered? In his fine house, or up there on the fortress wondering if they were all going mad?

He pounded the wet ground with his fist. Everything depended on Allday. He might have run into a guard-boat like the one confronted by *Achates'* cutter. Even now Keen would be weighing anchor, watching the flames on the severed boom, all he had to divide sea from rock.

Soon those flames would have died too.

A voice yelled a command and a loose volley of shots cracked up the slope towards the fortress.

Scott, *Achates'* third lieutenant and Keen's next most

experienced officer, yelled, 'Reload! *Steady*, lads!' He must have seen some movement at the fortress gates.

Bolitho tried not to think of Keen's helplessness as his ship tore free from the ground and began to claw her way round and into solid darkness. Short-handed because of the landing party, and with at least three of his officers out of the ship, it must be a living nightmare.

He saw Christy's eyes glow like twin matches and turned as a column of fire gushed from the end of the moorings.

Allday, in spite of all his doubts and arguments, had done it. The fire was burning brightly where the bargemen had lashed it to one of the buoys, and another would be ready when it died.

Then a cannon roared out like a thunder-clap. Where the ball went nobody saw. It had probably ripped over the very buoy which Rivers had indicated when he had made his casual threat.

Masters was crawling on the ground and when he saw Bolitho flopped down beside him. Now that he had done it he was unable to stop shaking with fear.

Bolitho looked at him and asked, 'What is the date, Mr Masters?'

Masters gulped and managed to reply, 'J-July the ninth, I believe, sir!'

He would have jumped to his feet if Christy had not dragged him down for his own safety.

Masters' voice cracked as he asked, 'I heard something! What's happening?'

Bolitho had heard it too. The faint rattle of drums and the frail sound of fifes.

He could see it as if he were there with them. His marines, marching along a rough road in this howling wind, the little drummer boys keeping an even distance behind their officers as if they were on parade. A road none of them had even seen, and some would never see it when daylight came.

Bolitho managed to say, 'The date is important. One we shall remember.'

He twisted his head to see another of Allday's blazing flares, but this time his eyes seemed blurred.

He drove the knuckle-bow of his hanger into the ground near his face and whispered, 'We shall win. *We shall win!*' It sounded like a prayer.

Keen ran up the poop ladder and clung to a rail as the wind drove along the full length of his ship, the sound rising and strengthening like some obscene chorus.

His mind reeled as he tried to calculate the time and distance he had left to bring *Achates* about once the anchor broke free. He could dimly hear the creak of the capstan, the hoarse shouts of petty officers as they waited for the moment.

Keen returned to the quarterdeck, his face stinging as if the flesh were raw. He saw the dark outline of the wheel and a handful of helmsmen, the master with a midshipman standing nearby. Seamen of the after-guard at the braces, their half-naked bodies shining in the gloom like wet marble.

Soon . . . soon. Now or never. Keen had read it often enough in the Gazette or some Admiralty report. One of His Majesty's ships driven ashore and lost. *A court martial later pronounced* . . . He stopped his racing thoughts and shouted above the din, 'Ready, Mr Quantock?'

The tall figure of the first lieutenant, angled like a cripple's against the sloping deck, staggered towards him.

'It's no use, sir!'

Keen faced him angrily. 'Keep your voice down, man!'

Quantock leaned forward as if to see him better.

'The master agrees with me. It's madness. We'll never manage it.' He was encouraged by Keen's silence. 'There's no shame in standing away, sir. There may still be time.'

'Anchor's hove short, sir!' The cry came like a dirge.

'*Time?* What has that to do with it, damn your eyes!'

Keen strode to the nettings and saw some seamen watching him anxiously.

Quantock persisted, 'Captain Glazebrook would never – '

Keen retorted, 'He is dead. We are not. Do you suggest that we abandon our admiral and all his party because *we* are at some risk? Is that what you are advising, Mr Quantock?' The release of his bitterness and anger seemed to help him. 'I'll see you, the master and all else in hell before *I* turn and run!'

He walked to the quarterdeck rail and peered aloft at the wildly thrashing canvas. They might lose a sail or a spar, perhaps the whole lot. But Bolitho was out there beyond the swaying poop. Pictures flashed through his thoughts. The Great South Sea. The girl he had loved, who had died of the fever which had almost done for Bolitho. In spite of his own despair Bolitho had tried to comfort him. Leave him now after what they had endured together? Never in ten thousand bloody years.

'Pass the word to the topmen, Mr Fraser. It will be close. Clear lower deck and put every available man on braces and halliards.' He grappled for the name of the lieutenant nearby. 'Mr Foord, prepare to drop the larboard anchor if the worst should happen.' It might hold her long enough to get some of the hands ashore.

He heard himself say calmly, 'Well, Mr Quantock?'

Quantock was glaring through the drifting spray.

'Aye, *aye*, sir.'

He snatched up his speaking-trumpet and strode to the side.

Keen gripped the smooth rail. How many captains had stood here? In storm or becalmed, entering harbour after a long and successful passage, or concealing fear as the deck had quivered and rocked to the roar of cannon fire.

Was he to be the last captain? He listened to the clank of pawls around the capstan, the crack of a starter across some-one's back as a boatswain's mate drove the men on the bars to greater efforts. Their weight and muscle to shift *Achates'* bulk against wind and sea.

He glanced once more at the crossed yards, the great rippling shapes of loosened sails where the topmen clung and waited to free them to the wind.

There was no sign of a light. The burning boom had vanished. Perhaps Allday had been prevented from reaching his objective. He would have given his life if so. One more picture rose in his mind. Of himself gasping and sobbing in agony. A mere midshipman with a great wooden splinter thrust into his groin like a spear. Of Allday, suddenly gentle, carrying him below and cutting the splinter away rather than trust his life to the ship's drunken surgeon.

'*Anchor's awei* . . . ' The rest was lost as the ship toppled to one side with waves rearing above the gangways and nettings like breakers on a reef.

'*Loose tops'ls!*'

The helmsmen slithered and fell but clung stubbornly to the big double wheel as the ship swung madly with the wind, the freed topsails crashing out from their yards, the sound of the gusts through canvas and shrouds drowning the cries of officers and seamen alike.

Keen forced his eyes to remain open as the sea dashed over the nettings and drenched him from head to toe. The water felt warm, jubilant in its efforts to throw the ship out of control.

He saw the *Sparrowhawk*'s midshipman, little Evans, clinging to a stay, his feet kicking at air as the deck plunged and yawed beneath him.

A dark object fell from the mizzen, hit the gangway with a sickening crack and vanished into the waves alongside. The man must have been torn from his precarious perch by the straining canvas. He had not even time to cry out.

Voices ebbed and died through the terrible chorus like souls already lost.

'More hands to the weather fore-brace there!'

'Mr Rooke, send two men aloft . . . '

'Take this man to the surgeon!'

'Lively there! The gig's breaking adrift!'

Suddenly the master shouted hoarsely, '*Answering*, sir!'

Keen turned and peered towards him. He could feel the wind flaying his mouth so that his lips were forced apart in a wild grin. But she *was* answering. With her main-yard braced hard round, the sails forcing her over so that the sea boiled through the sealed gun-ports in fierce jets, *Achates* was beginning to turn her full length into the teeth of the storm.

Broken rigging streamed down-wind like dead creeper, and Keen had already heard the rip of tearing canvas from overhead and knew that men were there to fight the damage with their bare hands.

'Nor'-east by north!' The man sounded breathless. 'Nor' by east!'

Keen gripped the rail until his fists ached. She was trying. Doing the impossible as with every second the wind drove her towards the blacker shadows of the land.

The yards creaked again and Keen watched the seamen straining wildly at the braces, some with their pale bodies almost touching the deck as they hauled with all their strength. Quantock's harsh voice was everywhere, harrying, threatening, demanding.

The deck seemed to lean forward and down in a great single thrust, and the sea roared through the beak-head and over the forecastle in a solid flood. Men tumbled and were washed aside like puppets, and it was a marvel that none of the guns was torn from its lashings. Keen had seen that too. A great gun thundering about the deck like an insane beast, crushing men who tried to snare it, smashing anything which stood in its path.

He watched with chilled fascination as the bows rose very slowly, the sea cascading away with a subdued roar. The ship was pointing towards the land. At the solid, unmoving barrier.

To confirm his disbelief he heard Knocker yell, 'Nor'-west it is, sir!'

There was still no signal. Nor would there be, he thought.

He should have felt despair for what he had done. Quantock had been right. There would have been no blame. Officially. He had been ordered to force the entrance rather than face the carefully sited battery in broad daylight. *Achates* was the only King's ship, Bolitho the only flag-officer here to act and decide. Nobody could have laid the blame on Keen's shoulder.

Now he might lose the ship and every man-jack aboard, and the island's defiance would remain as if they had never come to this damned place.

Yet in spite of the realization he was glad. He had tried. Bolitho would know it. And other ships would come to avenge them, British or French, it would make no difference in the end.

The lieutenant named Foord yelled wildly, 'The signal! Hell's teeth, the *signal*!' He was almost weeping with disbelief.

Keen said sharply, 'Control yourself, man! Mr Knocker! Bring her up a point to starboard!'

He tried to relax his limbs one at a time as he watched the hissing glow against the swift-moving clouds. Men ran to the braces again, and he heard the fore-topgallant sail boom out from its yard and knew that the topsail had been the one torn apart by the wind.

There it was. No mistake. Allday had done it.

'Nor'-west by north, sir! Steady as she goes!'

They seemed to be tearing through the water at a tremendous pace, like a runaway coach, its horses gone mad.

But Keen had heard something different in the gaunt sailing-master's voice. Not merely surprise or relief. Respect perhaps?

'Leadsmen in the chains!'

Keen pushed himself from the rail and walked to the opposite side to watch a leaping hurdle of breakers. The reefs looked close enough to touch with a pike.

He heard the cry of a leadsman but had no idea what the depth would be.

He saw the land suddenly close alongside, more spray, and felt the deck shiver as the keel ploughed into dangerous shallows.

Knocker was passing more helm orders, his voice suddenly

loud as the ship ran past the headland where the boom had once been.

There were vague explosions. Musket fire and the occasional boom of artillery. But it was unreal. Nothing to do with the plunging two-decker and her men.

Keen heard shouts from forward and then caught his breath as the ship gave a violent lurch. Then down the side he saw the dark outline of a small vessel, battered from her moorings by *Achates*, and capsizing slowly as they continued up the harbour.

The flare was still burning fiercely and Keen could see the flames reflecting on a paler shape nearby, Allday's barge. He snatched a telescope from a midshipman and trained it across the larboard bow.

In the reflected glow he could see the bargemen standing and waving their tarred hats as they saw the ship heading towards them. *Achates* must make quite a sight, Keen thought. Sails shining in the flare, while her hull remained locked in darkness.

'Prepare to shorten sail, Mr Quantock!'

Keen found that his whole being was shaking uncontrollably, like a man on the verge of death.

Then he saw the lights of the town for the first time, glittering through the spray like tiny jewels. They were almost there. It was incredible. Impossible, some would say.

Somewhere another cannon banged out, but Keen had no idea where the ball fell.

'Stand by to wear ship, Mr Quantock.'

There was still plenty of real danger. If the ship failed to respond this time they could drive on to the beach or become entangled with anchored shipping like a porpoise in a net.

Perhaps they had created their own trap? Keen found he could consider it without emotion. It would not matter now. If they could not leave, neither would anyone else. He pictured Bolitho's grave features and hoped he had seen *Achates* drive into the harbour like a phantom ship.

If it could only be settled in a battle of wills, he knew who would emerge the victor.

'Man the lee braces!' Quantock loomed towards him. 'I've ordered both anchors to be ready, sir, and put a lieutenant in charge of the compressor. In this gale the cable might part if . . . ' He left the rest unsaid.

Keen regarded him calmly. 'Carry on, if you please.'

There was no change in Quantock and Keen felt strangely glad. It seemed wrong that he should change in any way because of a single reckless act. When you considered it, Keen thought, there was no other description for it.

'Tops'l clew-lines!'

Keen watched the flurry of activity above the deck. Those men had done well, he thought. To preserve their lives, their ship and their pride as only sailors could.

'Helm alee!'

Once again the deck tilted over, Allday's barge swinging away from the jib-boom as if it had taken flight. But the wind and sea had lost their punch. Momentarily. They would bide their time. There was always another battle.

'Let go!'

Keen heard a splash and felt the planking quiver slightly as the second anchor banged against the hull as it swung from its cat-head in readiness to drop if the other failed.

Blocks squealed, and slowly but surely the unseen topmen kicked and fisted the rebellious canvas to each yard and secured it.

The motion eased immediately, and Keen said as calmly as he could, 'Lower the remaining boats. I want a warp run out from aft. Tell Mr Rooke to report to me.' He turned away from Quantock's bitter silence. 'I also want a muster of all hands immediately. Casualties and serious injuries too, if you please.'

A tiny figure appeared at his elbow. It was Ozzard, Bolitho's molelike servant.

'Here, sir.'

He held out a silver tankard, one of Bolitho's own.

Keen held it to his lips and almost choked on rum.

But it did what Ozzard intended and he handed him the tankard.

'That was thoughtful. Thank you.'

They both watched as the gig and then the jolly-boat were hoisted from the tier and swayed out above the gangway. More men were bustling aft while boatswain's mates bawled instructions for laying out a massive warp. Against the pale planking the huge rope looked like an endless serpent.

Ozzard asked timidly, 'Will he be safe, sir?'

Keen saw a lieutenant and Harry Rooke, the boatswain, hurrying towards him for orders, but there was something in Ozzard's voice which held him.

Safe? It was a word rarely considered in the King's service.

Faith had more meaning. Faith to enter a strange harbour despite the hazards and possible consequences. Faith of men like Allday who would risk anything because of Bolitho's word and reputation.

He smiled before turning towards his waiting subordinates.

'He will be expecting a lot from us tomorrow, Ozzard, *that* I do know.'

Ozzard bobbed and nodded. It was good enough for him.

9

A Close Thing

Bolitho felt a hand touch his arm and tried not to groan as the stiffness plucked at his wound. Had he really been asleep? The realization shocked him into immediate alertness.

'What is it, man?'

Lieutenant Mountsteven watched him curiously, as if he did not really believe he was sharing a small rough gully with his vice-admiral.

'Dawn soon, sir. I've roused all hands.'

Bolitho sat up and rubbed his eyes. They felt raw and tired, and he noticed for the first time that the wind had almost died.

Looking back, it still seemed unreal, an impossible hallucination. He peered over the edge of the ground and saw the vague glint of water, as if he expected to see *Achates* forcing the entrance, her sails bulging like metal breast-plates, burnished gold by the spluttering flares. *Achates* was only a small sixty-four, but in the eerie glare she had seemingly filled the harbour and had brought wild cheers and not a few tears from Bolitho's seamen.

Around him he heard men gathering up their weapons and recalled the Royal Marine corporal who had been sent by Captain Dewar to report that all his men were ashore and in position.

That too seemed like part of a dream, the corporal apparently unmoved and immaculate in his scarlet uniform.

He grinned, despite his anxieties. By comparison he felt like a vagrant in his stained shirt and his hair full of grit and blown sand.

The fortress was still lost in darkness, but the old volcano had a fine rim of grey light around its summit.

Mountsteven handed him a flask and said, 'I've put a good lookout to watch for the ship, sir. The marines will prevent any attempt to move a cannon from the town to fire on her.'

Bolitho held the flask to his lips and felt his eyes water as the raw brandy burned his tongue. So much depended on Rivers. Given time he could move his heavy battery to another wall where with ordinary shot he could pound *Achates* to fragments. With heated shot he could achieve it in minutes.

It was as if the whole island was unwilling to wake, to enter the new day. He doubted if Rivers had had much sleep, wherever he was.

He looked round as somewhere a cock crowed defiantly in the damp air.

The third lieutenant scrambled down the slope and said breathlessly, 'They're moving artillery in the fortress, sir. I put a picket as close as I could.' He too took the flask from the other lieutenant and raised it to his lips. He grimaced and added, 'But the gates are still shut.'

Bolitho nodded, his mind grappling with such frugal intelligence. Rivers must be regaining confidence, whereas the first excitement of the landing and breaking the boom was already fading with the dawn.

Bolitho stood up carefully and wiped his face with his sleeve. What a wretched situation it was. People in England would question the need for men to die for such a cause when the French would gather all the spoils anyway. He cursed angrily and knew he was thinking only of himself, of his hopes for a future with Belinda. No wonder youthful lieutenants like Mountsteven and Scott eyed him with some curiosity. He should have known, have remembered his own service as a lieutenant. Then he had never considered the personal problems of *his* superiors, their wives, or that they might be as apprehensive as their subordinates when the time came to fight.

He shook the mood aside like an old cloak. To live without Belinda would be unbearable. But to live without honour would be beyond him.

There was a startled challenge from the waterside and Bolitho heard Allday's voice, hushed but fierce as he retorted, 'It's me, you blind fool! Hold your noise or I'll spit you, so I will!' He stumbled down the slope and peered uncertainly at the three officers.

Bolitho smiled. 'You performed a miracle. It was well done!'

Allday seemed to realize that one of the dishevelled shapes was Bolitho and bared his teeth in the gloom.

'Thankee, sir.'

Scott said, 'Thought you might have run into a guard-boat, Allday.'

Allday looked at him as if to consider if a mere lieutenant was worth his attention, then said, 'We did, sir.' He drew his hand across his throat. 'No bother at all.'

The violent crash of a single cannon made several of the men gasp with surprise. Birds rose screaming and squawking in pale clouds from land and water alike, and as the sailors watched the smoke drift from the ramparts they all heard the unmistakable thud of a direct hit.

Bolitho fastened his sword-belt and snapped, 'They've found *Achates.*'

As if in answer to his words there was a swift response from the direction of the town. Musket fire for the most part, and then the sounds of horses clattering along a road.

Rivers' militia intended to attack them before they had found their proper bearings on the island, while a re-sited battery would concentrate on the anchored ship.

Bolitho said, 'Captain Keen will have to be quick. We must win him some more time.'

He peered round and noticed that already the landscape and the nearest huddle of seamen had grown sharper in the feeble light.

Mountsteven asked quietly, 'What do you intend, sir?'

'Flag of truce.' Bolitho saw his look of amazement and added sharply, 'Two volunteers, if you please.'

He tried not to flinch as the gun fired again. He did not hear the ball strike, but in a few moments the gunner would have his target in full view.

Allday said bluntly, '*One* volunteer. I'm comin', sir.'

Bolitho walked from his patch of cover and faced the track which wound its way up to the fortress. A bluff? He had nothing else to offer.

With Allday breathing hard at his side, and the boat-swain's mate, Christy, a step or so in the rear, Bolitho strode along the rough ground. Christy was carrying a shirt on a boat-hook as a flag of truce and was quietly whistling to himself as he followed his admiral. He had even managed to make a joke of the fact that the shirt belonged to one of the two midshipmen who were with the landing party. 'The only young gentlemen with one clean enough for the occasion,' as he had put it.

Bolitho was astonished that he could still raise a grin or two with his remark.

'*Halt!* That's far enough!'

Bolitho stood quite still, the fortress looming over him like a grey cliff. He thought he heard a scrape of metal and imagined a marksman taking careful aim at him, white flag or not. Again he felt the same bitterness welling up inside him. Who would care? Hundreds, thousands of sailors and soldiers had died all over the world for one cause or another, but who ever remembered why?

He cupped his hands. 'I want to speak with Sir Humphrey Rivers!'

There was a derisive chuckle. 'Don't you mean *parley*, sir?'

Bolitho pressed his hands tightly to his sides. He had been right. Rivers was inside. Otherwise the unknown men above the gates would have said so, to mock him for his mistake.

Allday muttered, 'I'll give that bugger *parley*!'

'Oh, it's you, Bolitho! I thought we had some beggars at the gates, what?'

Bolitho found he could relax now that he knew Rivers was really here.

'And pray, what can I do for you before I take you and your ruffians into custody?'

Bolitho felt his heart pumping against his ribs as if it was the only part of his body still able to respond. Surely the light was brighter? But for the storm the whole fortress would already be visible.

Somewhere beyond the wall he heard a man yell, 'Ready to fire, sir!'

But Rivers was enjoying himself. 'A moment longer, Tate! I must hear the gallant admiral's request.'

Bolitho said in a whisper, 'They cannot shoot while Rivers is there. The ship is in direct line with him.' He raised his voice again, 'I ask you to hold your fire and stand down your men. You have no chance of defeating us, and your people must know full well of the consequences for their actions against a King's ship.'

He tried to picture his words being passed from man to man behind that wall. But they were all islanders, and probably little better than pirates in times of war, although the more sensitive term 'privateer' had made their trade almost legal.

Rivers shouted angrily, 'God damn you, Bolitho! You had your chance, now you shall pay dearly for your bloody arrogance!'

Bolitho blinked as a shaft of bright sunlight pierced the ramparts of the fortress's central tower and laid bare the hillside behind him.

Bolitho heard some of the seamen calling from their hiding places and guessed the sun had also uncovered the anchored two-decker.

Rivers' voice rose higher still as he shouted, 'There's your target, lads! Make every ball tell. That captain is a bigger fool than his admiral!'

Bolitho turned very slowly and looked across the water to the white houses and the cluster of moored vessels. He found that he could ignore the chorus of jeers from Rivers' men as he saw what Keen and his depleted company had achieved in complete darkness. The long cable which had been run out to a mooring buoy from *Achates'* stern held the ship motionless, so that her whole broadside was exposed to the fortress battery. Keen had converted the ship from a living creature to a moored double battery. One side faced the town, the other commanded the anchorage and anything which tried to enter or leave. No wonder Rivers had mistaken their intentions.

Rivers yelled, 'I have a force of mounted men coming to deal with *you*, Bolitho. Your disgrace and ignominy after this reckless escapade will put paid to any future assaults on *my island*!'

Bolitho could see him framed against the washed-out blue sky, could feel the loathing in the man like something solid. He saw smoke rising lazily above the grey stones and knew they were heating shot to destroy *Achates*. There was no more time to spare.

He called, 'I shall return to my men, Sir Humphrey . . . ' He felt a nerve jump in his throat as he heard the far-off but familiar rumble. This time he dared not turn, dared not take his eyes from Rivers' silhouette as the muffled sound suddenly ceased.

Rivers exclaimed, 'What good can that do? Not one of her guns can even scratch these walls!' But he sounded less forceful, as if, like Bolitho, the sound of *Achates* running out her guns on both broadsides had released a memory.

'Do you have a telescope, Sir Humphrey?'

It was difficult to stay calm when every fibre made him want to charge at the gates and smash them down with his bare fists.

Rivers was already peering through a glass towards the motionless ship. *Achates'* total stillness made it somehow unnerving. Each sail neatly furled, not a soul moving above the black and buff hull.

Bolitho said, 'You will see a man in the mainmast cross-trees, a lieutenant to be exact. He too will have a telescope this morning, Sir Humphrey. Trained inland towards *your* house and estate.'

Rivers said, 'Don't play for time!'

'And after *that*, the town, Sir Humphrey, until not even a stone stands on end.'

The roar when it came was tremendous, thrown back from *Achates'* hidden side by the land, so that it echoed and re-echoed around the fortress as if the battery there had already opened fire.

Bolitho twisted round to watch the dense smoke moving away from the ship towards the shore, where moments earlier many people had been waiting to see the uneven battle.

Aboard ship Keen's officers would be passing instructions to the capstans, another turn on the massive warp to swing the ship further still towards the target.

He saw the scar on *Achates'* tumblehome where the first ball had found a mark. It was nothing to what heated shot would do.

A small pendant rose smartly to *Achates'* main-yard and flapped in the breeze.

Bolitho said flatly, 'The next broadside is laid and ready. It is your decision.'

Behind him he heard Christy murmur, 'Gawd.'

Allday said, 'The cavalry are comin', sir.'

Bolitho saw the cluster of horsemen cantering along the track which led from the town. They looked unruly, startled probably by the sudden blast of cannon fire. Mercenaries, local planters, militiamen, it did not matter. If they took control of the road and captured Bolitho's party it would mean another change of fortunes.

A bugle blared briefly and Bolitho saw the files of scarlet-coated marines emerge from the brush where they had lain in hiding and prepared for this final moment.

He saw the glitter of sunlight on the fixed bayonets, and could imagine Dewar and his lieutenant receiving the reports of the seasoned professionals like Sergeant Saxton.

The horses had gathered speed, the dust spewing away from the hoofs in a solid bank.

There was a ragged volley of shots, and Bolitho felt a cold grip in his stomach as three of the tiny scarlet figures fell across the track.

The marines seemed to take an eternity, the front rank kneeling beside their dead comrades while the rear rank took aim above their heads. More shots. This time it was a small drummer who fell.

Allday gasped, 'Jesus, why don't they shoot, damn them!'

Dewar's blade flashed down and the crash of muskets seemed as if a single shot had been fired.

Horses and men tumbled in confusion, but when the smoke cleared from the hillside the scarlet lines were unchanged. The horsemen were returning to the town, their dead and wounded left to their own resources.

Christy said fiercely, 'The gates are openin', sir!'

It was over. In twos and threes, and then in a flood, the fortress's garrison hurried into the sunlight, dropping their weapons as they ran.

Last of all came Rivers, swaying from side to side as if he were drunk.

But there was no slur in his voice as he faced Bolitho and said, 'I'll see you in *hell* for this!' He stared wildly at the lush green slope beyond the town. 'My house, my family, you fired on them without caring — '

Bolitho said sharply, 'By your orders some of my men have died today.' He tried to hold his anger under control. 'And for what? Because of your greed and ambition.' He turned away, afraid he would finally lose control. 'And have no fear, Sir Humphrey. While you were prepared to burn a King's ship to her water-line and murder every man-jack aboard if need be, Captain Keen took care to keep his guns *unshotted*. You were defeated by smoke, nothing more.'

It should have been a proud moment but Bolitho was sickened by it.

To Allday he said, 'We shall return to the ship. Dewar's men will take charge here.'

Allday gestured towards the stricken Rivers. 'What about 'im?'

'See that he is well guarded for his own safety.'

Allday glared as two seamen seized Rivers and hustled him back towards the fortress.

Almost to himself Bolitho added, 'It is always easy for the victor to exact revenge.' Then he clapped the burly coxswain on the arm and said, 'The sea is where I belong.'

Allday breathed out very slowly. It had been a close thing that time. He shivered despite the growing warmth. Getting past it. Leave it to the youngsters after this.

The delusion cheered him slightly and he quickened his pace.

The seamen stood on either side of the track and grinned as Bolitho walked amongst them.

Bolitho knew or could guess what they were thinking. *One of us*. Because he was as dirty and dishevelled as they were. Because he had been with them when the bluff could so easily have gone the wrong way.

There was so much to be done. The fortress to be occupied by Dewar's marines, the islanders to be sorted and placated. Despatches to be written. Explanations to be made.

Somewhere a wounded horse screamed in agony. Like a woman in terror. Mercifully it was silenced by a pistol shot.

Bolitho paused by the place where Dewar had made his stand. The drummer-boy lay on his back, his blue eyes and pinched features frozen at the moment of impact.

Allday thought he heard Bolitho murmur, 'Too young for this game.' Then he pulled out his handkerchief and laid it on the boy's face.

One of us. It seemed to mock him as he walked through the grinning, nodding sailors who had all expected to die on this fine morning.

I lead. They follow.

He stared across at the *Achates* and his flag which flapped occasionally from the foremast truck.

He saw the barge idling by some rocks ready to carry him

to the ship. He straightened his back and looked neither right nor left.

A lieutenant was standing in the stern-sheets, his hat in his hand. In a moment they would start to cheer. They were the victors, and that was enough for them. It had to be.

He hesitated and looked at Allday's homely face.

'Well, old friend, what are you thinking?'

Allday frowned, off-balance at this mood which he did not recognize.

Bolitho said quietly, 'I think I know anyway.' He faced the bargemen and forced a smile. 'Now let us find that other damned pirate!'

The lieutenant raised his cocked hat and the men began to cheer.

Bolitho sat down and looked at his torn breeches.

One of us.

Bolitho sat in his day-cabin and sighed as Yovell placed yet another copied letter before him for signature.

The fear and thrill of their attack seemed far behind them, even though it was still less than a week since he had faced Rivers outside the fortress. Their casualties had been mercifully few and had been buried on the hillside in the island's own graveyard.

Bolitho stood up and crossed restlessly to the stern windows and leaned over the passive water of the anchorage. The sill was hot beneath his palms, the sun high above the extinct volcano.

He saw *Achates*' guard-boat pulling slowly and with little enthusiasm in the blinding glare and could guess what they, like most of the ship's company, were thinking.

With their governor under arrest the islanders had settled down to await events. All resistance and hostility had ceased, and some of the local militia had been resworn to assist the Royal Marines mount guard on the fortress and battery. But it went deeper. It was a passive resistance, the townspeople taking pains to look away whenever a naval working party or sea officer walked past.

The sailors were at first hurt then resentful. Some had died, few really understood why, but they deserved better, they thought.

It was noon and the smell of boiling tar mingled with the headier aroma of rum as the daily ration was served to each mess throughout the ship. Fewer hammers broke the stillness now, and there was little to show of the damage made by the fortress's cannon, although one seaman had lost an eye because of a flying splinter.

There was a tap at the outer screen door and Keen entered, his hat beneath his arm. He looked less strained, Bolitho thought. He guessed that Keen had been dealing with his own procession of demands and reports. The surgeon and the first lieutenant, the purser and the master, they all paid their respects to the captain, if only to shift their own loads on to his shoulders.

'You sent for me, sir?'

'Sit down, Val.' Bolitho loosened his shirt for the hundredth time. 'How is the work progressing?'

'I turn the hands to work if only to keep their minds busy, sir. *Achates* is ready for anything. Bandbox neat, she is.'

Bolitho nodded. He had already noticed the new pride Keen had shown for his ship. Maybe her previous captain's example had haunted him and dominated the other officers from the grave.

Bolitho had heard of Keen's clash with Quantock before the headlong charge into harbour. It was hard to believe any of it had happened. But the Union Flag flew above the fortress, and to all outward appearances the island was as before.

Soon he would have to send a despatch to the French admiral whose ships lay waiting at Boston. If they were indeed still there.

Then the peace would shatter here and the pain begin all over again.

Keen watched Bolitho's grave features and said, 'The admiral at Antigua will send aid if you request it, sir.' He saw the line of Bolitho's jaw harden and added, 'But doubtless you have already considered that.'

'I was given this task, Val. Perhaps it is pride which stands in my way. Some might say conceit.' He waved down Keen's protest. 'We all have some. But I need eyes and ears, not another flag-officer to breathe down my neck. But for *Sparrowhawk*'s loss . . .'

They looked at each other. It still seemed as if Duncan was alive.

Keen said, 'Once we weigh and go in search of that damned ship the island could erupt. These people could starve out the garrison, but not the other way round. I think we should order a summary court martial and run Sir Humphrey up to the main-yard on a halter.' He spoke with unusual bitterness. 'Alive he is still a menace.'

They stood up as a single musket shot echoed across the water.

'Guard-boat. Must have sighted something.'

Keen snatched up his hat. 'I'll find out, sir.'

Bolitho took a telescope from its rack and waited for *Achates* to swing gently to her anchor. He watched the fortress swim into view, the upper ramparts half hidden in heat-haze so that the Union Flag seemed to be pinned to the sky itself. There was the headland and the tiny island and its Spanish mission beyond. Then he saw a solitary tanned topsail rounding the point before settling down on a final approach towards the anchorage.

The guard-boat, one of *Achates*' cutters, rocked on the swell, her oars protruding along either side like bleached bones.

A small brigantine. Probably some local trader. Her master would get a surprise when he saw *Achates*' bulk in the harbour.

Keen came back, his face moist with sweat.

'I've ordered the guard-boat to lead the brigantine to a buoy.' He waited for Bolitho to turn. 'She's been fired on to all acounts, sir. I'm sending the surgeon over immediately.'

'Fired on?'

Keen shrugged. 'That's all I know.'

'I see. Well, signal any local craft to stand away. I have an uneasy feeling about this.'

He raised his glass and steadied it on the brigantine as her flapping jib was taken in and she rounded smartly on to a mooring buoy.

He moved the glass carefully along the vessel's side. Black pock-marks marred her paintwork. Grape or cannister. Anything heavier would have sunk such a frail craft. The glass settled on two figures aft by the tiller. A big man in a blue coat with untidy grey hair. The other . . .

Bolitho exclaimed, 'God damn it, Val, it's young Adam! If he's taken any unnecessary risks, I'll . . . '

They faced each other and laughed.

'I'm a *fine* example for him, eh?'

It seemed an eternity for a boat to make the passage between *Achates* and the newcomer.

Bolitho replaced the glass on its rack. It would not do for Adam to think he was worried and over-protective. All the same . . .

Keen said, 'I'll go on deck and er, welcome them, sir.' He hid a smile as he shut the door behind him.

Adam entered the cabin, his features anxious and apprehensive.

'I'm sorry, sir — '

Bolitho strode to him and gripped his shoulders. 'You're *here*. That's all that matters.'

Adam looked round the cabin as if afraid of what he might see.

'The guard-boat, Uncle. They told me about the battle. How you had to fight your way into this place.' He lowered his eyes so that a lock of black hair fell across his forehead. 'I heard about *Sparrowhawk* too. I'm so sorry.'

Bolitho led him to a chair and said quietly, 'Never mind about that. Tell me about your troubles.'

It was an amazing story which the young lieutenant

blurted out. Just a few days ago, after riding out a fierce storm near the Great Bahama Bank, they had been confronted by a frigate. She had been Spanish and had ordered them to heave to and to await a boarding party. The brigantine's master had apparently been suspicious and when the frigate's boat had been almost alongside he had clapped on all sail and had headed away, a favourable wind taking him into some shallows too dangerous for the frigate to follow. But not before the Spanish boarding party had opened fire with swivels and a bow gun which had peppered the side and killed the brigantine's mate.

Bolitho listened without interruption. You were never safe. Not *really* safe. While he had been fretting over San Felipe's future, Adam had faced an unexplained attack and possible death.

He said, 'The vessel's master must be an audacious fellow. Courageous too. I should like to meet him.'

Adam looked at him, his eyes shining. He wanted, no *needed* to tell Bolitho about Robina, but after what he had seen and heard on his passage from Boston he would not spoil the moment for a fortune.

'He came over with me! He's here!'

Bolitho eyed him questioningly. 'Well, let's have him in.'

The sentry opened the screen door and stood aside to allow the visitor to enter. Only the marine's eyes moved beneath his glazed leather hat as he said, 'Master of the *Vivid*, sir!' The 'sir' was accompanied by a sharp tap on the deck with his musket.

Bolitho opened his mouth to speak and then stared with astonishment. The patched blue coat with old navy buttons sewn on the cuffs, the wooden stump which protruded from one of his trouser legs, none of these things could destroy the man's identity.

Bolitho hurried to greet him and held out both hands.

'Jethro Tyrrell. Twenty years, man. And here you are!'

He watched as Tyrrell put his head on one side and regarded him with mock amusement.

'A vice-admiral, they tell me.' He nodded slowly, his

untidy grey hair falling over his collar. 'Never knew the Admiralty had that kind'a sense!'

He released his grip and limped around the great cabin, his hand touching things, his eyes everywhere.

Bolitho watched him, the memories flashing through his thoughts like fiery pictures.

The little sloop-of-war *Sparrow*, his first command, and with Jethro Tyrrell, a Colonist officer, as his lieutenant.

It was painful to see his dragging stump, his worn clothing.

Tyrrell paused by Bolitho's coat which was tossed carelessly on a chair.

He touched one gold epaulette with his forefinger and said softly, 'As you say. Twenty years. You've done well, Dick. Real proud o' you.'

Even the soft Virginian drawl brought back a hundred more memories.

Tyrrell sat down carefully and adjusted his coat. 'I'd best be off. Just wanted to see you. Don't want to – '

Bolitho exclaimed, 'I was your commanding officer once, remember? You'll *stay here* and tell me everything. I tried to discover your whereabouts after the war.'

Tyrrell watched Ozzard bustling round him with goblets and bottles.

He said, 'When I was sent young Adam there as a passenger I knew I had to see you.' His eyes shone in the reflected sunlight.

'They were great days, eh?' He glanced at the spell-bound lieutenant. 'Real young terror he was. Younger than me too. Fought a duel for a girl who wanted him dead, and almost took on the Frogs single-handed.' He was smiling broadly but his eyes were incredibly sad.

Bolitho asked gently, 'What are you doing these days?'

'This an' that. I command the *Vivid*, but she's not mine, worse luck. Do a lot o' trading between the islands. The Dons and the King's ships are always after me as they think I'm a smuggler too. That's a joke. Look at me!'

The door opened and Keen entered warily.

Bolitho said, 'This is Jethro Tyrrell.' He looked at the grey-haired man in the chair. 'My first lieutenant in the *Sparrow*.' He smiled at Keen's surprise. 'Another war, Val, but a fine little ship.'

Tyrrell shifted in his chair, uncomfortable under their stares.

'Anyways, I hear you're having a spot of trouble here. Goin' to hand back San Felipe to the Frogs, right?'

Bolitho nodded gravely. 'News travels a long way.'

Tyrrell grimaced. 'Not fast enough, it seems. It's the bloody Dons you want to worry about. They intend to take this island.' He regarded their faces with quiet satisfaction. 'They will too if you're not damn careful. They've got eyes everywhere. They even tried to stop my *Vivid* to search her and see if I was carrying despatches or letters.' He glanced at Adam. 'My God, if they'd found him aboard they'd have murdered the lot of us, I shouldn't wonder.'

Bolitho leaned towards him. 'Is that really true? About the Spaniards?'

Tyrrell looked at him grimly. 'I need money to buy the *Vivid*. She's not much, but it would be a new start for me.' He turned his face away. 'Just as you want the ship which put down your frigate.'

He sounded hurt. Ashamed. But there was no doubting his sincerity.

Bolitho said, 'I'll help you, Jethro. I would have done anyway if I'd only known.'

'I had some pride, Dick. *Then* I did. Now I'm desperate. Lost my family, all gone. All I've got left is the sea, and I *need* a ship.'

Bolitho walked past him and then stopped with his hand on the big man's shoulder.

'You shall have it. Trust me.'

Tyrrell gave a great sigh. 'Then I'll take you to that bloody Spaniard.'

Bolitho looked at Keen. He seemed too stunned to speak.

Twenty years. It could be yesterday.

IO

The Face of Loyalty

'For God's sake close the skylight, Allday!'

Bolitho leaned over his chart again, his hands around neat calculations and soundings, San Felipe and the neighbouring shores of Cuba and Haiti.

With the stern windows shut and now the cabin skylight, the place was like a kiln. It was to no avail anyway, and Bolitho heard Black Joe Langtry's voice quite easily as the master-at-arms counted out the stroke of the cat-o'-nine-tails.

It was strange Bolitho had never accepted or grown used to it. A captain's last resort at maintaining discipline.

A roll of drums, a pause and then that awful crack of the lash across a man's naked back.

He stared hard at the chart until his eyes watered.

'*Ten!*' Langtry's harsh voice intruded again.

Keen would be up there with his officers, watching it. Hating it. But any King's ship sailing alone and without resort to other support was always in danger of exploding into chaos.

Three trusted seamen had deserted while working ashore for the purser, but had been hunted down and brought back by some of the local militia. They had apparently met some half-caste girls at one of the plantations. The rest needed little imagination.

Crack. 'Eleven!'

Now they were paying the price for their momentary pleasures. Keen had awarded the minimum punishment of twenty-four lashes apiece. But it was enough to turn a man's back into a tangle of raw flesh.

Bolitho thought of Tyrrell again. He was aboard his brigantine *Vivid* attending to storm damage and putting right the other scars left by the Spaniard's swivels.

It was unnerving that Tyrrell should appear like this. Memories of those far-off days together, of the little *Sparrow* and what she had meant to both of them.

Am I to be ever plagued by memory?

Just as the frigate *Phalarope*, which had been Bolitho's second command, had sailed in his squadron last year like a spectre from the past, now came *Sparrow*'s reminder to haunt him.

Was it really so? Was I happier then with less responsibility? Prepared to risk life, even lose it, rather than chance reputation as he was doing now.

The drums ceased and he realized the floggings had ended.

He knew Tyrrell, *really* knew him. Had been with him when he had been smashed to the deck and had lost his leg.

Now he was a shabby reflection of that other man. Outwardly he was no danger to anyone. He was just the sort of ship's master who would hear rumours about the movements and activities of men-of-war. Their nationality and colours mattered little to the master of a small trader. All were potentially dangerous. Seeking prime seamen, even through press-gangs, was no longer in use. Who would know or care until it was too late for the luckless sailor anyway?

Tyrrell had been unshakeable about the powerful two-decker. She wore no colours and carried no name, but Spanish frigates from Santo Domingo, even those from La Guaira hundreds of miles to the south'rd, knew her and kept their distance.

This mysterious ship, which had not hesitated to fire on *Achates* when Keen had outwitted her in the darkness and had butchered *Sparrowhawk*'s people without mercy, was in the Caribbean and its approaches for a purpose. A task in which she would risk anything if required.

He heard Allday open the skylight and knew that he, like Ozzard and everyone who came near, was being especially careful.

Bolitho looked at his big coxswain and shrugged helplessly. 'I do not know what is happening to me.'

Allday nodded his head and smiled. 'Waitin', that's what's wrong, sir.'

'I suppose so.'

Bolitho looked down at the chart again. It was a week since *Vivid* had sailed into the harbour and Tyrrell had re-entered his life. Without another ship Bolitho dared not leave San Felipe. An attack might be launched by Rivers' supporters, there were plenty of them in evidence. Bolitho could not blame them. They would have to quit their homes and their plantations when the French came. Perhaps Keen had been right. If they hanged Rivers it might end there.

But Rivers had powerful friends in America and the City of London. In Bolitho's eyes he was no better than a pirate. But a proper trial in London would be required by their lordships to prove it.

If Tyrrell was right and the unknown two-decker was preparing to mount an attack on San Felipe, it was folly to leave the harbour unguarded. *Achates* had proved what could be done when it seemed worth the risk.

The door opened and Adam walked into the cabin.

A full week since they had been reunited and yet they had said very little. Adam was keeping something from him. Or maybe he had been too busy and preoccupied to share the young lieutenant's confidences.

He said, 'Signal from the battery, sir. The brig *Electra* is standing into the bay. She should anchor within the hour.'

'Thank you, Adam.'

Bolitho's eyes moved back to the chart. He could picture the brig's commander clearly when he had described his discovery of the *Sparrowhawk*'s few survivors in an American trader. Napier, that was his name. He must have sailed under every inch of canvas to make such a fast passage to Antigua and then westwards to San Felipe. Dare he hope that *Electra* would be able to wait in the harbour as a show of authority? She was only a small brig, but she flew the same flag as *Achates*.

Bolitho suspected that many of the islanders would be happier if a King's ship was always here, rather than leave the door open for the French or, as Tyrrell had said, the Spaniards.

Bolitho walked to the windows and shaded his eyes with his forearm.

'Signal *Electra*'s captain to repair on board immediately he anchors.'

Adam smiled gravely. 'I have requested the battery to relay that signal already, Uncle.'

Bolitho turned and spread his hands. 'You'll make a fine commander one of these days, my lad.'

Keen entered the cabin and dropped into a chair at Bolitho's bidding.

'I wonder what news she brings us, sir?'

He took a glass of hock gratefully and held it to his lips. Ozzard had been keeping a special store of it in the bilges ever since the ship had left the Beaulieu River in Hampshire.

'Any news will be welcome. I sometimes feel like a man who has gone deaf.'

Keen said, 'Maybe their lordships will recall us.'

Bolitho said, 'Adam, make a signal to *Vivid*, better still, go across and speak with Mr Tyrrell. I'd like him aboard with me when we sail.'

Keen waited for the door to close and then put his glass down very carefully.

'May I say something, sir?'

'You disagree with my proposed strategy, is that it?'

Keen smiled briefly. 'You are taking a terrible chance. Two chances to be exact.' When Bolitho remained silent he continued, 'This man Tyrrell. How much do you know about him?'

'He was my first lieutenant . . .' Keen nodded. 'You mean that's not enough after twenty years?'

Keen shrugged. 'Hard to say, sir. He said himself he's desperate. He's lost his wife and family, even his reputation, because he fought for the King rather than Washington.'

'Go on.' Bolitho could sense Allday holding his breath. 'Suppose you meet with the Spaniard and bring her to action, what would we do if she hoists her true colours? Would you spark off a war?'

'Tell me about the second risk.'

Keen was perfectly right to point it out to him. But it made Bolitho feel more isolated than ever.

'The second one is that the Spanish ship, *if* she is still in these waters, might be waiting for you to leave harbour so that she can snatch *Achates'* place. You would have to fight your way back in. Not against a few stupid planters and the local militia, but a real ship, and the men to back up her authority. In my opinion, the risk outweighs the profit.' He dropped his eyes. 'I — I am sorry, sir. But it had to be said.'

Bolitho smiled sadly. 'I understand what it cost you. In truth, I do not know if a risk can ever be measured. I don't wish our people to die for no purpose. Nor do I want my own body divided between the wings and limbs tubs around the surgeon's table. I have everything to live for. Now. But . . . '

Keen grinned and took a refilled glass from Ozzard.

'Aye, sir, *but*. What a powerful argument that small word can raise against reason!'

Bolitho tapped the chart with his brass dividers.

'I believe that ship to be here, just as Jethro Tyrrell described. She has a sizeable company, so will require a good haven to shelter in while her captain seeks information about us. Beset as we are by enemies, that part will not be too difficult for him.'

Keen stood up and joined him by the table.

'*If* Tyrrell is right, it would make things very difficult in a war.' He ran his fingers along the islands. Puerto Rico, Santo Domingo, Haiti, even Cuba. 'The Spaniards would command all the approaches to the Caribbean and to Jamaica.' He nodded slowly, understanding spreading on his handsome features. 'And San Felipe stands astride the Windward Passage like a drawbridge. No wonder the French want the island for themselves. They need an ally, but they are not required to trust him!'

They were both studying the chart when a midshipman announced the arrival of *Electra* at the anchorage.

Keen buttoned his coat.

'I'll receive Commander Napier, sir.' He glanced at the table. 'I'm still not sure that I am convinced, sir.'

Bolitho smiled. 'You will be.'

He allowed Ozzard to assist him into his sea-going coat out of respect for *Electra*'s captain.

His body ran with sweat, and through the stern windows he saw the gentle rise and fall of the clear water and imagined himself swimming naked there. His thoughts turned instantly to Belinda. It only took a split second. Like dropping your guard through fatigue or over-confidence. The enemy's blade darting forward like a steel tongue. He had tried to occupy every moment of his time with his work and the puzzle which he must solve. But every so often he saw only Belinda and the distance which divided them like an eternal barrier.

He vaguely heard footsteps and lowered voices. He had to recover himself for their sakes as well as his own.

Soon now, probably very soon, they would have to fight. This was no haphazard scheme or piratical aspiration. The unknown ship had already proved that to be in the right was no protection. Too many had died already to support such an argument.

He faced the door. In any war the cannon was impartial. Its roar swept away saint and sinner with the same indifference.

Commander Napier, with a shining new epaulette fixed to his left shoulder for the occasion, entered and clicked his shoes together.

Bolitho took the heavy envelope from his hand and passed it to Yovell.

'You made a speedy passage, Commander Napier.'

Bolitho tried to contain his impatience as Napier was put in a chair and a glass of wine brought for him.

Napier said, 'English Harbour is almost empty of ships but for a third-rate which is refitting and two frigates. The admiral has taken the squadron to the Leeward Islands, sir. Commodore Chater is in temporary command.' He swallowed under Bolitho's grey stare. 'He sends you his respects and best wishes, sir.'

Bolitho heard Yovell breaking the seals on the canvas envelope and wanted to run and tear out the despatches from Antigua. But without the admiral there he was helpless. He knew a little of Commodore Chater. He was not one to risk the displeasure of his superior with some brave gesture.

Napier added huskily, 'I am commanded to place myself and *Electra* at your wishes, sir.' He screwed up his eyes as he tried to recall exactly what Chater had told him. 'When he learned of *Sparrowhawk*'s loss he wished to send some marines to enlarge your force.'

Bolitho nodded. 'But the marines have also sailed with the squadron, am I right?'

Napier replied miserably, 'Aye, sir.' Then he brightened and added, 'But I was ordered to embark a platoon of the Sixtieth Foot in their stead, sir.'

Keen, who had followed him aft, said quietly, 'That's something.'

Bolitho turned towards the windows while he tried to fit the pieces together.

Napier said brightly, 'But I expect you knew about the soldiers, sir. The commodore sent word with the courier-brig which sailed two days ahead of me.'

Bolitho swung round. '*What* did you say?'

Napier paled. 'The courier, sir. Despatches for the admiral at Antigua, others for you, sir.' He looked to Keen for comfort. 'From England, sir.'

Keen exclaimed, 'You were right, sir. They must have caught and sunk the courier-brig too.'

Bolitho grasped his hands behind his back and squeezed them until the pain controlled his dismay.

From England. With despatches. And letters. News of Belinda. And now . . .

He looked at Keen. 'So you are convinced?' He did not hear his answer.

To Napier he said, 'Have you a capable first lieutenant?'

Napier was completely lost. For hours he had rehearsed what he would say to Bolitho. He had had time to put on his best uniform. Now it had all shattered. Like opening a door to greet a friend and finding oneself confronted by a madman.

He managed to nod. 'Aye, sir. He is a good officer.'

'Just as well.' Bolitho looked at Keen. 'First opportunity tomorrow we will weigh and put to sea. In the meantime I shall endeavour to glean what I can from the gallant commodore's despatches. But before *that* . . . ' He crossed to the table and poured Napier another glass of hock. 'We shall all drink a toast. You too, Allday.'

Allday took a glass from Ozzard and watched the transformation in looks and tone.

Bolitho felt his mouth lift to a grin.

'A toast.' He raised his glass. 'To Mr Napier, the new acting-governor of San Felipe!'

'Sou'-west by south, sir! Steady she goes!'

Bolitho half listened to the helmsman's report but concentrated on the sprawling purple blur on the larboard horizon. It was afternoon and the sun still beat down on the slow-moving ship with relentless ferocity. But after the oppressive hostility in San Felipe it was like a tonic.

Bolitho could feel it in the ship around and beneath him, the cheerful banter of the seamen on deck. Mountsteven, who was officer of the watch, barely raised his voice as he supervised the final resetting of the fore-course.

Bolitho steadied his telescope and watched the vague suggestion of land, Haiti, which lay some fifteen miles to larboard. Despite the distance it had an air of menace. Whenever possible sailors avoided its shores with their tales of witchcraft and horrifying rites.

Achates had been delayed a further day in San Felipe for want of wind, but now with the prevailing north-easterly filling her topsails and courses she was standing down the Windward Passage as if she was enjoying it. Here the Passage between Cuba and Haiti was barely seventy miles wide, its narrowest part. In time of war it would be hard to force a convoy through, with San Felipe in enemy hands. The more he considered it, the less Bolitho could understand the reason for his orders.

He handed the glass to one of the midshipmen and began to pace slowly up and down the quarterdeck. He hoped he had not been too hard on Commander Napier. The latter appeared to be relishing his new, if brief, appointment as temporary governor. With his fourteen-gun brig anchored below the powerful battery, and a smart platoon of the Sixtieth Foot, or the Royal Americans as they were still known, in the fortress, he was able to present a show of strength.

He saw some marines having their muskets and equipment inspected by Lieutenant Hawtayne. He was glad they were back on board where they belonged. It seemed very likely they would soon be needed again.

He hid a smile as the marine lieutenant said in his piping voice, 'Smarten yourself up, Jones! You've *had* your rest ashore!'

Bolitho knew that the picture of the dead drummer-boy would last a long time in his memory.

He heard Adam's light step nearby and saw him waiting to speak.

'How is my flag-lieutenant today?'

Adam smiled. It was the moment.

'Miss Robina is a fine girl, Uncle. I've never met anyone like her . . .'

Bolitho let it pour out without interruption. So that was

the trouble. But for his own worries he would have realized that the ride to Newburyport would be a beginning rather than an ending.

'Have you asked her father for her hand in marriage?'

Adam blushed. 'It's far too soon, Uncle, that is, I hinted perhaps sometime in the future, that is, not the *too* distant future . . . ' His voice trailed away and he stared at the dark water abeam. Then he said, 'I know she won't have me, of course. Her uncle knows. He was glad to get rid of me aboard one of his vessels.'

Bolitho looked at him. *Vivid* was owned by Chase. It was strange that Tyrrell had not mentioned it.

'Let us walk awhile, Adam.'

They paced back and forth for several minutes while the ship moved and worked around them.

Bolitho said, 'You have a future in the Navy, Adam. A good one, if I have any say in the matter. You come of fine sea-going stock, but so have many others. Whatever gain you make, and whatever achievements you have won, you will have done so without the use of privilege, remember that. Yours will be a better Navy, or should be when young officers like you have positions of authority. We're an island race. We shall always need ships and those brave enough to fight them.'

Adam glanced at him. 'It is what I want. Have wanted since I joined your *Hyperion* as midshipman.'

Bolitho looked down at the gun-deck and saw the seaman who had lost an eye being greeted by some of his messmates as he swayed uncertainly past an eighteen-pounder. He was still unused to it. But with his black eye-patch to conceal the oakum which filled the empty socket he looked every inch a hero, and they were treating him as such.

Adam tried to find the words. 'Men like that one, Uncle. They mean a lot to you. They're not just ignorant hands, they *matter*, don't they?'

Bolitho faced him. 'They most certainly do. We must never take them for granted, Adam. There are plenty of others who do that!'

Adam nodded. 'When I sat in my father's old chair . . . '

Bolitho asked quietly, 'At Newburyport? Where his ship was once sheltered?'

Adam looked away. He had not meant it to slip out quite like that, or so soon.

'They showed me, Uncle. It was the family name, you see. Not common in New England.'

'I'm glad. You've seen more than I.'

He heard Keen approaching and was suddenly thankful. It was not just Hugh's memory, what he had done to their father when he had deserted to fight for the American rebels, not because of that or the shame which even Rivers had been quick to mention. Bolitho tried to face it. He was jealous. Hurt, even though it was ridiculous.

Keen touched his hat. 'Mr Tyrrell is in the chartroom with the master, sir. I think we should examine the next chart.' He glanced professionally at the clear sky. 'Should be able to maintain a fair speed all night at this rate.' He seemed oblivious to the awkward silence.

'Good, I'll come directly.' He nodded to his nephew. 'You too. It's all experience for whatever you intend.'

He hesitated outside the chartroom and said abruptly, 'Take charge, Val. I'm going aft. You can explain it all later.'

Adam asked anxiously, 'Are you feeling unwell, sir?'

Bolitho said, 'Just tired.'

He strode away and was soon lost in the shadows below the poop deck.

He was unable to face all of them crammed together in the small space of the chartroom. Knocker, the master, Quantock, Captain Dewar of the Royal Marines, and their assistants as well.

Bolitho had left another letter with Napier at San Felipe, and a copy to be sent by any other vessel which might happen to call at the harbour for supplies or water.

Not knowing about Belinda was tearing at him like claws. He had not realized how brittle his reserves had become. Not until Adam had reminded him of Hugh. *My father's old chair.*

Before, Hugh had remained misty and obscure. Now he was here amongst them. Fighting for his place.

Bolitho slumped down on the stern seat and stared at the glistening froth left by *Achates*' rudder.

Allday padded in from the dining space. 'Can I fetch you a glass, sir?' He was careful to keep his voice level.

'No, but thank you.' Bolitho twisted round to look at him. 'You are the only one who really knows me, do you understand that?'

'Sometime I do, an' then again sometime I don't, sir. By an' large I think I sees the *man* more'n others do.'

Bolitho lay back and breathed in the damp air. 'God, Allday, I am in hell.' But when he looked again Allday had vanished.

He watched a fish jumping astern. Who could blame Allday? He was probably ashamed of seeing his secret despair.

But Allday, as was his wont, had gone to his tiny, screened-off mess which he shared with his two friends, Jewell, the *Achates*' sailmaker, and the boatswain's mate Christy whom he had known in the *Lysander* at the Nile.

Three great tots of rum later he presented himself at Keen's cabin door.

The captain's clerk regarded him warily. 'What do 'ee want, Allday?'

The clerk winced as Allday breathed out the heavy fumes. 'Request to see the cap'n.'

It was unorthodox, and Keen was feeling weary after the discussion in the chartroom. But he knew Allday, and owed him his very life.

'Come in and close the door.' He dismissed his clerk and asked, 'What is it, man? You look like someone intent on a fight?'

Allday took another long breath. 'It's the admiral, sir. He's carryin' more'n his share. It's not fair . . . '

Keen smiled. So that was all. He had imagined something terrible had occurred.

Allday continued, 'I just wanted to say my piece, sir, seein' you're a decent man an' a real friend to 'im down aft. It's somethin' the flag-lieutenant said to 'im. I feel it in me bones. Somethin' which wounded 'im deeply.'

Keen was tired but he was intelligent and quick-witted. He knew he should have seen it. The unusual strangeness between the vice-admiral and his nephew.

He said, 'Leave it with me, Allday. I understand.'

Allday studied his face and then nodded. 'Had to speak, sir. Otherwise, officer or not, I'll put the flag-lieutenant across my knee and beat the hell out of 'im!'

Keen stood up. 'I didn't hear that, Allday.' He smiled gravely. 'Now be off with you.'

For a long while Keen sat at his table and watched the sun dying on the gently heaving sea.

He had a million things to do, for somehow he knew they would be called to fight very soon now. Like Allday, he thought, *in me bones*. The memory did not amuse him but he found that he was able to forget the conference, Quantock's silent disapproval and the man Tyrrell's brash promises to lead them to a place where they could hold an advantage against the other ship.

And all because of Allday. He had known Bolitho's coxswain on and off for eighteen turbulent years. Years of hardship and war, of momentary distractions and the incredible joy of staying alive when that seemed an impossibility.

One word stood out where Allday was concerned. *Loyalty*.

Keen reached wearily for the bell to summon his clerk.

He doubted if many people could describe what loyalty was, but he had been privileged to see what it looked like.

11

Revenge

'All hands, all hands! Hands aloft an' loose topsails!'

Bolitho stood at the quarterdeck rail and watched the dripping cutters being secured yet again on their tier. *Achates* had anchored for several hours while the boats had been lowered to examine an inlet where a ship might be concealed. As on all the other occasions, they had returned with nothing to report.

Bolitho shaded his eyes from the intense glare to look at the land. Santo Domingo was just a few miles to the north-west, then the Mona Passage, back to the northern approaches where they had started.

Two weeks wasted. Making use of winds which would barely move a leaf on an inland stream.

He watched the big topsails flapping and filling as the ship heeled slightly on her new tack.

Keen crossed the quarterdeck and waited for Bolitho to face him.

'With respect, sir, I think we should return to San Felipe.'

Bolitho replied, 'I know these waters well, Val. You can hide a fleet if need be. You think I'm mistaken, don't you?' He touched his crumpled shirt and smiled. 'I don't blame you. These past weeks have been hard on all of us.'

Keen said, 'I'm worried for you, sir. The longer we wait . . .'

Bolitho nodded. 'I know. My head on the block. I've always understood that.'

The shrouds creaked as the wind increased a little to fill the sails. High above the decks the extra lookouts strained their eyes and silently cursed their officers for their discomfort.

Bolitho heard the heavy tap of Tyrrell's wooden stump and turned to greet him. Keen made his excuses and moved to another part of the quarterdeck. His mistrust and growing suspicion were obvious.

Tyrrell glanced at Keen and said, 'Don't like me much, that one.' He sounded worried, less confident.

Bolitho asked, 'Are you still certain, Jethro?'

'She could have gone elsewhere.' He pounded his fist on the rail. 'But several friends told me she'd been usin' one of the inlets as a restin' place. She's nothin' to fear from the Dons. They *know* what she's about, I'm certain of that too.'

Bolitho looked at him thoughtfully. 'We're inside their waters now. I've no authority even to be here unless that damned ship is sheltering behind the Spanish flag.'

Keen returned, his face expressionless. 'We shall have to change tack again shortly, sir.' He purposely ignored Tyrrell. 'After that it will be a hard beat up to the Mona Passage. The wind is poor enough, but it seems intent on holding us back.'

Even as he spoke the fore-topsail flapped and banged against the shrouds and men scurried to the braces to retrim the yards yet again.

Tyrrell said suddenly, 'I know of a place. Give me a boat.' He was speaking quickly as if to stifle his own arguments against his suggestion. 'You don't believe me. I'm not even sure myself.'

They looked up as a lookout yelled, 'Deck there! Sail to the nor'-west!'

Keen murmured, 'Bloody hell! It'll be a patrol boat out of Santo Domingo!'

Tyrrell regarded him bleakly. 'They'll have been watchin' your fine ship for days, Captain, I'll wager a bounty on it!'

Keen looked away and retorted, 'You'd know about bounties right enough!'

Bolitho said sharply, 'Enough.'

He looked up at the masthead. A fine, clear day, the lookout would see better than anyone.

He cupped his hands and shouted, 'What ship?'

Bolitho was aware that several of the seamen nearby had stopped work to stare. An admiral, even a junior one, shouting? It must seem like heresy.

The lookout shouted down, 'Frigate, sir, by the cut of her!'

Bolitho nodded. A frigate. Keen was probably right. There was not much time. Two hours at the most.

He said, 'Heave to, if you please, and lower a cutter. Lieutenant in charge, and have the boat armed.'

Voices yelled around him and feet pounded across the sun-dried planking as *Achates* came reluctantly into the wind even as the boat was hoisted jerkily above the starboard gangway.

Knocker hovered at Keen's elbow and muttered, 'The inlet is a mere scratch, sir. Never get a ship in there!'

Tyrrell replied heavily, 'Your chart says that. I say different!'

Bolitho watched Scott, the third lieutenant, hastily buckling on his hanger while the wardroom servant followed him with his pistol and cocked hat. From fretting torpor to urgent activity, how often Bolitho had known and shared that.

'Cutter alongside, sir!'

There was a thud as a swivel-gun was mounted in the boat's bows, and two seamen began to ram a charge down its muzzle.

Bolitho said quietly, 'Did you always know about this inlet, Jethro? These past two weeks and before, you knew this was the place? Yet in a moment or two we would have changed tack and the opportunity would have been lost.'

Tyrrell said, 'You wanted that ship. I kept a bargain.'

Then he was gone, swinging his wooden leg in great strides as he made for the entry port.

Bolitho knew the truth at that moment, but something made him hurry to the nettings and call, 'Take care, Jethro! And good luck!'

Tyrrell paused, his big hands grasping the lines of the stairs down the tumblehome as he stared aft at the quarter-deck, his eyes watering in the sunlight. For just a few moments the years fell away and they were back in *Sparrow*. Then Tyrrell swung himself out and down into the cutter, his wooden stump jutting out like a tusk.

Keen murmured, 'I wonder.'

The cutter pulled quickly away from the side, the oars rising and dipping to a fast stroke, her coxswain standing upright behind the lieutenant as he headed for the shore.

Bolitho bit his lip. 'I trusted him. Perhaps it was too strong for him in the end.'

Keen shook his head. 'I don't understand, sir.'

Bolitho watched the boat swinging round in a tight arc as Tyrrell's arm pointed to larboard in a new direction. He could see the swirl of an inshore current, the way the trees and thick scrub ran down to the water's edge. It was hard to believe that the inlet was other than the chart had described.

There was a far-off bang and then the lookout called, 'Frigate's fired a shot, sir!'

Knocker remarked dourly, 'Couldn't hit Gibraltar from there!'

Bolitho glanced at Keen. Was it a warning to *Achates* to quit Spanish waters or a signal to someone else?

He said, 'I suggest you beat to quarters. Clear for action without delay.' He turned to watch the cutter's progress. 'We'll not be caught a second time.'

Around him men stood stiffly like crude statues, unable to believe what they had heard.

Then, as the drums rattled and voices barked hoarsely between decks, the truth became clear to everyone.

Keen folded his arms and looked down the length of his command. Men hurried along either gangway, tamping down the tightly packed hammocks in the nettings, while ship's boys dashed among the guns and spread sand which might prevent a man from slipping if the blood started to flow. Big Harry Rooke, the boatswain, was yelling at some of his own party as they scrambled along the yards to rig chain-slings to prevent the spars from falling on the men below. Others tore down screens between decks to transform the great space from small, individual messes and cabins into one open battery from bow to stern.

Quantock looked up from the gun-deck and touched his hat.

'Cleared for action, sir!' He had learned Keen's ways by now. Just as Keen had once learned them under Bolitho's command. 'Nine minutes, sir!'

Keen nodded. 'That was well done, Mr Quantock.'

But there was nothing between them, and neither smiled because of the small compliment.

Bolitho raised a telescope and watched the distant cutter. What Lieutenant Scott and the others must be thinking he could only guess. The roll of drums as *Achates* beat to quarters, the bang of a cannon, and all the time they were pulling further and further from their ship, their home.

He heard Allday give a discreet cough and saw him holding out his coat for him while Ozzard fussed around behind with his sword. Adam was here too, clear-eyed and looking incredibly young and anxious.

'Orders, sir?'

Bolitho allowed Allday to clip on the old sword and was saddened by Adam's formality.

He said, 'I am sorry, Adam. I should have known. You have every right to be proud. In your place I would have felt the same.'

The youthful lieutenant took half a pace towards him.

'I would cut off a hand rather than hurt you, sir. It was just that . . .'

'It was just that you wanted to share it with me and I was too busy to listen.'

Keen said, 'Ready, sir.'

He glanced from one to the other and felt strangely relieved. He looked directly at Allday but the coxswain did not even blink. Keen smiled. Allday was a fox.

'Very well.' Bolitho looked at his flag at the foremast truck. 'Run up the colours, if you please. And then, Mr Bolitho, make a signal. *Enemy in sight*.' He saw Adam's expression change from surprise to understanding as he added for the quarterdeck's benefit, 'We might as well give them the idea we are not totally alone, eh, lads?'

He looked at Keen. 'Let's be about it.'

Suppose there was nothing? That he had been wrong about Tyrrell, about everything else? He would be a laughing-stock.

He saw the signals midshipman, Ferrier, with his assistants, and little Evans from the *Sparrowhawk* busy at the halliards, and then as the bright balls of bunting dashed up the yard and broke to the breeze there was an excited cheer from the men at the upper-deck eighteen-pounders.

Most of them could not distinguish one flag from another. But to them it meant more than words. It was a symbol. A part of *them*.

Keen watched Bolitho's face and sighed. *I should have known*.

There was a sharp whiplash crack and several voices yelled, 'They've fired on the cutter, the buggers!'

Cheers one instant, fury the next.

Bolitho snatched a glass and watched the cutter coming about, the oars in momentary confusion as the water around it leapt with vicious feathers of spray. He saw a corpse pushed roughly over the gunwale to give more space to the oarsmen, and heard a loud bang as the cutter's swivel raked the trees nearest to the beach.

Keen was shouting, 'We may have to leave the cutter, Mr Quantock! But signal Mr Scott to return with all haste!'

He glanced at Bolitho but saw that he was standing by the nettings, his eyes fixed on the partly hidden inlet as if he was expecting something to happen.

The cutter was moving slowly now, and Bolitho knew that more than one of the seamen had been hit, probably by musket fire. He shifted his gaze from the lively current which betrayed the inlet and saw Tyrrell standing at the boat's tiller, waving a fist to drive the oarsmen to greater efforts.

The main-topsail lifted and cracked with sudden impatience.

Bolitho said, 'Be ready to get the ship under way again, Mr Knocker. We have a few minutes yet.'

Quantock said, 'The frigate's holding on the same course, sir.'

Bolitho felt his mouth run dry as something moved beyond and through a long bank of trees. Like a serpent's tail, yellow and red in the sunlight. The masthead pendant of a large ship, the remainder of her still hidden as she edged slowly through the concealed channel towards open water.

Then her tapering jib-boom and figurehead, blazing gold, and her forecastle and a tightly reefed topsail, her jib barely flapping as she moved sedately into the glare.

Another few moments and they would have lost her. They must have been holding their breaths as *Achates* had sailed past, laughed at their pathetic efforts to find them. Bolitho clenched his fists behind his coat tails. They would not laugh much longer.

The cutter was less than a cable away, and Keen said, 'Grapnel ready. No time to hoist the boat now!'

He tore his eyes from the other vessel as it moved from cover until she seemed to fill the shoreline.

'Hell's teeth, she's the one right enough!'

Bolitho lifted the old sword two inches from its scabbard and then snapped it down again.

'*Finally*, Captain Keen, you are convinced.'

He heard shouts as the boat's crew were hauled bodily up the side while the wounded were hoisted on bowlines, their anguished cries ignored in the haste to get them to safety.

Achates heeled more firmly in the wind, her hull brushing away the cutter like a piece of flotsam. Tyrrell remained standing at the tiller, his sole companion a dead seaman who crouched over an oar as if temporarily exhausted.

Bolitho exclaimed, 'Throw him a line! I'll not leave him!'

In his heart he knew Tyrrell intended to remain in the boat, to be carried away by the current. He had purposefully guided *Achates* from one false scent to another, and had even suggested that the boats should examine a cove directly alongside the other ship's real hiding-place. Nobody would ever have known. But something at the very last moment had persuaded him to act as he had.

Now the truth would come out. He would be lucky to escape with his life for what he had done.

Bolitho saw a heaving-line snake over the drifting boat, watched Tyrrell's uncertainty and anguish before he caught the line and took two turns around the abandoned swivel-gun.

Keen waited only long enough for Tyrrell to be seized by the waiting hands at the entry port before he yelled his orders and sent his men rushing aloft again to set the topgallant sails in what seemed like a rising wind.

Bolitho felt the ship shudder, the urgent clatter of blocks and rigging as *Achates* responded to the pressure.

Keen stared at him and said, 'What was the damn fool trying to do anyway? What chance will — ' But the rest of his words were lost in the jarring roar of gunfire.

Along the other ship's side the heavy muzzles were jerking back into their ports and suddenly the air above *Achates*' decks was filled with deadly iron. Several holes appeared in the tightly braced sails, and Bolitho felt the familiar jerk through his shoes as other balls struck hard into the hull.

He watched as Knocker's helmsmen took control and very slowly at first, and then more confidently, the ship pointed her bowsprit towards the land, the wind pushing her over with an invisible hand. The other ship was following suit to take the maximum advantage of the wind.

Had Bolitho ordered Keen to beat up the Mona Passage to take advantage of this same wind on the other side of the islands, it would have taken days to reach San Felipe. The ship which was now almost bows on as she clawed away from the shallows would have beaten them with time to spare. The little *Electra* would have fought to the finish, but nothing could have stopped the inevitable.

Keen held out his arm. *'Easy*, Mr Knocker! Easy now!'

Achates continued to turn, her sails bulging hard on the opposite tack as the seamen on braces and halliards threw their weight against the swing of the yards.

The master grunted over his shoulder and the helmsmen slowed the great spinning spokes of the wheel.

'Steady, sir! West by north!'

Bolitho licked his lips. The enemy's ports were at too extreme an angle to fire. She had made her challenge prematurely. But she was a well-handled ship and was already responding to the wind as she came about.

'Starboard battery!' Keen's sword came out of its scabbard with a hiss. 'On the uproll!'

Down the *Achates'* side and on the deck below the gun captains would be peering through their ports, trigger lines taut, as they watched their target swim into view.

The bright blade flashed down in the sunlight, and with a drawn-out roll of thunder the eighteen- and twenty-four-pounders of both decks hurled themselves inboard on their tackles.

The smoke billowed towards the bows and Bolitho watched as the enemy's rigging and canvas danced wildly under the onslaught. Tall waterspouts lined the enemy's bilge as other balls slammed hard down alongside, but she returned the fire even as she completed her manoeuvre.

Bolitho felt the deck shake and heard a terrible shriek from one of the hatchways.

Every gun crew was working like madmen, sponges, charges and rammers moving like parts of the men themselves. Finally those shining black balls from the shot-garlands, rammed home with a last tap for good measure. Each crew was racing its neighbour, and as every captain held up his hand Keen shouted hoarsely, 'Broadside! *Fire!'*

This time there was no mistake, and at a range of barely two cables it was possible to see *Achates'* weight of iron

smashing into the other ship's hull, splintering a gangway
and bringing down a tangled heap of rigging from the mizzen.

But the enemy's heavier thirty-two-pounders were already
reloaded and poking through their ports like angry snouts.
Again the stabbing line of orange tongues, the terrible com-
motion and crash between decks as many of the balls found
their mark.

Bolitho saw a man hurled from his gun, his face a mask of
blood. He also saw Midshipman Evans standing stiff and
unmoving as he stared at the other ship. If he was afraid of the
din of battle he did not show it, but in his pale features
Bolitho saw the enemy through the boy's own eyes. He was
remembering her as he had last seen her, when his ship had
been smashed and set ablaze, when Duncan had died beside
him.

Bolitho called, 'Walk about, Mr Evans!' He saw the boy
look at him without understanding and added, 'You are
small but still a prime target.'

Evans gave what might have been a smile and then went to
aid the fallen seaman.

The guns rolled inboard again on their tackles, the air
cringed to their explosions and men gasped in the dense
smoke and charred fragments which surrounded them.

Hallowes, the fourth lieutenant, strode behind the forward division of guns, his hanger across his shoulder as he
peered at his crews.

'*Stop your vents!*'

'*Sponge out!*'

Several men ducked as hammocks burst from the nettings
and metal screamed against one of the guns on the opposite
side. Two men fell, another limped away and crouched below
the gangway like a frightened animal.

'*Load!*'

Hallowes pointed at the crouching seaman and shouted,
'Back to your station, *now*!'

'*Run out!*'

Again the squeaking rumble of trucks as gun by gun the

ship presented her full broadside to the enemy. The latter had changed tack slightly and was converging on *Achates*, her guns firing again and again.

Bolitho watched Keen moving from one side of the quarterdeck to the other. More shots hammered the side, and there was a great chorus from the lower gun-deck and Bolitho knew that a twenty-four-pounder had been upended or, worse still, had broken away from its tackles.

Both ships were evenly matched. *Achates* mounted more guns, but the enemy's heavier broadside was taking a terrible toll. One lucky shot was all it would take. He stared at Keen's shoulders, as if to will him to act. *Close the range*, Val. Get to grips before he dismasts you.

More cries and screams echoed through the crash and recoil of cannon, and a marine staggered away from the poop nettings, his hands to his face, his chest punctured by flying wood splinters.

'Jesus, what a mess!' Tyrrell limped between the trailing tackles and pieces of torn rigging which had found their way through the nets overhead.

Bolitho said, 'Get below. You're a civilian.'

Tyrrell winced as a ball shattered on the breech of a quarterdeck nine-pounder and splinters cracked around them and flung two more seamen into a puddle of their own blood.

Keen turned round and glared at Tyrrell. 'What the hell are you doing here?'

Tyrrell showed his teeth. 'Get that bugger alongside, Captain, your people can't keep up this pace!'

Keen looked at Bolitho. 'They'll know it's your flagship, sir!'

So that was it. Bolitho pulled out his old sword. 'Put the helm over. We'll give them a fight,' he raised his voice, '*eh, lads?*'

He turned away as they cheered him. Half-naked, blackened by powder smoke, their sweat cutting channels through the grime, they were hardly the romantic heroes portrayed in the fine paintings he had seen in London.

He felt the madness welling up inside him. 'Lively there!'

The yards swung slightly as the helm went over, and within minutes the range had fallen to a cable, then half as much; then as the other ship's sails rose high above the nettings and muskets joined in the deafening onslaught, it was down to fifty yards and still closing.

The other captain had no choice. He could not turn and run. The land which had hidden him was now a deadly enemy, with breakers in plenty to show the lie of the reefs. If he tried to come about he would be all aback for those vital moments when Keen's gun crews would rake him from end to end.

There was a loud, splintering crack and voices yelled, 'Heads below there!' Part of the mizzen cross-jack yard ploughed through the nets, rebounded and crashed down in a welter of rigging, blocks and trailing canvas.

Bolitho felt a blow on the shoulder like an iron fist, then he was face down on the deck. His first thought was near to terror. Another wound. Fatal. Then he cursed into the smoke which had almost blinded him when his presence would be most missed.

He felt Adam holding his arm, his grimy face set in a grim stare, then Allday dragging something away from his back and easing him over on to his knees, then to his feet. A huge block, cut down by a shot through the mizzen rigging but swinging on its cordage like a bludgeon, had laid him low. He was not even cut, and he managed to force a grin as someone gave him his hat and another yelled, 'You'll show them buggers, sir!'

Bolitho faced the enemy, his eyes smarting, his shoulder throbbing from the blow. If it had struck his skull he would be dead at this very instant.

Musket shots punched into and through the packed hammocks, and wooden splinters flew from the quarterdeck or stood motionless like quill pens.

Axes flashed in the smoky sunlight, and more wreckage was hacked free and levered over the side with handspikes.

All the relentless gun and sail drill was showing its worth. When a man fell wounded, or was dragged away to await the surgeon's mates, another was instantly in his place from one of the opposite guns.

Now the marines could join in with their muskets, Sergeant Saxton counting out the time and tapping the deck with his boot as the ramrods rose and fell like one, and then as the muskets rose once more to the nettings he would shout, 'Take aim! Every shot a Don!' The crackle of musketry from the fighting tops showed that more marines were up there trying to mark down the enemy's officers.

Bolitho paced this way and that, his shoe catching a jagged splinter as the other ship's marksmen tried to hit him.

Closer, closer still, and the guns were thundering at almost point-blank range, their crews blinded and deafened as their feet and hands fought to keep control over their massive weapons.

'*Cease firing!*'

Quantock had to repeat the order before the last gun on the lower deck fell silent. As the enemy did likewise the other sounds broke through the stunned stillness. Men crying out in pain, voices calling for help, orders shouting for men to clear away the wreckage, to release the trapped wounded.

'*Hard over!*'

As the wheel went down *Achates'* jib-boom swept through the other ship's foremast shrouds like a battering ram. There was a terrible splintering sound and both hulls rocked together in a deadly embrace.

Men were running forward, leaving the guns to snatch up cutlasses and boarding pikes, axes and anything they favoured for hand-to-hand fighting.

Lieutenant Hallowes, his hat knocked awry, his hanger waving above his head, yelled, 'At 'em, lads!'

With a wild cheer the seamen raced to the point of collision to hack and slash their way across a glistening sliver of water.

Some were impaled by pikes as they clung to the boarding

nets, others were shot down by marksmen even before they had left their own ship. But others were through, and as more followed Bolitho saw the fourth lieutenant dashing on to the enemy's larboard gangway, hacking down a shrieking figure with his hanger and slashing aside another before he was overtaken by his whooping, battle-crazed men, their cutlasses already reddened from the first challenge on the forecastle.

The marines were bustling to the side, their faces grim beneath their hats as they fired into the men along the enemy's quarterdeck, reloaded with less precision than usual and fired again.

Captain Dewar drew his sword. 'Forward, Marines!'

The scarlet coats and white cross-belts vanished into the smoke, the boots slipping on blood, the bayonets thrusting away any resistance as they joined the others on the enemy's deck.

Keen had gone forward to encourage his men, and Bolitho heard the seamen cheering, 'Huzza, huzza!' and even though some were falling to the enemy's fire others were already fighting their way on to the quarterdeck.

There was a great cry from *Achates*' boatswain. 'Fire! She's afire!'

Bolitho said, 'I can see the smoke!'

Tyrrell gripped the rail as he stared at the enemy who were suddenly throwing away their weapons and screaming for quarter as the wild-eyed sailors tore among them.

Bolitho called, 'Mr Hawtayne! Have your bugler sound the retreat! Stand by to cast off!'

A sullen explosion shook both ships and more black smoke gushed from the forecastle. If the ship burst into flames *Achates* would suffer the same fate.

Keen came back mopping his face, his eyes seeking out his lieutenants and master's mates as the truth made itself felt in another deep explosion.

Dragging their wounded, and fighting off any of the enemy who tried to follow, *Achates*' boarding party returned to their own ship.

With her wheel either shot away or abandoned, the enemy two-decker began to drift down-wind as soon as the last line was hacked free. Corpses bobbed in the sea between them, and others hung from the rigging where friend and foe alike had been shot down.

'Get the fore-course on her! Reset the flying jib! Hands aloft and loose t'gan's'ls!' Quantock's harsh voice echoed through the confusion like a steadying force.

A great tongue of flame licked through the enemy's gun-deck and started an explosion among some broken charges. Men were running through the corpses and destruction and nobody appeared to be trying to save them or their ship.

As the wheel went over *Achates* turned slowly aside from her stricken enemy, laying bare the damage, the bloody streaks on the planking, the discarded weapons, and the guns which still smoked as if under their own command.

Another explosion boomed across the water and fragments of burning wood and rigging splashed dangerously close to *Achates* as she continued to gather way, her punctured and smoke-grimed sails filling to the wind.

More explosions, and this time a gout of fire and sparks spouted from the midships section and began to spread to masts and canvas, until everything was burning fiercely. Rigging and canvas became ashes in seconds, men, some on fire, were leaping into the sea, others splashed about looking for something to keep them afloat as the ship continued to blaze above them.

Bolitho watched the other ship die, but in spite of *Sparrowhawk* could find little satisfaction. His men were cheering, embracing each other. They had lived through it. One more time, and for some it had been the first battle.

The Spanish frigate, which had remained a silent spectator to the fight, was moving cautiously towards the burning ship. She was going to stand between *Achates* and her victim, an act which made her just as guilty. Dead men tell no tales.

There was a vivid flash and a boom which stopped all the cheers like an iron door.

The other ship was turning on to her side, her gun-ports alight like a line of angry red eyes.

She was breaking up, her heavy artillery tearing loose to add to the horror and agony of those still trapped below.

Bolitho saw Midshipman Evans watching the other ship's last moment. But there was no joy on his face, just tears, and Bolitho knew why.

He was not seeing the rightful destruction of a callous enemy. It was his *Sparrowhawk* he was watching.

Bolitho said quietly, 'Attend to Mr Evans, Adam. His storm is about to break.'

Keen joined him and touched his hat.

Bolitho said, 'What is the butcher's bill for all this?'

They both turned as the air shook to a final explosion, and like a gutted whale the enemy rolled on to her side and dipped beneath the surface.

Keen replied quietly, 'That might so easily have been us, sir.'

Bolitho handed his sword to Allday. 'I get your point, Val. Then our bill is not yet fully paid?'

12

The Letter

Napier, *Electra*'s youthful commander, stood exactly in the centre of Bolitho's day cabin while he completed his report.

Contrary to his orders, Napier had brought his brig to escort the battered two-decker for the last two miles of her passage into San Felipe.

Even as he had been piped aboard from his gig, Napier had seemed unable to prevent his eyes from probing around him. The sewn-up corpses awaiting burial, the tired, dirty sailors who barely glanced up from their countless tasks of splicing, stitching and hauling fresh rigging to the topmen on the yards.

Bolitho thought of those last moments. He still did not know the enemy ship's name. But soon he would, just as he would learn who had commanded her. The Spanish frigate had been careful to stand between the victor and defeated, to prevent, it seemed, any attempt to pick up survivors.

Napier said, 'Two Spanish men-of-war did stand inshore for a while. They were going to land a party at the island mission.'

He sounded surprised that Bolitho had not already questioned him about it. In fact, Bolitho was so fatigued he had barely skimmed over the commander's neatly written report.

Bolitho made himself stand and walk towards the open stern windows as *Achates* continued towards the island. He could still smell the heat and sweat of battle. The scent of death.

'What did you do?'

Napier relived his proudest moment as acting-governor.

'I warned them off, sir. Fired a shot from the battery to liven things along.'

Liven things along. Bolitho wanted to laugh, but knew if he did he might not be able to stop.

When and where would it end? Tyrrell had betrayed him, or had been about to. Now, not only the French were intent on San Felipe but the Spaniards also.

Keen entered the cabin and said, 'We are about to enter harbour, sir. The wind is steady from the sou'-east.'

He looked strained and extremely tired. He was feeling the ship's pain as if it were his own.

The pumps had barely stopped since the battle. *Achates* had taken two bad hits in her bilge. And a 'long nine', as a thirty-two-pounder was nicknamed, could do terrible damage. *Achates* was, after all, twenty-two years old. That represented a lot of miles under her keel.

'I'll come up.' Bolitho added bitterly, 'There may be some watching from the shore who will be disappointed to see us still afloat.'

He thought of the two Spanish men-of-war and their apparent intention to land men on what they still claimed as Spanish territory. But for Tyrrell's change of heart, the two ships would have been joined by the ship which now lay below a Caribbean reef.

Napier suddenly went pale. 'I – I do beg your pardon, sir. I had almost forgotten. There was a packet-ship from England.'

Bolitho stared at him and said sharply, 'Continue.'

Napier fumbled inside his coat and then produced a letter. 'For you, sir.'

He seemed to shrink under Bolitho's gaze.

Keen snapped, 'Come on deck, Commander Napier, I wish to discuss certain matters about docking my ship . . . '

But he paused at the door and glanced back at Bolitho. He was holding the letter with both hands, afraid to open it, afraid to move.

He turned and almost bumped into the flag-lieutenant. 'Not yet, Adam. There's a letter.'

In the gloom between decks Allday leaned on a blistered eighteen-pounder and peered through the gun-port to watch a green finger of land slide abeam. There were people there to watch the stained and battered ship sail past, but nobody waved or cheered.

To Allday it was just another landfall. He had been in so many harbours they had become merged and mixed in memory. He sighed. That letter was all that mattered for now. He could remember as if it was yesterday when together they had clambered into the overturned coach and found a beautiful woman more dead than alive. The resemblance to Bolitho's previous wife had been too much to believe.

He cocked his head as a gun boomed out from the old fortress. Better than any mock tears, he thought. A proper welcome, though there were too many jacks who would not hear the guns now or ever again.

He straightened his back as the door opened in the cabin screen and the scarlet-coated sentry snapped to attention.

Bolitho ducked beneath the deckhead beams and then saw Allday waiting for him.

He looked at Allday's anxious features and felt his own strength begin to ebb away. The careful composure he had tried to build up as he had read carefully through her letter, the moments of despair when his gaze had become misty, each was taking a toll now on his reserves.

He paused and listened to the guns, the jarring response from *Achates'* upper deck as she returned the salute.

Then he reached out and grasped Allday's hard hand.

Allday asked thickly, 'Is all well, sir?'

Bolitho squeezed his hand. It was somehow right that he should be here. The first to know.

'We have a *fine* daughter, Allday.'

How long they stood like this it was hard to tell. *Achates* changed tack around the point, and on the poop the marine fifers and drummers struck up a lively march, *Come cheer up my lads 'tis to glory we steer* . . . To Bolitho it could have been anything.

Allday nodded slowly, savouring the moment as he would retell it when he eventually put his feet ashore for the last time.

'And Ma'am, sir?'

'Very well.' Bolitho walked towards the sunlight. 'She asked to be remembered to you.' He quickened his pace on to the quarterdeck. Now he could face anything. *Do* anything. He looked at Allday's great beaming grin. 'She hopes we are not too bored by being employed in peacetime!'

Allday glanced up at the splintered cross-jack yard, the stains and marks of battle which were everywhere.

Then, despite the solemnity of the moment, a King's ship entering harbour, the salutes and the flag which dipped to *Old Katie* above the battery walls, he threw back his head and laughed.

Keen looked at him and then at Bolitho.

The reward for the victor was plain to see.

Captain Valentine Keen watched his superior with uncon-cealed surprise and admiration. Since *Achates'* return to San Felipe the work of repairs, the replacement of timbers and spars, had continued without a break. The facilities in Georgetown were poor, and they had been confronted by non-cooperation and hostility at every turn.

English Harbour at Antigua was the only suitable place for a proper refit, but Keen was resigned to seeing his ship put to rights in what amounted to primitive conditions. If *Achates* quit the island he had little doubt that an invasion of some kind would soon follow.

He knew that Bolitho had not spared himself. He had been ashore many times, had visited the ex-governor, Rivers, had even allowed him to return to his own home under open arrest, although Keen had voiced his disagreement on that score.

It was late August and the heat unbearable. But any day, at any hour, the fortress lookouts might report the approach of Spanish ships, French too for that matter, and *Achates* had to be ready for sea and prepared if need be to fight.

Electra had sailed that forenoon for Antigua. Despatches for the admiral, if he had returned, and others to be sent with all haste to the Admiralty in London. All this and a lot more had kept Bolitho working in his cabin until the middle watches, and yet he never seemed to tire or show his irritation at the delays and lack of help from the islanders.

The letter from his wife in Falmouth had done more for Bolitho than a hundred victories, or so it seemed.

Bolitho looked up from the litter of papers on his table. It had been something of a relief to send Napier to Antigua with his ideas and intentions which Sheaffe would eventually read at the Admiralty. He had committed himself. Right or wrong, he had made a decision. It was what he had veered away from previously. Now he was glad, even eager, to act with a freedom he had once found hard to express.

'Rivers has agreed not to interfere. Others can decide later what will become of him.' He saw the deep lines around Keen's mouth and was moved to add, 'It has been a difficult time for you, Val. I understand that.'

Keen shrugged. 'Mr Quantock, the master, Mr Grace, the carpenter, all are in rare agreement, sir. If this ship is called on to fight without proper attention in a dockyard she may suffer severe consequences.'

Bolitho nodded. 'I know that. You are also short-handed because of our losses and with no chance of replacements.'

Keen said, 'If we do not get support from other ships, sir, we will be hard put to defend ourselves, let alone this island.'

'I have sent a full report, Val.'

Bolitho leaned over the stern sill and took some deep breaths. The air was scalding hot and without movement. Better to be at sea, becalmed even. Anything rather than stay here and wait. He thought of Belinda's letter which he had read at the end of each demanding day. A daughter. He could

not visualize what she would be like. Belinda had written of
her love, of her hopes, but he could read between the lines
too. The birth had not been easy for her. It was just as well
that she still believed his mission to be one of diplomacy and
not one of danger.

Keen asked abruptly, 'What about Mr Tyrrell, sir?'

Bolitho bit his lip. He had sent Tyrrell over to his brigantine as soon as *Achates* had moored. They had spoken very
little. Guilt or defiance, it was hard to tell. Yet.

He said, 'I shall see him directly, Val. I need his *Vivid*. She
is all I can find at present.' He smiled at Keen's surprise. 'I
intend to purchase her anyway, so she might as well sail
under our flag for the present.'

'If you think that's wise, sir.'

'Wise? I am not certain of anything. But what I do know is
that it will take several months to complete repairs on my
flagship. In the meantime we may be attacked by the Dons. I
cannot in all sensibility agree to hand over the island to the
French until we have settled this matter once and for all. If
there was any last minute conflict the French would be quick
to blame us, accuse us of provoking a war so that they could
not take over what is rightfully theirs.'

He watched Keen's face. He was unconvinced.

'I have this feeling, Val. That I was sent here to perform an
impossible task. But if I am to be a scapegoat then I want to
rest on my own decisions, not on those made by people who
have never heard a shot or seen a man die.'

Keen nodded. 'Well, sir, I shall back you to the limit and
beyond, but that you already know.'

Bolitho sat on the stern seat and plucked at his shirt to gain
an illusion of coolness.

'When you attain flag-rank, Val, I hope you will
remember all this. It is far better to sail in the line of battle
with every enemy muzzle trained on the flagship than to sort
through the dung of diplomacy. In a moment I shall speak
with Jethro Tyrrell. He is a man who lost everything, but
who once gave so much for the flag he honoured. He was a

true patriot, but was branded a traitor by his own people. He has lived with bitter memories, as a wolf will live off scraps. But he still cares, and at that moment when he was about to betray us he stood firm and led us to the enemy. In his eyes it was madness. What is honour to him? It has done precious little to repay his sacrifices. He thought instead of saving us from harm, so that when we returned here the island would be under Spanish colours and it would be too late for me to do anything but report failure.'

Keen shook his head. 'Will you trust him again?'

'I hope to.'

Bolitho looked at the glittering water, the small vessels pinned down on their reflections by the glare.

'Rivers is a rogue. He became rich by offering favours to the scum of the Caribbean. Slavers, soldiers of fortune, pirates, all have paid him his dues. He has property in the South Americas, but needed his power as governor to take full advantage of the profits. I found some evidence in the fortress, but that is but the tip of an iceberg. I loathe him for his greed, but I *need* him if only to give some credibility to our being here.'

Keen listened to the renewed thud of hammers and the squeak of tackles as more cordage was hoisted aloft. He had had his own doubts from the beginning about sending a small two-decker to perform the work of a squadron. What was the matter with England? Instead of showing pride for past victories she seemed to cringe for fear of upsetting old enemies.

Keen would have hanged Rivers and anyone else who had shared in the deaths of his sailors and marines. The consequences could wait.

Bolitho had risen to his feet and was shading his eyes to watch the distant fortress. When he spoke he sounded untroubled, although his words held the impact of iron shot.

'You see, Val, I believe the United States are more concerned with improving their relations with the South Americas, the Spaniards and Portuguese. So Rivers' appeal for their protection rather than French reoccupation must have received a warm reception. I also believe that Samuel Fane, and certainly Jonathan Chase, have no illusions about the French, should there be another war in Europe.'

Keen stared at him, his tiredness forgotten. 'You mean that the United States' government connived with the Dons!'

'Not directly. But when you put your hand in a fox's hole you must expect to be bitten. The Spanish government could not afford to become openly involved so they employed a powerful privateer for the purpose. With *Sparrowhawk* destroyed and local shipping too frightened to move, there was only *Achates* to prevent the seizure of San Felipe. Chase must have known about Tyrrell's past connections with me, just as he was well aware of his desperate need of a ship. The rest we can guess, but nobody had allowed for Tyrrell's old loyalty.'

Keen looked astounded. 'If you say so, sir. It is precious flimsy evidence to support your reputation at any future enquiry.'

'I agree. So we shall have to manufacture some.' Bolitho looked at him calmly. 'I'll see Tyrrell now. Please ask my flag-lieutenant to join me.'

Later, as Tyrrell limped into the cabin and lanterns were being lit for an early dusk, Bolitho faced his old lieutenant with a sense of sadness as well as determination.

Tyrrell took a proffered chair and laced his powerful fingers together.

'Well, Jethro.'

Tyrrell smiled. 'Well, Dick.'

Bolitho sat on the edge of the table and regarded him gravely.

'As these are British waters for the present I am using my authority to commandeer your vessel and place her under our colours.'

He saw a momentary start but nothing more. Tyrrell was too tough to be budged by one shock.

'Also, I am placing her under the temporary command of

my nephew, who in his capacity of flag-lieutenant will carry a despatch with him to Boston.'

Tyrrell stirred and showed a first hint of uneasiness.

He exclaimed harshly, 'An' me? You intend to string me on the main-yard, eh?'

Bolitho pushed a letter across the table. 'Here is my authority to purchase the *Vivid* once you have returned to San Felipe. You see I kept my word. She'll be yours.'

He was barely able to watch Tyrrell's anguish, but continued, 'I have spoken with Sir Humphrey Rivers. To spare his own shame, and possibly his life, he will give me all the information I need about that Spaniard. If he changes his mind he has a choice of charges. Treason or murder. He will hang for either.'

Tyrrell stared at him then rubbed his chin. 'Chase will never agree to part with the *Vivid*.'

'I think he will.'

Bolitho looked away. It was all Tyrrell could think of. A ship of his own. A last chance.

Tyrrell stood up and looked around like a man already lost. 'I'll be on my way then.'

'Yes.' Bolitho sat and leafed through some papers. 'I doubt we shall meet again.'

Tyrrell turned almost blindly and started for the door. But Bolitho got to his feet, unable to play it out to the end.

'*Jethro!*' He walked round the table and held out his hand. 'You saved my life once.'

Tyrrell looked at him searchingly. 'An' you mine, more'n that.'

'I just want to wish you good luck, and I hope you find whatever it is you're looking for.'

Tyrrell returned the grasp and said gruffly, 'There's none like you, Dick, nor never will be.' There was emotion in his voice now. 'I lived all those years again when I met your nephew. I knew then I couldn't go through with it, though God knows this island is not worth the dyin' for. But I know you, Dick, and I know your values. You'll not change.'

He gave a wide grin and for a brief moment he was the same man. The one in the little sloop-of-war in these very waters.

Then he limped away, and Bolitho heard the midshipman of the watch calling for a boat alongside.

Bolitho leaned against the bulkhead and looked at his hands. They felt as if they were trembling.

Allday emerged from the adjoining cabin as if he had been lurking there to protect him from attack.

'That was *hard*, Allday.' He tried to hear the dragging thump of Tyrrell's stump leg. 'I fear it may be harder on young Adam.'

Allday did not understand what he was talking about. The man called Tyrrell had been an old friend of Bolitho's, so everyone said. But to Allday he had seemed like a threat, and for that reason he was glad to be rid of him.

Bolitho said, 'I feel different, knowing that I have a daughter.'

Allday relaxed. The mood was past.

'One thing's for certain, sir. She'll be a welcome change. Two Bolithos on the high seas are enough for anyone, an' that's no error.'

For a brief moment he thought he had gone too far, but Bolitho looked at him and smiled.

'Well, then, let's broach a bottle and drink the young lady's health, eh?'

On the poop Adam heard Allday's laugh through a skylight and gripped the netting with sudden excitement. Across the darkening water he could see the *Vivid*'s riding light, the faint glitter of a lantern from her tiny cabin.

Soon, far sooner than he had dared to hope, he would see and hold Robina in his arms. He could feel her kiss as if it had just been placed on his mouth, smell her perfume as if it was here on deck.

He was glad that Bolitho had seen fit to trust his old friend. It would be interesting to listen to his stories again once they had set sail from San Felipe.

The first lieutenant was doing his evening rounds of the upper deck and saw Adam's silhouette against the sky.

Quantock clenched his fists. It was unfair. He should have been given charge of the *Vivid*, no matter how brief it was to be. Damn them all to hell. If *Achates* returned to England in her present state she would likely be paid off like most of the fleet. Quantock knew he would be thrown on the beach to join the ranks of unwanted lieutenants without any chance of employment.

He swore at the evening sky. *Damn peace!* In war there was risk, but at the same time there was always a chance of promotion and honour.

The Bolithos and those like them had always had it. He peered around the deserted deck. My turn will come.

Achates swung quietly to her cable and, like the men who lay on the orlop within the surgeon's call, nursed her own wounds of battle.

In her crowded mess between the great guns below deck the seamen and marines sat by their glimmering lights and yarned with each other, or consumed their carefully hoarded rum. Some with tarred hands surprisingly gentle carved small and intricate models or scrimshaw work. One seaman who had the gift of being able to write sat beneath a lantern while one of his messmates stumbled through a letter for his wife in England. In the Royal Marines' quarters, or the barracks as they were known, the men worked on their kit, or thought of that last battle, and the next which, although nobody mentioned it, they knew was inevitable.

Down on the orlop where the air was thick as fog, James Tuson, the surgeon, wiped his hands and watched as one of the badly wounded had his face covered and was carried away by the loblolly boys. He had died just a minute or so ago. With both feet amputated it was better so, Tuson thought.

He looked along his small, pain-wracked command. Why? What was it all for?

These sailors did not fight for flag or King as so many landsmen fondly believed. The surgeon had been at sea for twenty years and knew this better than most. They fought for each other, the ship, and sometimes for their leader. He thought of Bolitho standing on deck, his stricken expression as these same men had cheered him for taking them into hell. Oh yes, they would fight for *him*.

As he ducked beneath the massive deck beams he felt a hand touch his leg.

Tuson stooped down. 'What is it, Cummings?'

A surgeon's mate raised a lantern so that he could see the wounded man better. He had been hit in the chest by an iron splinter. It was a marvel he had survived.

The man called Cummings whispered, 'Thankee for takin' care of me, sir.' Then he fainted.

Tuson had seen too many men crippled and killed to feel much emotion, but this sailor's simple gesture broke through his guard like a fist.

When he was working he was too busy to care for the crash and rumble of guns on the decks above. The procession of wounded men always seemed as if it would never end. He rarely even looked up at his sweating assistants with their wild eyes and bloodied aprons. No wonder they call us butchers. A leg off here, an arm there, the naked bodies held on the table while he worked with blade and saw, his ears deaf to their screams.

But *afterwards*, at moments like these, he felt differently. Ashamed for the little he could do for them. Ashamed too for their gratitude.

The surgeon's mate lowered the lantern and waited patiently.

Tuson continued along the deck and tried to shut from his mind the tempting picture of a brandy bottle. If he gave in now, he would be finished. It was what had driven him to sea in the first place.

Somewhere in the gloom a man cried out sharply.

Tuson snapped, 'Who was that?'

'Larsen, sir, the big Swede.'

Tuson nodded. He had taken off the man's arm. It sounded

as if it had grown worse, maybe even gangrene. In which case . . .

He said briskly. 'Have him brought to the table.'

Tuson was calm again. In charge. He watched the figure being carried to the sick-bay. A Swede. But in a King's ship nationality did not count.

'Now then, Larsen . . . '

Bolitho was with Keen on deck when the brigantine *Vivid* slipped her mooring and tacked slowly towards the harbour entrance.

He raised a telescope and scanned the little vessel from bow to stern and saw Adam standing beside Tyrrell's powerful figure near the tiller, his uniform making a smart contrast with the men around him.

Whatever he found in Boston might hurt him, but would not break his heart. Bolitho knew he must not interfere, must face the risk of turning Adam against him when he would have offered anything to prevent it.

Keen was reading his thoughts. 'He may not even see the lass, sir.'

Bolitho lowered the glass and allowed the brigantine to become a small model again.

'He will. I know exactly how he feels. Exactly.'

The headland slid out to shield *Vivid* from view. Only her topsail and driver showed above the land, and then as she changed tack again they too were gone.

Keen respected Bolitho in everything, but he could not understand why he had bothered to pay good money to give Tyrrell the *Vivid*. He should have felt lucky to be spared the hangman's halter. Then he looked at Bolitho's profile and saw the sadness there. Whatever there had once been between him and Tyrrell would not be shared with anyone, he thought.

Bolitho turned his back to the sea.

'Now we must prepare the defences of this island, Val.' He

pounded his fist into his other hand. 'If only I had some more ships I'd stand out to sea and meet them gun to gun.'

Keen said nothing. Bolitho was certain of an attack. The Peace of Amiens meant nothing out here, especially to the Spaniards. He looked at the glistening horizon and wondered. But for Tyrrell's change of heart they might be out there now, and San Felipe under another flag. Rivers had played a dangerous game by setting one against the other, but it seemed to Keen that only *Achates* would pay for the consequences.

Bolitho clapped him on the arm. 'Why so grim, Val? Never turn your face away from what is inevitable.'

He seemed in such high spirits Keen was shaken from his apprehension immediately.

He said, 'Where would you like to begin, sir?'

It was infectious. Keen had watched it happen before so many times. When he himself had been nearly killed in battle, that too had been described as a time of peace.

'We will obtain some horses and ride around the island. Check each vantage point against Mr Knocker's chart and any local map we can discover.' Bolitho pointed at the haze around the old volcano. 'The island is like a great juicy bone, Val. And now the hounds of war are taking up their positions around us.'

He had seen the anxiety on Keen's face, and if he was dismayed at the prospect of fighting an undeclared war over San Felipe, so too would be most of his ship's company.

Bolitho did not really need to ride round the island, he could picture its strength and its weakness as he had gauged it on the charts. But he needed Keen and the others to know he was determined to stand firm. To hold the island until he was certain in his mind of the right course to take.

The wound in his thigh throbbed and itched in the humid air and he wanted to rub it.

Why was he troubled by the prospect of a siege or an open attack? Was it because of Belinda, or was it the chance of action which drove him on?

He thought suddenly of Sir Hayward Sheaffe's quiet room at the Admiralty. It seemed like another world now, with the fortress and the spent volcano shimmering across the placid water. But Sheaffe's words were quite clear, as if he had just uttered them. 'Their lordships require a man of tact as well as action for this task.'

Bolitho thought of Midshipman Evans' expression when the nameless two-decker had burst into flames. Of the shocked surprise on the dead marine drummer's face. He thought too of Duncan and others he had not even known.

The man of tact would have to step down for a while.

13

A Holy Day

Adam Bolitho stood by a window in Jonathan Chase's study and stared at the unending ranks of white horses across Massachusetts Bay. Just an hour ago he had been brought ashore in *Vivid*'s boat and had been met by Chase's astonished agent. In fact, *Vivid*'s return to Boston under British colours had caused quite a stir along the waterfront.

It was like part of a dream. Chase had made him welcome at his house, but had seemed restrained, cautious even, as Adam had given him the big sealed envelope from his uncle.

He shivered, conscious of the New England weather, the restless change in the September Atlantic. He thought of San Felipe and felt strangely guilty. The worst part was that it did not seem real, any of it. He was here, and Chase had mentioned before he had left in some haste to read Bolitho's letter that Robina and her mother were also in Boston and might be expected shortly.

Adam turned and looked at the fine room with its paintings and nautical relics. The right place for a man like Chase, he thought, an ex-sailor, ex-enemy too, who now had his roots here.

He thought of the ten days' passage from San Felipe to Boston. How different from that other occasion when he had yarned away the hours with Jethro Tyrrell. This time, despite the cramped conditions of the brigantine, he had barely spoken to Tyrrell, and then only on vague matters of navigation and weather.

And why had his uncle made the offer to purchase *Vivid* for him, and why should Chase be prepared to sell? None of it made much sense, but then none of it seemed to matter now that he was back here with the prospect of meeting Robina again.

'I am sorry for keeping you waiting.'

Chase was a powerfully built man and yet he had re-entered the study as noiselessly as a cat.

He seated himself carefully in a chair and said, 'I have read your uncle's letter and have ordered that the other one which he enclosed be carried immediately to Sam Fane at the capital.' He regarded the lieutenant thoughtfully. 'Strange he should send you.'

Adam shrugged. He had not really considered it before.

'I was available, sir. Captain Keen needs all his own officers aboard the flagship.'

'Hmmm. Your uncle once told me he hates politics, but he seems to understand them well enough.' He did not explain but continued, 'As you will have observed when you entered Boston Harbour, the French men-of-war have gone. News travels on the wind. The French admiral will have no wish to insist on receiving San Felipe from the British until the position is made clear.'

'But the French and Spanish governments have been allies more often than not, sir.'

Chase smiled for the first time. 'The French would need Spain as an ally if there was another war. If there is to be any conflict over San Felipe the French intend it shall not be of their making. It would suit them very well if your ships withdraw under a cloud after they have repulsed any Spanish claims to the island. *Then*, and only then, the French admiral will see fit to assume control and install a governor.'

Adam said, 'I think it wrong to gamble with people's lives in this fashion.'

Chase nodded. 'Possibly, but San Felipe is a *fact*. In war or peace it commands an important sea route. The government of my country would prefer to see it in friendly hands, better still, under our own protection. That was what Sir

Humphrey Rivers suggested. As Vice-Admiral Bolitho's aide, you will of course know all about it. I can see that you are as sharp as your uncle in such matters, and you will have realized that Rivers, despite all his claims of loyalty to King George, is hell-bent on being his own man. He played a dangerous hand by discussing the island's future with Spain or, to be precise, with the Spanish captain-general at La Guaira. A secret shared is no longer a secret.' He gave a heavy sigh. 'Anyway, it is impossible to share anything with a tiger.'

He watched Adam's reactions and saw that he had his full attention.

'I can speak freely to you because neither of us has any control over the affair. I was aware of the Spanish interest because I trade with both the captain-general at La Guaira and his neighbour in Caracas. They have always thought their own government to be out of touch with their expanding empire in the South Americas. Every week the slave ships bring more labour for the mines and the plantations, and they probably pass the great galleons of Spain on passage home loaded to their deck beams with gold. San Felipe's position has threatened their freedom of movement in the past. They intend it shall not happen again.'

Adam had a sudden picture of *Achates* at San Felipe with some of her yards sent down for repair work being carried out by the ship's company which really needed the proper skills of a dockyard.

He exclaimed, 'That two-decker . . .'

Chase smiled gravely. 'The one you sunk? Oh yes, Lieutenant, I heard all about that from my own sources. *Like the wind*, remember? She was the *Intrepido*, and was refitted at Cadiz and armed to be a match for anyone foolhardy enough to interfere with her intentions. A privateer, a hired adventurer, call him what you will, but her captain was ordered to sweep aside all opposition and take command of the island. Later a proper governor would be installed and the Spanish flag would be raised, to, I suspect, small interference from either the British or the French. Your government would be too embarrassed to waste more time and lives on a lost cause, and the French would raise no objection as it would put Spain under obligation for any future strategy on their part.' He leaned back in his chair and added, 'Does that explain?'

Adam nodded, confused and sickened by the apparent simplicity of such cruel logic.

Chase said, 'But things are never what they seem. The Dons thought like the Dons. Quick, clever, ruthless, but they had failed to take your uncle's stubbornness into their scheme of things. Nevertheless, he is the one I pity. He is the one man who stands between the Spaniards and their claim to San Felipe. I believe all this was known when he was sent here in the first place. I mean no disrespect, but the British can be devious in their negotiations. What does honour matter to some when it concerns events on the other side of the world, eh?'

'I cannot *believe* it, sir. My uncle will stand firm.'

Chase looked concerned. 'Of course, I'm sure of that if nothing else. But without the islanders to back him, what can he do? Stand and fight?'

Adam clenched his hands so tightly that the pain made his eyes smart.

'He will!'

Chase looked away, as if unable to watch his despair.

'Then God help him.'

The door swung open and Adam heard the girl ask excitedly, 'Where have you hidden him, Uncle? And what is all this *stuff* about you selling the *Vivid*, she's a favourite of yours!'

She turned and saw him by the window and gasped with surprise.

'You really are here!' She ran to him and kissed him lightly on the cheek. 'Now everything is wonderful!'

Adam did not dare to touch or hold her, and could see the anguish on Chase's grim features across her shoulder.

Chase said heavily, '*Vivid* has always been on the small side for my fleet. Tyrrell has earned her twice over.'

He kept his eyes on Adam's and said nothing about Bolitho's money.

He moved towards the door, his face still on the young couple by the window.

There was no easy way, and his tone was almost brutal as he said, '*Vivid* must weigh before nightfall. Lieutenant Bolitho here will have important news for his uncle, isn't that so?'

Adam nodded slowly, hating him, yet admiring him at the same time.

For how long they stood together he did not know. He held her to him, murmuring lost words into her hair, while she clasped his shoulders as if still unable to realize what was happening.

Then she leaned back in his arms and stared at him as she asked, '*Why?* What does anything matter now? We shall have each other! Everything we've ever wanted! So *why?*'

Adam brushed a strand of fair hair from her eyes, all his hopes and happiness spilling away like sand in a glass.

'I have to go back, Robina. Your uncle knows why. He can explain better than I.'

Her eyes flashed with sudden anger. 'How can it concern you? You are only a lieutenant, why should he discuss such things?'

Adam held her firmly as she tried to force herself away.

'There has been a lot of fighting. Our ship sank an enemy but we were badly damaged too.' He felt her arms go limp as his words struck home. 'My uncle discovered what dangers threatened the island, and who was behind them. He sent me here to give his despatches to your uncle, so that this information could be sent to your president.'

She watched his eyes and his mouth as he spoke. 'But why should it involve my uncle or any of my family?'

Adam shrugged wretchedly. 'Because they were involved. They knew the Spanish intentions long ago, your uncle as good as told me just now. Apparently it would not suit your government to have either the French flag or ours flying above San Felipe. But now that my uncle has brought it into the open, nobody else will dare to interfere.' He could not hide the bitterness even from her. 'So my uncle stands alone to act as he must.'

She stepped away, her eyes towards the floor as she said in a small voice, 'Then you do not intend to make your life here among us?'

'It is not like that! I love you with all my heart.'

'And yet you deny me this?'

Adam moved towards her but she took two paces away.

'It's my duty – '

She looked at him again, her eyes hot with tears. 'Duty! What do I care about that! We are both young, like this country, so why should you throw your heart away for a meaningless word like *duty*!'

Adam heard Chase in the passage-way, and other, lighter footsteps, Robina's mother.

They both appeared in the doorway, Chase's face stern and determined, the woman's pale with anxiety.

Chase asked bluntly, 'You told her then?'

Adam met his gaze evenly. 'Some of it, sir.'

'I see.' He sounded relieved. 'Your Mr Tyrrell seems eager to leave. The wind's backing . . . ' His voice trailed away.

'Thank you.' Adam turned and looked at the girl, the others unimportant and misty as he said, 'I meant every word. One day I'll come back and then . . . '

She dropped her eyes. 'It will be too late.'

Chase took his arm and accompanied him through the beautifully panelled entrance hall. A black footman opened the outer door and Adam saw the cold blue squares of sea and sky beyond it, mocking him.

Chase said quietly, 'I'm sorry, I really am. But it's all for the best, you'll see that one day.'

Adam walked down the steps and saw Tyrrell waiting by the gates. He watched the lieutenant's face every foot of the way and then with his swinging, limping gait fell in step beside him.

'You decided then?'

'It was decided for me.' Adam could barely see where he was walking in his despair and pain.

'I ain't so sure about that, Lieutenant.' Tyrrell shot him a glance. 'I can guess how you feel.'

Adam looked at him, his voice angry. 'Why the difference? On passage here you barely said a word?'

Tyrrell grinned. 'Just wanted to be sure about you. You could'a stayed put right here.'

He quickened his pace as his eyes found the moored brigantine.

'But, like me, Lieutenant, you couldn't bargain away your loyalty.'

They stood together on the jetty and waited as a boat cast off to collect them.

Once Tyrrell looked at Adam's face and then across to his new possession. Tyrrell knew all about having a broken heart. He had learned it in a dozen ways. But a ship of your own was something else.

He clapped the lieutenant roughly on the shoulder.

'Come along, young fella, we'll catch wind *and* tide for once.'

Adam hesitated and looked back but the house was completely hidden from view.

He repeated what he had told her just moments earlier. 'I love you with all my heart.'

He had not realized he had spoken aloud, and Tyrrell was moved to say, 'You'll soon forget. Only dreams last forever.'

Bolitho climbed the last of the stone stairs to the fortress's battery parapet and discovered that he was not even breathless. It must be the change from shipboard life.

It was early morning, the air cool and damp from a heavy overnight downpour. It was so typical of all the islands hereabouts, he thought. Drenching rain at night and yet within an hour or two of sunrise the place would be bone-dry again.

Lieutenant George Lemoine, who commanded the platoon of the Sixtieth Regiment of Foot, touched his hat and smiled.

'I heard you were up and about early, sir.'

Bolitho leaned on the parapet and stared down at the shining harbour. A lot of the anchorage was still in shadow, but soon the sun would appear around the old volcano and the ships, like the town beyond, would quiver in another morning haze. He could see the black and buff lines of *Achates'* gun-decks, and wondered if Keen was still fretting about mounting lists of needs for his command.

They were running short of fresh stores. Even drinking-water had to be man-handled in casks by the seamen. There was still no sign of cooperation from the islanders, who showed their resentment by pleading poverty even when it came to fresh fruit or juices for the sailors.

Bolitho had done all he could to get to know the islanders. As admiral in command, governor and in charge of the island's defences he had seen the hopelessness of the situation. The planters and traders resented the fact that they could not move their vessels in or out of harbour, while ships which called at San Felipe to collect cargoes had to be checked before they could be allowed to anchor. It needed a full garrison and several ships to perform what Lemoine's soldiers and the marines had to carry out unaided.

Bolitho breathed in deeply. He saw his barge tied to the fortress's jetty where he had first met Rivers over three months ago. Down there too was the point where Rivers' men had fixed their boom, where *Achates* had burst through in pitch-darkness. Battles fought, men dead and wounded, probably a trifle to the planners in government and Admiralty.

Now it was late September, and Adam should be back at any moment. He thought of his purchase of *Vivid*. Reward or bribe? He still could not be sure of his own motives.

He thought too of Falmouth. Autumn. Red and brown leaves, the smell of wood smoke in the evenings. Resolute, cheerful people, now at peace because of ships like *Achates*.

He had received no more letters from Belinda, but then there had been no news from any direction. The island seemed as if it were totally isolated, even though the lookouts had sighted the topsails of unidentified men-of-war on the horizon on several occasions.

Perhaps it was all over before it had begun? *Achates'* unexpected discovery of the hidden two-decker and putting her to the bottom within the hour might have killed all the ardour for an attack.

But uncertainty had made him restless and often unable to sleep. He had taken to riding around the island while it was still cool, or visiting the fortress if only to show the soldiers he had not forgotten them.

He wondered if the news of what had happened had reached the streets of London and the countryside. Would Belinda understand what was really happening? There would be those ready enough to describe his efforts as a reckless adventure to cover up the loss of Duncan's *Sparrowhawk*.

A sentry shouted, 'Gunfire, sir! To th' east'rd!'

Lemoine tensed. 'By God, he's right.' He cupped his hands. 'Corporal of the guard! Sound the alarm!'

Bolitho watched the red-coated soldiers running from their cave-like quarters below the battery walls.

It was probably nothing, or a show of impudence by some passing Spanish vessel. But they could not take chances.

He looked round and saw Midshipman Evans' shadowy figure below the watch-tower, already removing a telescope from its case.

It was uncanny how the boy followed him and seemed able to guess what he was going to need next.

But it was still too dark around the point to see anything. Or was it? There it was. A flash reflected on the belly of a low cloud. Then another. Not enough for a sea-fight. More likely a chase.

He said, 'Mr Evans, pass word to the guard-boat. Warn the ship. And my compliments to Captain Keen, and tell him we may have company before the day's out.'

He saw Crocker, *Achates'* most senior gunner's mate, hurrying along the upper battery, some soldiers panting behind him.

Crocker was probably the oldest man in the ship, and with his white hair in a spiky pigtail, and strange, loping gait, he was quite a character. His left eye was almost sightless, he had been part-blinded by a splinter when he had been not much older than Adam. But his right one was as keen as steel, and he could manage, lay and train any gun better than a full crew. He also knew how to heat shot, and Bolitho thought he could already smell the acrid fumes from one of the ovens behind the parapet.

Crocker seemed surprised to see his vice-admiral on the wall. He knuckled his forehead and twisted his head round to get a better view. It made him look even more villainous, and Bolitho was able to appreciate why all the gun captains feared his wrath.

'Good mornin' fer a shoot, sir!'

Bolitho smiled. 'Be ready.'

Lemoine watched the man lope away with his helpers.

'He's certainly kept my men on the bustle, sir!'

Somewhere in the town a church bell chimed. It sounded strangely sad on the damp air.

Bolitho trained his telescope towards the ship once more.

'What was that, Mr Lemoine?'

The lieutenant hid a yawn. He had been awake until the early hours playing cards unsuccessfully with his second in command.

'A lot of the islanders are Catholics, sir. The bell is for early mass.' When Bolitho remained silent he added helpfully, 'An important celebration for them, sir. St Damiano's Day.'

Lemoine had not wasted his time in the regiment, Bolitho thought. Some would never bother their heads with matters outside their own ordered world.

There was another thud of gunfire. They must be trying to prevent a ship from entering harbour. He thought of Adam.

No, not him. Tyrrell was too old a hand to be caught at this early hour.

He moved his glass again and saw the opposite headland shaking itself from the shadows. He could see the leap of surf around the reefs, and the further necklace of rocks by the point named Cape Despair, probably with some justification.

Feet clattered on the stairs and a runner barked out his report to Lemoine who in turn said, 'Message from your flagship, sir. All boats lowered and patrols alerted.'

Bolitho could see them in his mind. Small pickets of marines, backed up by volunteers from the local militia. A puny enough force, but properly used it could prevent any attempt at landing men through the reefs. There was only one safe way, and that was the one which Keen had used. And old Crocker with his heated shot would do his best if the enemy tried to force the entrance.

Sunlight ran down the slopes and laid bare the water at the harbour mouth. Bolitho trained his glass again and saw the guard-boat moving slowly below the land, a midshipman in the stern-sheets, probably enjoying his own freedom of command.

Lemoine said, 'There she is, sir!'

The ship appeared around the headland, sails emptying and then refilling instantly as she changed tack. She was a large vessel, and Lemoine said, 'Indiaman, sir, I know her, she's the *Royal James* and was in Antigua several months back.'

Men were leaning through the gun embrasures, and others ran along the jetty below to see what was happening.

Bolitho made up his mind. 'I'm returning to the flagship, Mr Lemoine. You know what to do here.' He was halfway down the stairs before the lieutenant had time to reply.

The bargemen came to life, and Allday jumped to his feet as Bolitho appeared half-running through the gate.

'To the ship, Allday.'

He ignored their startled glances and tried to discover what was troubling him. The Indiaman should be able to reach safety unless her pursuers gained a lucky hit and brought down a vital spar or two. But with this powerful south-east wind the other ships would soon have to stand away from a lee shore or face the havoc of the guns. In broad daylight Crocker could not miss.

The oars rose and fell, and with each powerful stroke the barge seemed to fly across the water as if eager to lift over it.

Bolitho seized Allday's arm. 'Alter course! Steer for the headland!' When Allday hesitated he shook it and shouted, 'I must be blind! Lemoine told me without knowing it. This is a very holy day!'

Allday swung the tiller so that the barge heeled over, but not a man aboard missed his stroke.

'Aye, if you says so, sir.'

He thinks I'm mad. Bolitho said urgently, 'And yet on this St Damiano's Day there was not a single movement from the mission!'

Allday stared at him blankly.

Bolitho looked around for the guard-boat but it was too close inshore, near the entrance, and every eye would be watching and waiting for the *Royal James* to burst into view round the point.

Bolitho banged his hands together. *I should have seen it.* 'Are the men armed?'

Allday nodded, his eyes slitted against the early sunlight. 'Aye, sir, cutlasses and three pistols.'

He darted a glance at Bolitho's face, knowing something was about to happen, yet held back from asking in front of the bargemen.

'It will have to suffice.' Bolitho pointed at a tiny patch of sand. 'Beach her there.'

As the bargemen tossed their oars and the boat glided into the protection of a high slope of land it seemed suddenly peaceful.

'Clear the boat.' Bolitho climbed over the side and felt the sea tugging at his legs as he waded ashore. Cutlasses and three pistols against what? He said, 'Send a man to fetch the patrol from the point. Tell him to stay out of sight.'

Allday watched him anxiously. 'Is it an attack, sir?'

Bolitho took one of the pistols and then picked up a heavy cutlass from the pile of weapons on the beach. Now, of all times, he had come ashore unarmed.

'The mission. I feel there is something wrong.'

The men gathered up their weapons and followed him obediently up the steep slope and across the long piece of headland.

The wind was quite strong, and Bolitho felt the sand whipping from the tough gorse and scrub which always looked so inviting from seaward.

He saw the huddled buildings of the mission on the little islet, the deserted beach, the air of utter desolation. Not even any smoke to betray a fire or sign of life.

He heard far-off cheering, the voices thinned by the wind, like children at play. He paused and looked across the harbour entrance and the old fortress with the flag curling above it. The shouts were most likely from the guard-boat as the big Indiaman suddenly loomed above the headland and headed towards safety.

There was a large boat towing astern, but other than that few hands on deck to shorten sail once the ship had reached the anchorage. At that moment he saw the guard-boat sweep into view, the midshipman raising a speaking-trumpet to his lips as he shouted at the incoming ship.

Bolitho tore his eyes away and looked at his handful of seamen. Keen and the others could take care of the *Royal James* now. He had seen the raked sails of a frigate rounding-to as she stood away from the land as her quarry slipped beneath the fortress battery.

Allday said, 'The boats have gone, sir.'

Bolitho stared at the little islet. It was true. The fishing boats had vanished. Perhaps that was the simple explanation for it. The monks or missionaries had gone fishing. Food must often come before prayer.

'*Look*, sir!'

Allday's cry made him turn towards the nearest line of

rocks. They were no longer deserted but alive with scrambl-ing, running figures, the sunlight glittering on swords and bayonets.

'Soldiers!' Allday raised a pistol, his chest heaving with alarm. 'A hundred o' the buggers at least!'

There were a few shots, distant and without menace until the balls whined overhead or smacked into the hard sand.

'Take cover!'

Bolitho saw the bargeman with two marines from a patrol running along the edge of the land. One fell instantly, and the others vanished from sight.

Then there was a muffled explosion. It was more of a feeling than a sound. As if all the air had been sucked from your lungs.

As Bolitho rolled on to his side and looked back to where they had left the barge he saw the *Royal James* give a great convulsion. Then every gun-port along her side burst open, but instead of muzzles he saw searing tongues of flame shooting out, then leaping above to lick and consume sails and spars with terrifying speed. The boat which had been towing astern had cast off and was being rowed back towards the entrance.

Allday whispered, 'A fire-ship!'

Bolitho saw his eyes gleam in the growing wall of fire, could even feel the heat across the water like an open furnace as the wind fanned the towering flames and drove the aban-doned ship unerringly up the harbour. Straight for the moored *Achates*.

More shots ripped above the headland, and Bolitho heard the yells of the oncoming soldiers.

Without *Achates* there was no hope, no protection, and the fortress battery had guarded her killer from destruction.

Allday peered at him, his eyes wild. 'Fight, sir?'

Bolitho hung back. Was that all there was to it? To die here on this desolate place for nothing? Then he recalled the drummer-boy as he had covered his face.

He stood up and balanced the heavy blade in his hand.

'Aye, fight!'

On either side of him the bargemen stood up and shook their cutlasses.

Bolitho tried to shut out the terrible roar of flames and fired his pistol at the line of soldiers. There was no time to reload. There was no time for anything.

He bounded across some loose stones and hacked aside a man's sword with such force that he fell headlong down the slope.

The clash of steel on steel and a few haphazard shots, it was less then enough. Bolitho felt figures pressing around him, staring eyes, teeth bared in hate or desperation, as the over-whelming number of soldiers drove them back towards the water. He slashed out with all his strength and saw a man's face open from ear to chin, felt his cutlass jar on ribs as he knocked down another's guard and drove the blade into him.

He heard a gasp and with horror saw Allday fall among the struggling, stabbing figures.

'*Allday!*'

He knocked a soldier aside and tried to reach him. It was no use. Not for a gesture. His own pride.

Bolitho dropped his blade. '*Enough!*'

Then ignoring the levelled weapons he fell on his knees and tried to turn Allday on to his back. At any second he expected to feel the hot agony of steel enter his body, but he no longer cared.

The soldiers stood motionless, either too stunned by the ferocity of the brief action or too impressed by Bolitho's rank, it was impossible to tell.

Bolitho bent over him to shield his eyes from the glare. There was blood on his chest, a lot of it.

Bolitho said desperately, 'You're safe now, old friend. Rest easy until . . .'

Allday opened his eyes and looked up at him for several seconds.

Then he whispered, 'Hurts, sir. Real bad. Th' buggers have done for poor John this time . . .'

A seaman dropped beside him. 'Sir! Th' Dons are runnin' away!'

Bolitho glanced up and saw the soldiers running and limping towards the rocks where they had left their boats.

It was not difficult to find the reason. A line of horsemen, with Captain Masters of the San Felipe Militia, were cantering over the sky-line, sabres drawn, their approach all the more menacing because of the silence.

Masters wheeled his horse and dismounted, his face shocked beyond belief.

'We saw what you tried to do.' The words fell out of him. 'Some of us decided to head them off.'

Bolitho looked at him, his eyes seeing nothing but the man's shadow and the great pall of smoke from the chaos in the harbour.

'Well, you're too late!'

He prised the cutlass from Allday's hand and flung it after the disappearing soldiers.

He felt Allday grip his wrist, and saw him looking at him again, his eyes tight with pain.

Allday muttered, 'Don't take on, sir. We beat th' buggers, an' that's no error.'

Boots pounded over the sand and more red coats appeared on every side.

Bolitho said, 'Take him *carefully*, lads.'

He watched four soldiers carry Allday down towards the barge. There were explosions in the distance and voices were calling from every direction. They needed him. There was no time for grief. He had heard that often enough.

But he hurried after the soldiers and gripped Allday's arm.

'Don't leave me, Allday. *I need you.*'

Allday did not open his eyes but seemed to be trying to smile as they lowered him into the boat.

When Bolitho reappeared above the beach the sunlight glanced off his bright epaulettes and a few militiamen gave a cheer.

One of the bargemen, his wounded arm tucked inside his shirt, paused to glare at them.

'Cheer, yew buggers, will yew? 'Cause yew'm safe fer a bit?' He spat contemptuously at their feet. He jerked his head towards Bolitho's shoulders. "E's worth more'n yew an' the whole bloody island!'

Bolitho strode through the scrub, some of which had been set alight by drifting sparks from the fire-ship.

Another attack might come at any moment. Keen would be needing help. But nothing seemed to have any substance.

Allday could not die. Not like this. His was the strength of an oak. *He must not die.*

14

No Better Sentiment

There were cries of horror and dismay as the harbour entrance was suddenly filled with flames and billowing black smoke. To any sailor fire was one of the greatest enemies. In storm or shipwreck there was always a chance. But when fire rampaged between decks, where everything was tarred, painted or tinder-dry, there was no hope at all.

Lieutenant Quantock dragged his eyes from the blazing Indiaman and shouted, 'What shall we do, sir?' Hatless, and with his hair blowing in the wind, he looked wild and totally unlike *Achates'* normally grim-faced second in command.

Keen gripped the rail and made himself face the oncoming inferno. *Sparrowhawk*, the Spanish privateer and now his own *Achates*. There was no time to kedge the ship along the harbour. Anyway, most of the boats were away on picket duty.

He could feel Quantock staring at him, sailors nearby frozen in various attitudes of alarm and disbelief. One moment they had been jubilant as the Indiaman had passed beneath the battery's defences. The next, and the enemy was right here among them and intent on burning them alive.

Keen knew the signs well enough. Hesitation, then panic. Nobody could be asked or commanded to stand and await death like a beast at slaughter.

Thank God he had had the ship cleared for action after Midshipman Evans had brought the message from Bolitho.

'Mr Quantock! Load and run out the larboard battery, both decks!' He punched the lieutenant's arm. *'Move yourself!'*

Calls trilled and men jerked from their various stances to

obey the order. With trucks squeaking on both decks of *Achates*' larboard side, the one which lay helpless to the fire-ship, the guns were run out.

Keen felt the smoke stinging his eyes as he tried to gauge the progress of the other vessel. Her sails were charred remnants and her foremast was burned to a stump. But the wind was all she needed to carry her to her victim. Even as he watched he saw the Indiaman brush almost gently against a moored topsail schooner. Just a mere touch and in seconds the vessel was fiercely ablaze, her anchor-watch splashing in the water alongside.

'Ready, sir!' Quantock sounded desperate.

Keen found himself thinking of Bolitho. Where was he? Had he gone with some of the patrols to repel an attack from one of the beaches? He tightened his stomach muscles. Maybe Bolitho was dead.

'As you bear!'

He walked to the quarterdeck rail and looked at his gun crews, as he would if they were engaging a living enemy.

'Fire!'

In the confined harbour the roar of the broadside was like a giant thunder-clap. Keen watched the mass of iron show its passage across the water like an opposing wind, felt the deck sway over as if the ship was trying to free herself and escape.

He saw the fire-ship stagger, spars and burning fragments fall around her in tall columns of steam.

'Reload! Steady, men!' That was Mountsteven with his guns.

Keen shouted, 'Mr Rooke! Send some hands aloft to douse the sails. Put some others along the gangway.'

The boatswain nodded and hurried away bawling orders. He knew that buckets of water hauled to the upper yards, or flung down over the exposed tumblehome would be next to useless. Like trying to put out a forest fire with a mouthful of spit. But it kept them busy and occupied. No time to feel terror, no time to abandon ship until the last, disciplined moment.

'Fire!'

Keen saw the broadside smash into the Indiaman's forecastle and felt sick with despair as great gouts of flame burst through the holes made by the iron shot.

The master said in a whisper, 'We'll not stand her off, sir.'

Keen did not look at him. Knocker was a careful man and had probably unshipped his chronometer so that it would not go down with the ship.

Keen looked at the grim-faced gun crews with their rammers and sponges, the menacing way that the smoke was curling between the ratlines and shrouds as if the rigging was already ablaze.

He could do nothing to save her. This fine ship which had seen and done so much. *Old Katie*, they called her. And now . . .

Quantock raised his speaking-trumpet. '*Fire!*'

Tuson, the surgeon, hovered by the ladder, and Keen said, 'You wish to get your wounded on deck?'

That, if anything, might snap the last strand of order. There were not any of Dewar's marines aboard to prevent the stampede once it began. He saw the grateful look in Tuson's eyes and was glad of what he had done.

Goddard, the quartermaster, yelled, 'Look yonder, lads!'

The Indiaman had bumped against another moored craft and that too was well alight, sparks shooting from her hold and adding to the horror.

But it was not that which Goddard had seen.

Keen stared until his eyes throbbed with pain as the little brigantine *Vivid* nosed through the smoke and falling fragments, her yards braced as she overreached the other vessel.

Quantock said hoarsely, 'Christ Almighty, she must have followed her through the entrance! It'll be her turn to burn in a moment!'

Keen tore the telescope from a midshipman's fingers and trained it on the advancing wall of flames. In the lens it looked even worse, terrifying, and Keen could feel his mouth and throat going dry as he watched.

He saw Tyrrell's big frame by the tiller as he steered his *Vivid* closer and closer to the other vessel's starboard bow. Through the haze of smoke and whirling smuts he looked as if he would never budge. Even now the sails were swinging and snapping in the wind, although how Tyrrell's men could find the strength to work at halliards and braces against that heat was a miracle.

Keen heard shouts from the gun-deck as the first of the wounded were brought from the orlop but did not turn away from the awesome sight in the harbour. He imagined he could feel the heat and knew he could not delay the order to abandon much longer.

'Secure the guns, Mr Quantock.'

He expected a chorus of insults at the absurdity of his order, but instead he heard the squeak of trucks and hand-spikes as the eighteen-pounders were secured at their ports.

There was a mingled groan as the *Vivid*'s masthead pen-dant vanished in a puff of smoke. Any second now and all the care in the world would not prevent her taking fire.

Keen saw the two vessels lurch together, the impetus of *Vivid*'s full set of sails swinging the fire-ship slightly to larboard.

Lieutenant Trevenen murmured thickly, '*Vivid*'s afire, sir.'

Keen watched the flames jumping like terrible demons from rigging to rigging, multiplying and spreading until the fore-course was reduced to ashes.

But *Vivid* was holding her way against the other, heavier hull, pushing her round. There were men too at the point where both vessels were locked together, and moments later Keen saw a splash as one of the Indiaman's anchors was released from the cat-head. Given time the anchor cable would burn through too, but as the flukes dragged along the harbour bed the fire-ship's shape began to lengthen as she took the strain of the cable.

Her smouldering mizzen and yards cracked and fell in

charred fragments alongside and Knocker gasped, 'She's *aground*, by God!'

Keen nodded, unable to speak. Tyrrell probably knew the harbours hereabouts better than most, and had gauged his action to the second, so that the blazing Indiaman was already pushing herself firmly into the shallows.

Keen heard himself say, 'Send every boat you can, Mr Quantock.'

Vivid was blazing fiercely. It was almost impossible to see which vessel was which. There was still danger, the ship might refloat herself, or a fragment might drift down on *Achates*.

Keen turned and looked at his command. But whatever happened they had stood firm. Like Bolitho had told them. Together.

They were staring up from the gun-deck and watching him. Because of the smoke, and the carefully rationed water aboard ship, they looked more like a mob of filthy buccaneers than jack-tars.

They were cheering now, waving their fists and capering as if they had won a great battle. He saw Quantock looking at him, his eyes bitter. The sailors had at last discarded their dead captain and had adopted Keen.

Keen grinned at them and felt like weeping. Then he made up his mind.

'Call away the gig. I'll fetch Tyrrell myself.'

They found Tyrrell and most of his small crew clinging to a spar and half an upturned boat.

And there too was Adam Bolitho, half-naked and with a livid burn on one shoulder.

Tyrrell allowed himself to be hauled into the stern-sheets where he slumped and looked across at the remains of his brigantine.

She was already burned to the water-line. Unrecognizable.

Keen said, 'I'm sorry for what happened and the way I treated you. It was a close thing. You lost your ship but you saved mine.'

Tyrrell barely heard him. He put his arm around Adam's shoulders and said roughly, 'Seems to me, you an' me both lost somethin', eh?'

As the gig approached *Achates'* side the seamen ran along the gangway and swarmed into the shrouds to cheer as Tyrrell looked up at them.

Keen said, 'They're grateful to you.'

'Quite right too.'

Tyrrell looked at his wooden leg; even that had been charred by the blaze. What was the point of going over it again? If *Achates* had not been here when the attack had started, none of this would have happened. He looked at his beloved *Vivid* as she broke in halves and slipped into the shallows in a rising cloud of steam. And *Vivid* would still be his.

He felt the young lieutenant's hand on his arm as he said quietly, 'We'll both get another chance one day, Jethro.'

Tyrrell bared his teeth. 'Sure as hell hope so. Can't spend the rest of my days lookin' after you!'

Keen stood by Bolitho's table and watched him with concern. He had noticed that Bolitho had been studying the day's log of events but that his eyes rarely moved.

Keen said, 'Mr Mansel, the purser, reports that fresh fruit and vegetables have been coming on board from the town, sir. It is still arriving. They don't seem to be able to do enough for us now.'

Bolitho smoothed out the papers on his table. *Now*. That word said so much. He heard Ozzard tiptoeing behind him to close the stern windows as dusk filled the harbour with shadows once more. But there were still a few sparks and glowing embers to mark where the fire-ship lay in the shallows. It was only this morning when he had passed the time with Lieutenant Lemoine at the fortress.

Keen knew Bolitho needed to be alone but was unwilling to leave him. He recalled his own shock when the barge had hooked on to the chains and he had seen Allday carried aboard as if already dead.

All his other feelings had been scattered like the ashes of the fire-ship.

Pride in his men, of what they had done in spite of the terrible danger. A deep, inner satisfaction that he had not broken under the strain. Neither seemed to count any more. Allday had become part of his life too. In fact, when he thought about it, most of the people he knew and cared for had been helped and influenced by Bolitho's coxswain.

At times like this Allday would have been the one to enter the cabin and gently hustle away unwanted visitors, like his dog had once done when he had been a shepherd in Cornwall.

Now he lay in Bolitho's own sleeping quarters, a sword-thrust in his chest which had even shocked the taciturn surgeon.

Keen tried again. 'We took several prisoners, sir. The crew of the fire-ship, some soldiers from the mission too. You were right. They are all Spaniards from La Guaira. After this the Dons will never dare to attack San Felipe. The whole world will know what they did. I would give little hope for their heads when their King is told of their bungling.'

Bolitho leaned back in his chair and rubbed his eyes. He could still smell smoke. Could see Allday's attempt to smile just for his benefit.

He said, 'Tomorrow I will draft a report for Sir Hayward Sheaffe.' London would be grey and wet in September, he thought vaguely. 'After that it will be up to Parliament.'

His words seemed to mock him. What did any of it matter?

'But for the moment it can wait.'

He looked up sharply but it was only one of the duty watch pacing the poop overhead.

Tuson was a good surgeon in spite of his early record. He had already proved that several times over. But if only . . . He cut his thoughts short.

He said, 'I was sorry to hear about Jethro Tyrrell's loss.'

'He took it well, sir.' Keen hesitated. 'He was asking if he might visit you.'

The adjoining door opened and Adam stepped noiselessly into the cabin.

Bolitho asked, 'How is he?'

Adam wanted to comfort him but said, 'He remains unconscious, and Mr Tuson says his breathing is poor.' He looked away. 'I spoke to him but . . . '

Bolitho got to his feet, his limbs heavy. There were lights in Georgetown, and he wondered if the people were still standing quietly on the waterfront as they had since the action. Sharing the pain or the guilt he did not know, or care.

Adam was saying, 'Allday and I were once taken prisoner together, sir.' He was speaking to Keen but his gaze was on Bolitho. 'Afterwards he said to me it was the only time he had ever been flogged. He seemed to think it was a bit of a joke.'

Keen nodded. 'He would.'

Bolitho clenched his fists. They wanted to help but they were ripping him apart.

He said abruptly, 'I'll go to him. You both get some rest. Take care of that burn, Adam. In this climate . . . ' He did not go on.

Keen led the way from the cabin and said softly, 'Hear the silence? And they say that ships are only wood and copper!'

Adam nodded, glad of the darkness below the poop. Bolitho had told him to take care of his burned shoulder. He was incredible.

Bolitho opened the small door and stepped into the sleeping-cabin. The ship was so still at her moorings that the cot barely moved.

Tuson was holding a small bottle up to a shuttered lantern but turned as Bolitho entered.

'No change, sir.' It sounded like a rebuke.

Bolitho looked into the cot where he had fretted over the months since hoisting his flag above *Achates*.

Allday was heavily bandaged and had his head on one side as if to breathe better. Bolitho touched his forehead and tried not to show his anguish. The skin felt like ice. As if he was already gone.

Tuson said quietly, 'Narrowly missed the lung, sir. Thank God it was a clean blade.'

He watched Bolitho's shadow rear across the massive timbers and added, 'Would you like me to stay, sir?'

'No.' He knew Tuson had plenty of people awaiting his care. 'But thank you.'

Tuson sighed. 'I'll come when you need me.'

Bolitho followed him into the cabin. 'Tell me.'

Tuson slipped into his plain blue coat. 'I don't know him as well as you, sir. He seems strong enough, but it is a bad wound. Most would have died there and then. I am deeply sorry.'

When Bolitho looked again Tuson had gone. Down to the bowels of the ship, to his sick-bay and solitude.

Ozzard hovered nearby. 'Anythin', sir?'

Bolitho looked at him. So small and frail. He too was feeling it badly.

'What was Allday's favourite drink?'

Ozzard's watery eyes lit up. 'Well, rum, sir. Always liked a wet.' He fumbled with his hands. 'I – I mean, *likes* a wet, sir.'

Bolitho nodded. Even that was typical. In moments of crisis and danger, disappointment or celebration, he had often offered Allday a glass or two of cabin brandy. And all this time he had preferred rum.

He said gently, 'Then fetch some, please. Tell the purser I want the very best.'

He was sitting beside the cot, the cabin door half open to catch some air, when Ozzard returned with a copper jug. In the cabin's heat the rum made his head swim.

Bolitho tried to concentrate on what he must do tomorrow, on the ship's affairs, on Tyrrell's future. But he kept seeing Belinda's lovely face when they had made their last farewell. How she had told Allday to look after him and Adam.

He heard the muffled trill of a call, the distant patter of bare feet as the duty watch was turned to for some task or other.

The voyages they had done together. And just last year when they had both been prisoners of war in France when Allday had carried the dying John Neale in his arms, it had been his strength and confidence which had held them and had given them courage.

He remembered his own early days as a midshipman and lieutenant when he had fondly believed that the admiral in his quarters was beyond pain and protected from personal doubts.

Bolitho heard the squeak of a fiddle from the forecastle and pictured the off-watch hands enjoying the cool evening air.

He saw himself in the mirror above the little desk and looked away. What price your vice-admiral now?

He took a clean handkerchief and dabbed it in a glass of rum, then with great care he wiped a little of it on Allday's mouth.

'Here, old friend . . . ' He bit his lip as the rum trickled unheeded down Allday's chin. There was a bright scarlet stain in the centre of the bandages. Bolitho restrained the urge to yell for the sentry to summon the surgeon again. Allday was fighting his own battle. It would be cruel to make him suffer further.

Bolitho stared at Allday's homely face. It looked older, and the realization made him get to his feet, too stunned to accept what was happening, yet unwilling to share it with others.

He clenched his fists and peered around the small cabin like a trapped animal. There was nothing he could do. Barely seeing what he was doing he held the glass to his lips and swallowed the rum, the fire on his tongue and throat making him gasp and retch.

Then he waited until his breathing had returned almost to normal. He saw Ozzard's small shadow through the open door and said in a voice he barely recognized, 'My compliments to the surgeon . . . '

Ozzard seemed to shrink even smaller as Bolitho's words reached him.

'Quick as I can, sir!'

Bolitho swung round as one of Allday's hands groped over the side of the cot.

'Yes, I'm *here*!'

He held it between his own hands and stared fixedly at Allday's face. It was set in a frown, as if he was attempting to remember something. His hand had no more strength than a child's.

Bolitho whispered, 'Easy now. Don't let go.' He tightened his grip but there was no response.

Then Allday opened his eyes and stared at him for what seemed like minutes without any sign of recognition. When he spoke his voice was so small Bolitho had to bend over him until they touched.

Allday murmured, 'But you don't like rum, sir, you never have!'

Bolitho nodded. 'I know.' He wanted to talk, to help him, but the words would not come out.

Doors banged open and feet pounded on companion-ladders, then Tuson, with Keen and Adam behind him, burst into the cabin.

The surgeon pressed his hand on to Allday's chest, oblivious to the blood on his cuff. Then he said, 'Breathing's a whole lot better.' He sniffed. 'Rum, was it?'

Allday was unable to focus properly but he needed to speak, to reassure Bolitho in some way.

'Could do with a wet, sir.'

Tuson stood aside and watched gravely as the vice-admiral put one hand under the coxswain's head and held a glass to his lips. He knew that if he lived until he was a thousand he would never forget this moment.

He said, 'Leave him now.'

He watched as Bolitho dashed some water from a bowl on to his face, the way he was trying to prepare himself to confront the others in the cabin.

Tuson said quietly, 'Never mind about them, sir.' Afterwards he was surprised he had dared to address his admiral in such a fashion. 'It'll do no harm for them to see you have feelings too. Just a man like the rest of us.'

Bolitho took another glance at Allday. He looked at rest.

He said, 'Thank you. You will never know . . . ' He left the sleeping-cabin to face the others.

Tuson looked at the rum on the desk and grimaced. Allday should be dead. All his experience pointed to just that. He began to snip at the bloodied bandages.

Then even Tuson's severe features broke into a smile. *Could do with a wet indeed.*

In the great cabin they sat or stood in total silence as Ozzard brought some wine.

Then Keen raised his glass. 'This happy few, sir.'

Bolitho looked away. There was no better sentiment

15

Last Farewell

The weeks and then months which followed the attack on the harbour seemed to Bolitho like a slow record of Allday's fight against death. Any progress was often marked by an immediate set-back, and Bolitho guessed that he was fretting about his inability to move, his 'uselessness', as he put it.

A few vessels visited the island, and slowly but surely things returned to normal. There were no more attacks, and traders reported that they had not sighted any Spanish men-of-war or suffered further interference.

In October that year two hurricanes struck San Felipe with a ferocity which made a military attack puny by comparison. Great tidal waves had threatened *Achates* and destroyed smaller vessels, and torn the roofs off many of the houses. Plantations were laid to waste, and several people had been killed or badly injured, their livelihoods destroyed.

But it was the turning point between the islanders and the *Achates'* company. Without the disciplined efforts of the seamen and marines it seemed unlikely that anything of value would have been saved. The ship, once a symbol of law and oppression, had taken on a new guise, that of protector, so that for the officers and men alike the daily routine was less demanding.

Three months to the day after being cut down by a Spanish sword Allday walked across the *Achates'* quarterdeck for the first time. Ozzard went with him, but Allday, true to his fashion, would not lean on him for support.

Bolitho made a point of being on the poop and watched

while Allday moved into the sunlight, his feet unsure and dragging, as if he had never walked a ship's deck before. Bolitho noticed too that several of Allday's friends were much in evidence, as they had been throughout his struggle to survive. But they understood and were careful to keep their distance, outwardly engrossed in their various trades.

Bolitho heard Adam's light step beside him and said, 'I never thought I would see this day, Adam.' He shook his head. 'Never.'

Adam smiled. 'He's doing well.'

Bolitho saw Allday reach the quarterdeck rail and grasp it with both hands as he took several breaths and looked down at the gun-deck.

Scott, the third lieutenant, who was in charge of the watch, took elaborate care not to see him, even walked to the compass and peered at it as though the ship was at sea and not alongside.

Bolitho turned and looked at his nephew. All these weeks and they had barely discussed Boston and what had happened there, although Tyrrell had told him the bones of the matter.

He said quietly, 'What we have done here is important, Adam. I put my views to the Admiralty, my beliefs as to what should happen here after we have gone.' He shrugged. 'I have to believe they will act upon them. Too many have suffered and died to throw it all away. I used to hear my father say we in England are so often like that. We do not take proper care of what we have won with blood and sweat.' He gestured towards the anchorage. 'Just a pair of frigates here and the Dons would never have attempted to seize the place. Likewise the French would have looked elsewhere to make a bargain.'

'Suppose their lordships still insist on handing over the island, Uncle?'

'The Spanish attack should have shown them the importance of San Felipe. If not, then I have failed here.' He touched his arm impetuously. 'But it was wrong to use you the way I did. I knew that Chase would trust you, would tell you what I needed to know. But as a result you lost a chance to win his niece. I cannot forgive myself for that.'

Adam moved his shoulder and felt the burn beneath his shirt. He gave a rueful smile. 'We were nearly too late anyway, Uncle.'

They both looked at the charred fragments in the shallows. Sea-birds were perched in rows on the blackened ribs of the fire-ship, and weeds grew where Tyrrell had driven his brigantine to her destruction to save them all.

Adam hesitated. 'At least I saw my father's house.'

Bolitho glanced at him and was glad that the jealousy had gone.

Adam sounded far away. 'I told her I would return some day.'

'Perhaps we shall go together. When that happens you can take *me* to see Hugh's old house.'

They looked at each other, sensing the bond between them. It was as if Hugh was very much here with them. Like this island, Bolitho thought, without threat or hostility.

He tensed as Allday swayed after releasing his grip on the rail.

Then Allday looked up to the poop and grinned. He had known they were there all the while, Bolitho thought.

He said, 'Without Allday . . . ' He did not need to go on.

The midshipman of the watch clattered up the poop ladder and touched his hat.

Bolitho looked at him. 'Well, Mr Ferrier, are you going to tell me about the sail?'

The midshipman flushed, his carefully worded speech scattered.

'I, er, the captain sends his respects, sir, and a courier-brig has been sighted to the east'rd.'

Bolitho nodded. 'Thank you. It is a while since I "enjoyed" the midshipman's berth, Mr Ferrier, but I have not yet forgotten how to read a signal.'

Adam exclaimed. 'You knew? And yet you carried on talking to me as if the brig and her news are of no importance!'

Bolitho watched the midshipman pausing to speak with two of his friends. The story would be enlarged somewhat by tonight, he thought.

Ferrier was the senior midshipman, and the brig's arrival would affect him too. Homeward bound and a lieutenant's examination, the young could always find room for optimism.

He said simply, 'It was important that we should talk. As to the rest, I shall have to fall back on Thomas Herrick's Lady Luck.'

Bolitho moved to the rail and looked along the upper decks. Men were on the gangways or working high overhead on the yards. But their eyes were towards the harbour entrance, and Bolitho could guess what many of them were thinking. They had been glad to leave England and the humiliation of being thrown on the beach like so much unwanted top-hamper. Now, after what they had seen and done together, they would be eager to return to their homes.

Bolitho thought of Falmouth, what they would say when they met again, whenever that might be? Of his very own daughter. What name had she chosen for her?

He said, 'I'm going below. My compliments to the officer of the watch and please tell him to keep the people working. I don't want any long faces if the news is bad.'

Adam stood back and touched his hat. It was difficult to know which tack his uncle would take next.

Bolitho hurried into his cabin and saw to his astonishment that Allday was hard at work putting a shine on the old sword.

'You should be resting, man! Will you never do as you are told, dammit?'

But for once his mock anger failed to have the right effect.

Allday ran the cloth once more along the blade and then looked at him squarely.

'The surgeon says I'll not be the same again, sir.'

Bolitho walked to the open stern windows. So that was it. He should have guessed. He had seen that Allday was unable to straighten his back properly. As if the deepness and pain of his chest wound prevented it.

Allday added quietly, 'Not much of an admiral's coxswain I'll be an' I wanted . . .'

Bolitho looked at him and said, 'You've earned your time ashore in comfort more than anyone I know. There's a place for you at Falmouth, but you know it.'

'I know, an' I'm grateful. It's not just that.' He looked at the sword. 'You won't need me any more. Not like this.'

Bolitho took the sword from him and laid it on the table.

'Like what? A bit knocked about, is that all? You'll be your old mutinous self in no time, you see.' He rested his hand on his shoulder. 'I'll never sail without you. Not unless you wish it. You have my word.'

Allday stood up and tried not to grimace as the pain probed through him.

'That's settled then, sir.'

He moved from the cabin, his feet dragging on the painted canvas.

His determination, his pride were as unbeatable as ever, Bolitho thought sadly. And he was *alive*.

Later that day, as the sun dipped towards a placid sea, Bolitho stepped into *Achates'* wardroom. After his own and Keen's cabins it seemed small and overcrowded, he thought.

Quantock said stiffly, 'All officers and senior warrant officers present as ordered, sir.'

Bolitho nodded. Quantock was a cold fish, even the action had not changed him. Nor would it now, he decided.

He heard his nephew close the door behind him and said, 'Please be seated, gentlemen, and thank you for inviting me here.'

It had always amused him. Any senior officer, even Keen, was a guest in his ship's wardroom. But had anyone ever denied one an entrance, he wondered?

He glanced around at their expectant faces. Sunburned, and competent. Even the midshipmen who were crammed right aft by the tiller-head looked more like men than boys now. The lieutenants and the two Royal Marines, Knocker, the priest-like sailing-master, and Tuson, the surgeon, he had grown to know and understand them in the time they had carried his flag at the fore.

Bolitho said, 'You will know that the courier-brig brought despatches from England. Their lordships have given full consideration to the reports on San Felipe, and to the large part your efforts played in an otherwise difficult mission.'

He saw Mountsteven nudge his friend the sixth lieutenant.

'Furthermore, I have been advised that French interference in the Mediterranean, and their pressures on His Majesty's Government to evacuate Malta in accordance with the *same* treaty which obliged us to hand this island to them, makes further negotiations impossible. As a direct result, gentlemen, all French and Dutch colonies which we had agreed to restore will now be retained. That, of course, will apply to San Felipe.'

It seemed impossible. In the neatly phrased despatches it was still hard to compare the complex negotiations which had swayed back and forth across Europe while *Achates* had been fighting for her very survival.

Bonaparte, now named Consul for life, had annexed Piedmont and Elba and showed every intention of retaking Malta once the British flag came down in the name of independence.

Bolitho saw the excitement transmit itself around the wardroom. So much for the Peace of Amiens. The signatures were barely dry on it.

He said, 'I am ordered to remain here until sufficient forces are despatched from Antigua and Jamaica to reinforce the garrison.'

He saw Keen drop his eyes. He knew what was coming next.

'The recent governor will be replaced as soon as possible. Sir Humphrey Rivers will be returning to England to stand trial for treason.'

He could find no satisfaction in that. After the luxury and

wealth of his little kingdom he would be taken home in a King's ship, the first of any size which could be made available. And after that, with this totally unexpected shift of events, he would very likely hang.

He looked from face to face and added, 'You have performed very well, and I should wish you to carry my thanks to the people also.'

Keen watched as Bolitho smiled for the first time since he had begun to speak. Whatever anyone else might think, Keen could see plainly enough where the strain and responsibility had made their mark.

Bolitho said quietly, 'And after *that*, we are going home.'

Then they were all on their feet shouting and laughing like boys.

Keen opened the door and Bolitho slipped away. He had two letters from Belinda, and now there was time he would re-read them from the beginning.

Keen and Adam followed him up the companion and then Keen asked, 'Will it be war, sir?'

Bolitho thought of the young and jubilant faces he had just left behind, of Quantock's sour disapproval.

'There is little doubt in my mind, Val.'

Keen stared around in the gloom, as if already preparing his ship for another battle.

'God, we've hardly recovered from the last one, sir!'

Bolitho heard Allday's unfamiliar dragging footsteps and turned towards his cabin with its motionless scarlet sentry.

'Some never will, my friend. It's too late.'

Keen sighed and said, 'Join me, Mr Bolitho, and share a glass. Doubtless you'll be getting a command of your own if war does come about.' He gave a smile. 'Then you'll discover what hardship really means!'

Aft in his cabin Bolitho made himself comfortable in a chair and opened the first letter.

Going home. They would have been surprised had they known just how much it meant to their vice-admiral.

Then he listened to her voice again as it lifted from the page.

My darling Richard . . .

'See that these letters are put aboard the packet with the others, Yovell.'

Bolitho listened to the squeak of tackles through the cabin skylight, the stamp of feet on deck as another net of fresh food supplies was hoisted above the gangway.

After all the waiting it was difficult to accept that the moment had arrived. Not that time had been allowed to drag on their hands, he considered.

A smart frigate and two bomb-vessels were now anchored below the battery, and a big armed transport had brought more soldiers as promised to reinforce the garrison. He smiled at Lemoine's reaction when a full colonel had taken charge.

'I was just getting a taste for power, sir,' the lieutenant had said.

He heard Allday coming through the dining space and looked up to greet him. Allday had made great strides where his health was concerned and the colour had returned to his face. But he still could not straighten his shoulders, and his smart blue coat with the gilt buttons seemed loose on his big frame.

It must be close on six months since he had been struck down, three since the brig had arrived here with the Admiralty's final instructions on the island's future.

Bolitho said, 'It will be spring in England when we reach there. A year since we left.'

He watched Allday's expression but he merely shrugged and replied, 'Probably all have blown over by that time, sir.'

'Maybe.'

He was still brooding. More afraid of the land than the hazards at sea. Allday had once told him that an old sailor was like a ship. Once tied up and unwanted, and with nothing useful to do, both were doomed.

And Allday had been a lot younger when he had said it.

Calls shrilled along the upper deck and voices barked commands as some marines marched to the entry port.

Bolitho stood up and waited for Ozzard to bring his dress-coat. The new governor had arrived in San Felipe aboard the frigate. A small, birdlike man, he seemed dull by comparison with Rivers.

His warrant made it clear that Rivers was to take passage in *Achates*. A cruel twist of fate for both of us, Bolitho thought.

As Keen had remarked, 'Why this ship, damn his eyes? A plague on the man!'

Ozzard patted the gold-laced coat into place and eyed the epaulettes with professional interest. He reached for the fine presentation sword on its rack but dropped his hands as Bolitho gave a quick shake of the head.

He waited for Allday to take the sword and clip it to his belt. As he had always done.

Bolitho had written to Belinda about Allday's courage and the price he had paid for it. She, better than anyone, would know what to do. In a fast packet his letters would reach home long before *Achates*.

'Thank you. I shall go and meet our, er, guest.'

He glanced quickly round the cabin but Ozzard had already gone.

'Ready, Allday?'

Allday made to straighten his back but Bolitho said, 'Not yet. It takes time.' He watched his despair. 'As it did when I nearly died, remember? When you cared for me every hour of the day?'

He saw something of the old sparkle in Allday's eyes.

'I'll not forget that, sir.'

Bolitho nodded, moved by Allday's pleasure at the memory.

'Flag at the fore, remember that too? I'll see you an admiral's coxswain yet, you scoundrel!'

They went on deck together and Bolitho saw Rivers waiting by the entry port flanked by an escort of soldiers. He wore manacles on his wrists, and Lieutenant Lemoine, who was in charge, said hastily, 'My colonel's orders, sir.'

Bolitho nodded impassively. 'Sir Humphrey is under my protection, Mr Lemoine. There will be no irons here.'

He saw Rivers' look of extraordinary gratitude and shock. Then he watched as his eyes moved up the foremast truck where the flag lifted in a fresh breeze. As a vice-admiral himself he was probably hanging on to this moment as his other world fell in ruins.

'Thank you for that, Bolitho.'

Bolitho saw Keen frowning in the background and said, 'It is all and also the least I can do.'

Rivers looked across at the waterfront. People had flocked there to watch him leave. No cheers, no rebukes either. San Felipe was that sort of place, Bolitho thought. With a stormy past and a future just as uncertain.

Why should I care? Even feel sorry for the man, he wondered? A traitor, a respectable pirate who had caused too many deaths because of his own selfish greed. Rivers had two sons in London, so it was likely he would be well defended at his trial. He might even talk his way out of it. After all, if war came, the island's security owed much to him, whatever the true reasons had been.

In his heart Bolitho knew that the real blame lay with powerful men in London. Who had allowed Rivers to extend his role here for his own advantage.

Keen watched Rivers being escorted below and said, 'I'd have put him in the cells.'

Bolitho smiled. 'When you've been a prisoner, Val, and I hope that never happens to you, you'll understand.'

Keen grinned, unabashed. 'But *until* then, sir, I don't have to like him!'

Ferrier, the senior midshipman, touched his hat to Keen.

'Mr Tyrrell's come aboard, sir.'

Bolitho turned. He had imagined that Tyrrell had stayed ashore for most of the time since *Vivid*'s loss because he did not want to talk about it. Or, independent to the end, he had been seeking a berth in some other vessel.

He had heard *Achates* was sailing very soon. The whole island seemed to know. There would likely be a few more babies on the plantations, black and white, after *Achates* had crossed the ocean. It was good to hear the seamen calling out to the people in the boats in the harbour and along the waterfront. The yards of the ships were festooned with coloured streamers, and every inch of space had been filled with fresh fruit and gifts from the islanders who had once hated and feared them.

He saw Tyrrell's shaggy head appear above the ladder to the quarterdeck and walked to meet him.

'Thought I'd make a quick farewell, Dick. To you an' the youngster. Next time he an' I meet he'll be a post-cap'n.'

Like Allday, he was finding it hard, and at any second he would blunder away on the wooden pin which he hated so much.

Bolitho tried to gauge the moment, knowing that any careful speech would be taken as charity, even condescension.

'Will you go back home now, Jethro?'

'Got no home. All gone, dammit, I told you!' He relented immediately. 'Sorry about that. Bein' with you again has unsettled me quite a bit.'

'Me too.'

'Really?' Tyrrell stared at him, wary of a lie.

'I was thinking . . . ' Bolitho saw Knocker from the corner of his eye hurry to the first lieutenant, who in turn looked at the captain. Bolitho knew why. He had felt the shift of wind on his cheek even as he had been speaking with Rivers. It was not much, but with the winds here so perverse it must not be wasted. But just as when Ferrier had come to tell him about the brig's arrival, so now he would not break the spell by looking up at the masthead pendant. He continued, 'There's England, you know.'

Tyrrell threw back his head and laughed. 'Hell, man what are you sayin'? What would I do over there?'

Bolitho looked past him at the shore. 'Your father came from Bristol. I recall you telling me. It's not all that far from Cornwall, from us.'

Tyrrell watched the sudden activity as the relaxation on deck changed to purpose and movement. He knew all the signs. A ship leaving was nothing new. But homeward bound . . .

He said desperately 'I'm a *cripple*, Dick, what th' hell use am I?'

'There are plenty of ships in the West Country.' He dropped his voice. 'Like *Vivid*.'

He saw Keen moving nearer. It could not wait.

Bolitho said, 'Anyway, I want you to come.'

Tyrrell gazed around as if he could not trust his own judgement.

'I'd work my passage, I'd insist on that!'

Bolitho smiled gravely. 'It's settled then.'

They shook hands and Tyrrell said, 'By God, I'll do it!'

Bolitho turned to his flag-captain.

'You may get the ship under way when it suits.'

Keen yelled, 'Hoist all boats inboard! Both watches of the hands, Mr Quantock!'

He looked at Bolitho and the one-legged man by the quarterdeck rail and shook his head.

Men were dashing aloft and out along the yards, and with her capstan manned *Achates* shed her ties with the land and moved slowly out to her anchor.

Adam said excitedly, 'Hear them, Jethro? They're cheering us!'

Along the waterfront the handkerchiefs waved and voices echoed across the water as the great capstan continued to clink round.

Tyrrell nodded. 'Aye, lad, this time they are.'

Captain Dewar marched across the deck and touched his hat with a flourish.

Keen caught the mood too. 'Very well, Major, you may play us out if that was what you were about to suggest?'

Bolitho found that he was gripping the worn rail with unusual force. He had seen it all before countless times, but somehow this was quite different.

'Anchor's hove short, sir!'

'Loose the heads'ls!'

Bolitho turned and saw Allday beside him. *His right arm*.

'Man the braces there!' Quantock strode about, his head jutting forward, immersed for the moment in the complexities of his trade.

'Anchor's aweigh, sir!'

It was not a blustery departure, with the ship heeling over under a pyramid of canvas. With all the dignity of her years *Achates* swung slowly across the wind, the sunlight glancing off her figurehead, the armour-bearer, and along her sealed gun-ports and freshly painted tumblehome.

'Get the t'gan's'ls on her, Mr Scott! Your division are like old women today!'

The sails hardened and shivered at their yards, and with barely a ripple below her dolphin-striker *Achates* glided towards the harbour mouth.

Bolitho watched the narrow strip of water. It looked no wider than a farm gate. A glance at Keen's tense features told him that he was remembering that wild charge through it in total darkness.

'Steady as you go!' That was Knocker. Even he seemed different as he called, 'Mr Tyrrell, you may be able to offer some local knowledge. If so, I'd be obliged.'

Here was the fortress. The sloping track where the marine drummer had died, where Rivers had made his greatest mistake.

The flag above the old battery dipped in salute and Bolitho saw a line of redcoats on the jetty, bayonets fixed, colours lowered, as *Achates*' topgallant sails made little patches of shadow on the fortress wall.

Allday murmured, 'They'll not forget *Old Katie* in a hurry.'

He turned his head to listen as the small cluster of fifers and drummers broke into *The Sailor and His Lass*.

Once Bolitho saw him thrust one hand to his wound, and then he removed it from his fine blue jacket and laid it on the rail beside his.

As if, like the island, he was leaving the pain astern.

16

The Secret

Bolitho walked up the slippery planking and gripped the nettings at the weather-side of the quarterdeck.

The ship was plunging and shuddering as rank after rank of waves surged against her quarter in an unbroken attack.

Bolitho watched as the bows dropped yet again and the sea thundered over the forecastle and cascaded along the upper gun-deck like a flood, breaking over the guns before surging away through the scuppers until the next onslaught.

In spite of the savage movement and damp discomfort Bolitho felt a sense of exhilaration, the nearest thing he could remember since his last command as post-captain.

How different was the Atlantic's grey face to the waters around San Felipe. Lines of angry, rearing waves, their crests like broken yellow teeth.

Achates was making the best of this unexpected storm under jib and close-reefed topsails and was as steady as could be expected. Nevertheless, during the time he had been on deck Bolitho had seen the boatswain and his men floundering amongst the surging water to secure lashings on boats and guns, or to fight their way aloft to repair broken cordage.

Keen was here too, his tarpaulin coat flying in the wind as he bent over the compass and had a shouted conversation with the master.

How perverse the weather had been since the day they had set sail from San Felipe. The breeze had dropped almost as soon as the island had vanished below the horizon. They had been becalmed for days before they had been able to spread

more sails again. It had taken more time then to recover what
they had lost on the lazy currents and tides.

Now, deep into the Atlantic, they were seeing its other
face. The ship was standing up well in spite of her repairs,
many of which had been makeshift because of the lack of a
dockyard. It was just as well, he thought grimly. The nearest
land was Bermuda some two hundred miles to the north-
west.

Here was another. He held his breath as the sea boiled over
the weather-gangway and swept some seamen aside like
twigs on a flooded stream. He looked up at the tightly
braced yards, the reefed canvas like grey metal in the dim
light.

Stooping shadows waited for the right moment before
dashing from one handhold to the next. A few noticed him at
the weather-side and probably thought him crazy for leaving
his fine quarters.

Keen staggered towards him, his face shining with spray.

'Mr Knocker says it cannot last more than another day,
sir.' He ducked as a solid sheet of water deluged over the
quarterdeck and ran down the ladders on either side.

'How is Sir Humphrey taking to all this?'

Keen watched two of his men as they dragged some fresh
cordage towards the mainmast in readiness to haul it aloft to
the topsail yard. He relaxed slightly as they scampered into
the ratlines before the next incoming sea could sweep them
away or smash them senseless into one of the guns.

He shouted, 'Well enough, sir! He spends much of his
time writing.'

Bolitho tucked his chin into his cloak as the spray and
spindrift dashed down from the poop. Preparing his defence. Making a last will and testament. Probably just to
keep his mind away from the miles as they dragged beneath
Achates' scarred keel.

The officer of the watch moved hand over hand along the
quarterdeck rail and yelled. 'Time to call the first dog-watch,
sir!'

Keen grinned into the storm. 'God, it looks more like midnight!'

Bolitho left him and groped his way aft beneath the poop, where by contrast it seemed almost quiet, the sounds of sea and wind muffled and held at bay by the ship's massive oak timbers.

But in the cabin it was just as lively, with water spurting through the sealed gun-ports and the gallery on the weather-quarter. Every lantern swung in a wild dance, and the cabin furniture did all it could to tear itself from Ozzard's storm-lashings.

Ozzard appeared from his pantry and clung to the screen for support. His face was pale green, and Bolitho did not have the heart to ask him for something hot to drink.

'How is Allday?'

Ozzard gulped. 'Resting, sir. In his hammock. He had a large tot of – ' But even the memory of the neat rum was too much and he fled, retching, for the door.

Bolitho went into his sleeping-cabin and grasped the side of his swaying cot. Where Allday had almost died.

He waited for the deck to rise again and then hoisted himself, fully clothed, into the cot.

He hated being out of things, it was the part of his flag-rank which he found least acceptable. Strategy was one thing, but at times like these, as the ship fought her natural enemy without respite, he felt little better than a passenger.

Bolitho kicked off his shoes and grimaced at the shadows which loomed and died around him like macabre dancers.

But if the ship foundered, passenger or not, it would be better if the people saw their vice-admiral fully dressed.

During that night the storm blew itself out and the wind, although still strong, veered to the south and enabled Keen to set more sails and his men to carry on with their repairs. Between decks the trapped water and scattered possessions were cleared away, and when breakfast was piped the galley funnel was pumping out its usual plume of thick, greasy smoke.

Bolitho sat at his table, drinking scalding coffee and munching thin strips of pork fried pale in biscuit crumbs. It was one of his favourite meals at sea, and none could serve it better than Ozzard.

Despite the foul weather and unavoidable delays they should sight the Lizard, the southernmost tip of Cornwall, in fourteen days.

He was surprised that it should make him feel so nervous, unsure of himself. All he had longed and hoped for and yet he was as unsettled as a callow midshipman.

He got up and walked to the mirror above his desk. He was a year older. The lock of hair which hid the cruel scar above his right eye was still black, and yet he was sure there were some grey strands too. He tried to shrug it off. The youngest vice-admiral on the List, apart from Our Nel, that is. But he found no consolation. He was forty-six and Belinda ten years his junior. Suppose . . .

Bolitho turned almost gratefully as Keen entered the cabin, his hat beneath his arm.

'Have some coffee, Val, what — ' He saw the grim expression on Keen's face and asked, 'Trouble?'

Keen nodded. 'The masthead has reported drifting wreckage to the nor'-east. Victim of the storm, I expect, sir.'

'Yes.' He pulled on his faded sea-going coat. 'Not the packet which set sail before us?'

'No, sir. It would mean too much drift.' He watched Bolitho curiously. 'If we change tack to examine the remains we will lose valuable time, sir.'

Bolitho bit his lip. He had once seen a drifting boat with only one man alive in it. All the rest were corpses. He thought of little Evans, how he must have felt in his drifting boat, his ship gone, his companions wounded and dying around him. What must it be like? The last one alive, like the man he·had seen all those years ago?

He said, 'There's always a chance, Val. Alter course and send a boat away when you consider it near enough.'

An hour later, as *Achates* shortened sail and tacked uncomfortably close to the wind, the quarter-boat pulled swiftly towards the great spread of bobbing flotsam and broken timbers.

It had seemed an eternity before they had got near enough to examine the storm's success. In such Atlantic weather it seemed likely that several ships had shared this one's fate.

Bolitho had stood on the poop with a telescope and had watched the remains spreading out across *Achates*' bows, tragic and pathetic.

She had not been very large, he thought. She had probably been struck by one gigantic wave across her unprotected poop, driven over before she could recover.

Keen lowered his glass. 'There's a boat, sir!'

Bolitho moved his own glass and stared at the swamped, listing thing which had once been a long-boat.

Keen exclaimed, 'They're alive! Two of them anyway!'

Lieutenant Scott, who was in charge of the quarter-boat, was already urging his oarsmen to greater efforts as he sighted the survivors.

Bolitho heard Tyrrell's wooden stump on the wet planking and asked, 'What do you make of it, Jethro?'

Tyrrell did not even hesitate. 'She's a Frenchie. Or was.'

Keen steadied his glass and said excitedly, 'You're right! They're no merchant sailors either!'

Bolitho saw Tuson and his mates waiting by the entry port, a tackle being rigged to haul the survivors aboard.

Bolitho asked, 'Who speaks the best French in *Achates*?'

Keen did not falter. 'Mr Mansel, the purser. Used to be in the wine trade before the war.'

Bolitho smiled. He had heard slightly differently, and that Mansel had in fact been a smuggler.

'Well, tell him to be ready. We may be able to discover what happened.'

There were ten survivors in all. Knocked, dazed and half-blinded by the mountainous seas, they had lost hope of rescue so far from land. Their vessel had been the brig *La Prudente*, outward-bound from Lorient to Martinique. Their

commander had been swept overboard, and their senior
lieutenant had managed to clear away one boat before he too
had died from a blow on the head from some falling wreckage. The dead lieutenant was still in the boat, his face very
white beneath the water which filled it almost to the gun-
wales.

The coxswain of the quarter-boat yelled, 'Shall I cast 'er
off, sir?'

But Lieutenant Scott snatched a boat-hook and dragged
the dead lieutenant towards him.

The survivors must have been too shocked and weak to
push their officer over the side, Bolitho thought. He watched
them being carried and helped to a companion-way. They
still did not seem to know what was happening.

Keen said, 'Mr Scott has found something, sir.'

He could not hide his eagerness to get under way again, to
fight back to their original track.

The dead officer rose above the gangway, water running
from his mouth and his uniform as he swung above the
gun-deck like a felon on the gallows.

Scott hurried aft and touched his hat. 'He had this tied to
his waist, sir. I saw it when the boat tilted over.'

Bolitho looked at Keen. It was like robbing the dead.
The French lieutenant lay on the deck, his arms and legs
stretched out, one eye part open as if the light was too strong
for him.

Black Joe Langtry, the master-at-arms, covered the corpse
with a piece of canvas, but not before he had removed a pistol
from the man's belt. It had probably been his only means of
maintaining some order on that terrible night when his ship
had been overwhelmed.

Keen said, 'All the same, sir. Lorient to Martinique.'

Bolitho nodded. 'My thoughts entirely.'

It took a few moments to open the thick canvas envelope
and break the imposing scarlet seals.

Bolitho watched the purser's lips move as he scanned the
carefully worded despatch which was addressed to the

admiral in command of the West Indies Fleet at Fort de France.

No wonder the dead lieutenant had tried to save the package.

The purser looked up from the table, uncomfortable under their combined gaze.

He said, 'As near as I can tell, sir, it says that upon receipt of these orders hostilities against England and her possessions will be resumed immediately.'

Keen stared at Bolitho. 'That's near enough for me!'

Bolitho walked to the stern windows and watched the quarter-boat being warped round in readiness for hoisting. It gave him time to think, to weigh chance and coincidence against a small act of humanity.

He said, 'For once a storm was a friend to us, Val.'

Keen watched as Bolitho tipped a handful of pistol balls from the envelope, to carry it to the sea-bed rather than let it fall into the wrong hands. But the lieutenant had been killed before he could act, and his men had been too ignorant or too frightened to care.

Keen said, 'So it's no longer just a threat. It's war.'

Bolitho smiled gravely. 'At least we know something which others do not. That is always an advantage.'

With her yards retrimmed and her helm hard over *Achates* turned her jib-boom away from the drifting pattern of flotsam and the waterlogged boat which would sink in the next storm.

That evening at dusk the dead lieutenant was buried with full honours.

Bolitho watched with Adam and Allday close by as Keen said a few prayers before the corpse was dropped alongside.

The next Frenchman they met would not be so peaceful, Bolitho thought.

'Well, Sir Humphrey, I believe you wish to speak with me.'

Bolitho kept his tone level but was shocked to see the

change in Rivers' appearance and demeanour. He looked ten
years older, and his shoulders were bowed as if he was
carrying a great burden.

Rivers seemed surprised when Bolitho indicated a chair for
him and sank into it, his eyes wandering around the cabin
without recognition.

He said, 'I have written down all I know of the plot to seize
my — ' He faltered. 'To seize San Felipe. Rear-Admiral
Burgas, who commanded the squadron at La Guaira, was to
govern it until Spanish ownership was recognized.'

'Did you know about the Spanish mission, that it might be
used to shelter an invading force?'

'No. I trusted the captain-general. He promised me more
trade along the Spanish Main. I could see nothing but
improvement.'

Bolitho took the papers from him and scanned them
thoughtfully.

He said, 'These might help with your defence in London,
although . . . '

Rivers shrugged. '*Although*. Yes, I understand.'

He looked at Bolitho and asked, 'If you are in England
during my trial, would you be prepared to speak for my
defence?'

Bolitho stared at him. 'That is an extraordinary thing to
request. After your action against my ship and my
men . . . '

Rivers persisted, 'You are a fighting officer. I want no
defence for what I did, but understanding of what I had been
trying to do. To keep the island under the British flag. As it is
now, thanks to you.'

When Bolitho remained silent he continued, 'After all,
had the Dons made their move before you came, my actions
might have succeeded, and I would have been seen in a very
different light.'

Bolitho eyed him sadly. 'But they did *not*. You must know
from past experience, Sir Humphrey, that if a captain fires
upon or seizes an enemy ship, or what he believes to be a foe,

only to discover when he reaches port that their two countries are at peace, what then? That captain could have had no way of knowing the facts, and yet . . . '

Rivers nodded. 'He would be blamed nevertheless.' He stood up. 'I should like to return to my quarters now.'

Bolitho rose too. 'I have to tell you that we shall be in sight of land within the week. After that your affairs will be taken out of my hands.'

'I understand. Thank you.'

Rivers walked to the door and Bolitho saw two Royal Marines waiting for him.

Adam, who had been present throughout the brief interview, said, 'I feel no sorrow for him, Uncle.'

Bolitho touched his scar beneath the rebellious lock of hair.

'It's too easy to judge.'

Adam grinned. 'If you had been appointed governor, Uncle, would you have behaved as he did?' He saw Bolitho's confusion and nodded. 'There you are then.'

Bolitho sat down. 'Young devil. Allday was quite right about you.'

Adam watched him, his features suddenly serious.

'I was glad to join you as your flag-lieutenant, Uncle. Being with you for such a long period has taught me a lot. About you, about myself.' He looked wistfully around the cabin. 'I shall miss the freedom more than I can say.'

Bolitho was moved. 'The same applies to me. I was warned against bringing you. Too close, Oliver Browne said. Perhaps he was right in some ways, but when we reach Falmouth things will – '

They both looked up at the skylight as a lookout's voice pealed down, 'Deck there! Sail to the sou'-east!'

Bolitho stared at the square of blue above the skylight. He felt his heart quicken, an unexpected dryness in his throat. Like the hunter caught off guard when he needed his vigilance the most.

He crossed to his chart on the table and examined it,

following the neat calculations, the unerring line which led all the way to the Cornish coast. It was unlikely that a merchantman would be outward-bound from either England or France if war had just been declared. It would take time for the rules to be accepted or broken.

'I'm going on deck.'

He strode to the door and out into the sunlight. The sea was lively with white-caps, and the wind still steady from the south so that *Achates* had her yards tightly braced to hold her on a starboard tack.

Men stood about in small groups or stared up at the seaman in the mizzen cross-trees.

Keen cupped his hands. 'Mizzen topmast-head there!'

'Sir?' The man peered down at his captain far below.

'What does she look like?'

'Man-o'-war, sir!'

Keen beckoned impatiently. 'Get aloft with a glass, Mr Mountsteven, that fellow is a madman!'

He saw Bolitho and touched his hat. 'I beg your pardon, sir.'

Bolitho looked at the empty sea, suddenly apprehensive. Did going home mean so much? Was it that different now?

Keen said, 'From the sou'-east, it seems, sir. Too far out for the Bay.'

Mountsteven had reached his precarious perch beside the lookout.

He yelled, 'She looks, sir, like a whacking frigate!' A pause. 'A Frenchie, I'd suggest!'

Bolitho made himself walk calmly to the quarterdeck rail as the conjecture buzzed around him like a swarm of hornets.

A French frigate standing well out to sea, probably steering north for the Channel or the tip of the Bay, Brest perhaps?

He thought of the dead lieutenant, the envelope, the little brig on passage from Lorient to Martinique.

'Deck there! There's another sail astern of her, sir!'

Knocker, who had silently appeared by the wheel,

muttered, 'Pork and molasses! More bloody trouble, I'll be bound!'

Keen said, 'She's on a converging tack, sir. She'll have the wind-gage, by God.'

Bolitho did not turn but stared along the full length of the deck. So near and yet so far. Another two days, maybe less, and they would have met with ships of the Channel Fleet as they endured the weary task of blockade duty.

He said, 'The Frenchman is taking a chance, Val.' He turned and saw understanding on Keen's face. 'Maybe they do not know the news, as *we* would not but for loss of *La Prudente*.'

Midshipman Ferrier, who had swarmed into the weather-shrouds at the first sighting report, yelled, 'I can see the first one, sir! A big frigate! I can't make out the other but — '

Mountsteven's voice cut him dead. 'Second one is a ship of the line, sir! A seventy-four!'

One of the helmsmen sucked his teeth. 'The bastards!'

Bolitho took a telescope and climbed up beside the mid-shipman.

'Where away, Mr Ferrier?'

Then he saw the leading Frenchman, her topgallant sails like gold in the sunlight. Even as he watched her outline changed slightly. He remarked half to himself, 'She's setting her royals.'

Bolitho climbed down to the deck and looked at his nephew.

'As *you* will know, a frigate's job is to sniff out danger and identify strangers.'

Adam nodded. 'Then they cannot know about the war.'

Bolitho tried to clear his mind. The pattern was all wrong. The French ships were closing rapidly with the southerly wind well in their favour.

He snapped, 'Ship's head, Mr Knocker?'

'East-nor'-east, sir! Full an' bye!'

Keen murmured, 'If I let her fall off two points or so they'll suspect something, that we're trying to keep clear of them.

On the other hand, sir, a change of tack would give us a few extra knots.'

A change of course away from the enemy, setting more sail, either of those would arouse the interest of any frigate captain, let alone one with a seventy-four in close company.

'Continue as we are, Val. They'll be watching us too, remember.'

Keen glanced up at the masthead pendant. 'But for the damned weather we'd have been at anchor by now.'

Six bells chimed out from the forecastle and Bolitho saw the purser emerge with his clerk in readiness to issue the rum to each mess. He thought of Allday, how the rum had touched him like a memory.

'I suggest you send the people to their messes, Val. The galley can serve a hot meal a little earlier today.'

Keen hurried away and spoke to Quantock by the rail, and seconds later the calls shrilled between decks and the sailors grinned at each other because of the unexpected break in routine.

Bolitho took the telescope again and sought out the other vessel. One of the newer French frigates, he decided. Forty-four guns. He could just discern her hull now as it lifted on a long roller before dropping again in a great welter of spray. She was flying.

Bolitho listened to the subdued chatter of the men on watch. The prospect of a sea-fight did not seem to be troubling them. They had already dispatched a Spanish two-decker and had captured an island. A French frigate would be simple compared with that.

Keen joined him again. 'They might stand away when they know our flag, sir.'

'Very well. Run up the colours.'

But when the scarlet ensign broke from the gaff nothing changed other than Mountsteven reporting that the frigate had hoisted her tricolour.

Tyrrell appeared on deck, his jaw working on a piece of salt beef.

He squinted up at the mizzen truck and asked, 'D'you reckon you could get me up yonder, Cap'n?'

Keen stared at him, his mind grappling with other problems.

'Bosun's chair, d'you mean?'

Tyrrell glanced at Bolitho and grinned. 'Just had a thought. You recall that seventy-four in Boston, the one which was supposed to be doin' the parley. Could be her. If so, she'll likely not know about the war yet.' He grinned more widely. 'Now, that'd be a terrible shame, eh?'

They had forgotten about Mountsteven but his voice made them all remember as he called, '*Third* ship, sir! 'Nother frigate, I think!'

Keen said softly, 'Jesus!' Then to the boatswain he said, 'Assist Mr Tyrrell aloft, if you please.'

Many of the watch on deck turned to stare and to follow Tyrrell's jerking progress up the mizzen-mast, his wooden stump clicking against halliards and spars.

Keen dropped his voice. 'Three to one, sir. The odds are formidable.'

Bolitho handed his glass to a boatswain's-mate. 'Do you suggest we run?'

Keen said, 'I'll run from nothing, sir. But I cannot answer for the ship's state if we are called on to fight.'

Bolitho watched the frigate's outline alter again as she changed tack until she was pointing directly towards him.

He said quietly, 'It's another war, Val, not some petty quarrel. With half the fleet still laid up, England has never been less prepared. If our people are expected to endure a long, bitter conflict they will need victories, not leaders who turn and run away because the odds are *formidable*!'

He turned and studied Keen's concern. 'We've no choice, Val. The frigates will be round us like hounds after a stag. That would give the seventy-four time to close the range and finish the fight. If we are to be beaten, I'd prefer it to be facing the enemy, not being chased until the wind has gone out of us.'

Bolitho faced Tyrrell as he was lowered carefully to the deck.

'Damn near cut myself in half.' Tyrrell glanced at them questioningly, then added, 'She's the same one right enough. Must have gone south when she quit Boston. Rear-admiral's flag at the mizzen.'

Bolitho said, 'Then she's the *Argonaute*, a new third-rate. I know her admiral from times past. Contre-Amiral Jobert. One of the few of the old Royalist navy to escape the Terror. A good officer.'

He knew that the others nearby were listening to him despite their efforts to conceal the fact. Trying to discover what was about to happen. What would become of them.

He said lightly, 'I shall go aft and have a bite to eat, *then* we can clear for action.'

Bolitho strode beneath the poop and knew his casual comment about food would spread through the messes like wildfire. He could almost hear it. Nothing to worry about, lads. The admiral's having his grub.

He barely saw the sentry who flung open the screen door for him and he did not stop until he reached the stern windows. When he leaned over the sill he could just discern the frigate's topsails. An hour or more yet to wait. Maybe nothing would happen. Why must they fight if only to die? Who would blame him for standing away from the odds which were bearing down on him?

He felt his chest and the urgent hammering of his heart. Was it fear? Is this what it is like? That one action too many. God alone knew it had happened often enough to far better men.

Bolitho wiped his face with his shirt cuff and turned blindly into the cabin again.

Fear of losing something so precious he could think of nothing else beyond it.

He had been hoping too hard and too much. A weakness when so many were depending on him.

What were hopes anyway? In the roar of a broadside they counted for very little.

Ozzard entered the cabin with a tray.

He said, 'Fresh chicken, sir.'

Bolitho watched him as he laid the tray carefully on the table. So the ship's purser had had hopes too. He would not have sacrificed one of the ship's own stock of chickens otherwise.

Ozzard watched him patiently. 'A glass of something, sir?'

Bolitho smiled. Poor little Ozzard. Trusting and loyal. It never seemed to occur to him that before evening he might be dead.

He said, 'Yes, Ozzard. Some of your special hock.'

As he hurried away Bolitho buried his face in his hands.

The French admiral had obviously not heard about the outbreak of war. Otherwise he would certainly have changed his formation, ready to attack from three bearings at once. *Achates* could fire on and possibly cripple the leading frigate before her captain realized what was happening, and then thrust on to attack the seventy-four. Still bad odds, but some improvement.

He recalled his own fury and disbelief when the Spanish two-decker had attacked *Achates* and destroyed *Sparrowhawk*, how they had all cursed her for her cowardice and deception.

Could he now bring himself to act in the same fashion?

Honour. The word seemed to echo around the cabin like a taunt.

He looked at the old family sword on its rack and remembered how his father had handed it to him instead of to Hugh. Hugh was the elder son and should have had it. But his disgrace, the shame which had followed Bolitho like an evil spirit even as far as San Felipe, which had broken their father's heart, had put the sword into his trust.

Bolitho said, 'Then so be it!' The choice had never been his, and his mistake had been to believe otherwise.

When Ozzard returned with a bottle from his cool store in the bilges he found Bolitho as he would have expected, calm and outwardly untroubled.

Things could not be so bad after all.

17

Fair Warning

Bolitho stepped over some trailing lines and walked to the weather-side of the quarterdeck. The French frigate was much nearer but had shortened sail as if uncertain what to do next. He estimated that she was about half a mile from *Achates'* starboard quarter.

He heard men crawling about the deck behind him, as if the best part of the ship's company had suddenly become cripples.

It was essential that the ship should be cleared for action without all the obvious bustle and movement which the French lookouts would immediately recognize.

Keen was saying to the boatswain, 'You shall send your people aloft to rig chain-slings only when we begin to engage.'

Big Harry Rooke rumbled something in reply and Keen rapped, 'They've no choice, man. One stupid move now and we'll be feeding the fish before dusk!'

He turned and saw Bolitho watching him.

'Mr Quantock is sorely ashamed of his record, sir. Twenty minutes to clear for action!' His attempt to joke seemed to steady him and he added, 'What are your orders for this memorable day, sir?'

Bolitho pointed. 'In a moment we will alter course three points to lee'rd. It is my guess that the frigate will close the range to take station on our quarter again. But he'll be much nearer.'

If only his heart would settle. The tension might so easily reveal itself in his voice.

Keen looked past him at the frigate's shortened pyramid of canvas. 'She's new, like the third-rate. Probably to impress the Americans.' He did not conceal the bitterness. 'Whereas our masters thought fit to send the oldest sixty-four still in service!'

Bolitho walked to the rail and glanced along the gun-deck and the black eighteen-pounders. Their crews were stripped for battle and were concealed beneath the gangways or huddled against their guns with their tools and weapons.

'It will have to be quickly done, Val. The French seventy-four is well astern of us now. But it will take time. They'll be ready for us after we show our intentions.'

Keen nodded, his mind working on the next manoeuvre and the one after it. 'The third French vessel is smaller. Mr Mountsteven thinks she is a twenty-six-gun frigate. As I recall, she will be the *Diane*, a real veteran by comparison.'

Knocker turned the half-hour glass by the binnacle and said, 'Ready, sir.'

'Pass the word to the lower gun-deck.'

Keen looked round as Allday appeared from the poop. He was carrying Bolitho's old sword and his features were stiff as if to conceal the pain of his wound.

Bolitho held up his arms so that he could clip the sword into place.

Allday muttered, 'You should not be wearin' them epaulettes today, sir.' He shrugged and gave a brief grin. 'But I've sailed with you often enough to know better'n to argue, I suppose.'

Bolitho looked at the Frenchman's sails. He saw sunlight lance from a levelled telescope in her foretop. At any second they might see something suspicious and beat to quarters.

But he said, 'Take care of yourself, Allday. No risks today.'

He touched his arm, and two of the quarterdeck powder-monkeys nudged each other, the enemy forgotten as they shared something private.

Allday eyed him bleakly. 'Don't insult me, sir. If them

buggers come at us, they'll find me ready enough, an' that's no error!'

Bolitho smiled. 'I also know better than to argue, old friend.'

He swung away as Keen said, 'They've made a signal to the *Argonaute*, sir!'

Midshipman Ferrier lowered his big signals telescope and said, 'It's code, sir.'

Bolitho said, 'Alter course.'

Ready and waiting, the helmsmen put the wheel over, and while others ran to trim the yards, Knocker reported, 'Three points it is, sir! Nor'-east by north!'

Bolitho could feel the difference as the wind thrust more forcefully into *Achates*' canvas.

Keen said, 'Recall Mr Mountsteven from aloft. I had all but forgotten him again.'

'The Frenchie's changin' tack, sir.'

Bolitho held his breath as the powerful frigate turned a point or so towards *Achates* and at the same time spread her main-course and driver.

Keen slammed a fist into his palm and exclaimed, 'He's overhauling us, sir.'

A marine dropped something on the poop as he crawled closer to the hammocks and Sergeant Saxton snarled, 'I'll skin you alive if you make another move!'

Bolitho watched the frigate and saw the clear spray bursting over her beak-head and bowsprit. If she continued to overhaul them she would pass down the starboard side at less than half a cable's distance.

He raised the telescope and saw intent faces staring across the lively water, strangely alien after the familiar ones he met every day.

'Stand by on the gun-deck!'

Keen folded his arms and stared at the enemy. As soon as *Achates* changed tack again she would be laid hard over to leeward by the wind. But her sudden manoeuvre would carry her across the frigate's bows. It was now or never, for in a matter of minutes both vessels would collide once *Achates* began to turn.

'Man the braces!'

Bolitho gripped the old sword and pressed it against his leg.

'*Now!*'

The big wheel squeaked violently as the helmsmen threw their weight on the spokes, and as the yards began to shift with the wind two more ensigns were run up to the main and mizzen trucks.

'Open the ports! Lively there! *Run out!*'

Bolitho watched the frigate and could not take his eyes from the towering mass of sails and rigging as she swept towards *Achates'* side.

He heard a trumpet and pictured the wild confusion aboard as the vessel they had been stalking suddenly turned like a lion at bay, her guns bared, each one double-shotted, every captain seeking his own target.

Keen yelled, '*As you bear!*' His arm flashed down. '*Fire!*'

For an instant Bolitho thought he had left it too long. That he should not have wasted valuable time by hoisting his battle ensigns. If their roles had been reversed . . .

His mind cringed as the eighteen-pounders of the upper battery hurled themselves inboard, while from the lower gun-deck the heavier roar of the twenty-four-pounders shook the ship from truck to keel.

Men stumbled about in the choking smoke as it was swept through the open ports and above the gangway while *Achates* exposed her broadside to the wind.

At such a close range the effect was immediate and terrible.

The frigate's foremast and main-topmast staggered under the onslaught of the double-shotted guns. Then spars, sails and rigging joined together in one great avalanche of destruction which thundered over the bows and sides, hurling spray into the air and dragging the hull round.

'Sponge out! *Reload!*'

Keen shouted, 'Stand by to come about, Mr Quantock.'
He did not need telling the need for haste.

As the helm went down again and *Achates* surged round
into the wind, Bolitho was grateful that they had not made
more sail. In such a stiff wind the ship might have been in
irons, or worse, dismasted.

Gun by gun along the starboard side the captains were
holding up their hands as each barrel poked its muzzle
through a port.

The frigate was still floundering down-wind under the
dragging weight of fallen spars and sails, but Bolitho was not
deceived and knew what could happen once that wreckage
was hacked away.

'Main-tops'l braces there! Heave! Put your backs into it!'

Achates continued to turn, the frigate suddenly appeared
above her starboard bow as if she and not the little two-decker
was moving.

To any inexperienced eye it would look like chaos. The
boatswain and his party swarming out on the topsail yards to
rig the chain-slings, while below them their ship pirouetted
around her masts to cross the enemy's stern.

'Starboard battery! *Ready!*'

Keen had his hand in the air and did not even blink as here
and there along the enemy's side a gun fired in defiance. But
for her it was already too late, and as *Achates* crossed the
frigate's starboard quarter even those guns fell silent, unable
to traverse enough to find a target.

Bolitho saw a ripple of musket fire from the poop and
mizzen-top and instant response from Dewar's sharp-
shooters.

He felt something like sickness in his stomach as *Achates*'
jib-boom passed the frigate's stern. He saw her glittering
cabin windows, her name, *La Capricieuse*, in gold letters
across her counter.

Then *Achates*' starboard carronade belched fire from the
forecastle and the enemy's stern and poop appeared to open
like an obscene cave. When the carronade's massive ball burst

within the crowded hull its packed charge of grape would transform the gun-deck into a slaughter-house.

Men, weapons, the rudder, everything would be blasted aside and incapable of movement for many hours.

Keen cupped his hands. 'Get the royals on her, Mr Quantock!'

He had no time to wait and worry about the carronade's harvest. The frigate was out of the fight.

Once again *Achates* clawed her way round to hold the wind on her quarter. It was as if nothing had changed. Not a man lost, not a scratch on wood or canvas.

Bolitho climbed the poop ladder and levelled his glass to seek the French seventy-four. Even in distance she looked fierce and enraged, he thought. She was spreading more sails, and had hoisted a signal to her yards for the benefit of her remaining companion.

He heard Knocker shout, 'East-nor'-east, sir!'

The Frenchman was steering north-east. Again they were on a converging tack. But the *Argonaute* held the wind-gage and would probably try to cripple her enemy by dismasting or by tearing down her rigging with chain-shot while keeping at a safe distance.

Bolitho trained the glass on the dismasted frigate. It must have been a terrible shock. Bolitho remembered his time as a prisoner of war in France. Never again, he had vowed then.

Keen touched his hat. 'All guns loaded and ready, sir.' He glanced aloft. 'Mr Rooke has even managed to rig his nets and slings.'

Bolitho smiled. 'I *know* it was a risk, Val.'

Keen looked away. 'You gave them fair warning. They'll not need it this time.'

He stared hard at the French seventy-four. Just over a mile distant, while the little frigate was standing away from her heavy consort and tacking down-wind to be ready to dash down and harry *Achates* from another angle. After seeing the fate of *La Capricieuse* it was unlikely she would force home an attack yet.

Bolitho also watched the French flagship and felt the nearness of their contest like claws in his loins. She was new, big and better armed. But *Achates* was more agile, and had proved her worth a hundred times over.

Keen was thinking aloud. 'If he holds the wind we cannot reach him, sir. Whereas he can move in when he pleases or chance some long shots which might score a serious hit.'

'I agree.' Bolitho climbed up to the nettings and peered over them. 'The other frigate, the *Diane*, she's steering for the west'rd, next she'll come about after us.' He shot him a grim smile. 'To snap at our heels!'

Keen nodded. 'She could do some damage if we were already engaged with the *Argonaute*, sir.'

Bolitho stepped down. 'Tell me what you think. Shall we use the *Diane* as bait?'

Keen's eyes lit up. 'Go for the frigate, sir?'

Bolitho nodded. 'Contre-Amiral Jobert is, I believe, an honourable sailor. I cannot see him standing by while his remaining frigate is attacked by a ship of the line!'

Bolitho looked at the sun. Only an hour since the car-ronade, the Smasher as it was termed, had blasted away the other frigate's resistance.

He said, 'You have a gun captain named Crocker. I met him at the fortress. A fearsome fellow but, I understand, the finest of his trade.'

Keen said, 'Lower gun-deck, sir. I'll send for him.'

Crocker came aft, his good eye shielded from the sun. After the cool gloom of the lower gun-deck he was finding it irksome. He knuckled his forehead and gazed at Bolitho, his deformed figure at odds with the scarlet-coated marines nearby.

Bolitho said, 'I want you to take charge of the two stern-chasers. We shall have company there directly, and when I give the word I want you to damage her badly enough to cause concern to her admiral.'

Crocker twisted his head further as if to fix his good eye on him.

'*Sir?*'

Keen said wearily, 'Just do it, Crocker. The French seventy-four will close the range when her admiral sees what is happening.'

'Oh, I *see*, sir!'

'Pick all the men you want, but I need that frigate winged.'

Crocker showed his uneven teeth. 'Bless you, sir, I thought you was makin' do with the little 'un!'

He loped away with his strange swinging gait, and Keen said, 'If we let the Frogs get alongside, old Crocker will frighten them to death!'

Bolitho loosened his neckcloth and looked at the sky. Sea-birds floated high above the embattled ships, indifferent, and coldly watching for the gruesome scraps which would soon be theirs.

He thought of Belinda, the green slope below Pendennis Castle where she could watch and wait for the ships to pass.

He heard Adam say, 'It won't be long.'

Bolitho looked at him. Was he afraid? Resentful that he might die so young?

But the lieutenant saw his glance and said, 'I'm *all right*, sir. I shall be ready.'

Bolitho smiled. 'I never doubted that. Come, Adam, let us take a walk together. It will pass the time.'

The swivel-gun crews and marine marksmen in the tops peered down as the vice-admiral and his youthful aide walked up and down the quarterdeck, their shadows passing over the naked backs of the seamen at their tackles with their rammers and charges.

Midshipman Ferrier lowered his glass for the hundredth time, his eye sore from staring at the oncoming seventy-four. It seemed such a short while ago that he had been thinking of home, of the chance to take his lieutenant's examination. In that towering pyramid of sails and the double line of guns which glinted in the sunlight like black teeth, he saw his hopes already gone. Now the thing which worried him most was whether or not he could stand up to what lay ahead.

He saw Bolitho pass by, speaking with his nephew, the way the flag-lieutenant was smiling at something he said. When he raised his telescope again his fear had gone.

On the lower gun-deck Midshipman Owen Evans peered through the gloom until he found Lieutenant Hallowes who was in charge of the twenty-six cannons here and ran to pass a message from the captain.

Hallowes listened to what the midshipman reported and remarked laconically, "Pon my soul, Walter, we're goin' for the frigate first!'

His assistant, the fifth lieutenant, laughed as if it was the greatest joke he had ever heard.

Evans paused at the foot of a ladder, his eyes taking in the red-painted sides, the shining skins of the men by the open ports, the air of watchful tension. Every man had his ears covered by his neckerchief. In this confined space the roar of the twenty-four pounders could deafen anyone in minutes.

Evans stared at his hand on the scrubbed woodwork. It was shaking uncontrollably, as if it had a will all of its own.

The shock made him look round at the gun-deck again. It was unlike the other times when he had been on deck near the vice-admiral when the Spanish ship had burst into flames after that fierce battle. Or even when he had taken command of *Sparrowhawk*'s boat. It was nothing like it at all.

Scenes flashed before his eyes. His pride and excitement at being accepted as midshipman in a fine frigate like *Sparrowhawk*. His first uniform made with loving care by his own father. Evans came of a large family, but he was the only one who had chosen the sea rather than tailoring.

Foord, the fifth lieutenant, saw the boy hesitating by the ladder and snapped, 'Move your feet, lad. There'll be messages aplenty in a moment or two!' Foord had once been a midshipman in this very ship and was only nineteen himself. He added in a gentler tone, 'What is it, Mr Evans?'

Evans stared up at him. 'Nothing, sir.' But his mind was screaming instead, *I'm going to be killed. I'm going to die.*

Foord watched him run up the ladder and sighed. Probably still thinking about Captain Duncan's death, he thought.

On the orlop deck beneath Foord's feet, Tuson, the surgeon, walked slowly round his makeshift table, his eyes taking in the array of glittering saws and probes, the empty 'wings and limbs' tubs, the leather strap to wedge between a man's teeth. The great jar of rum to ease the agony. Away from the slowly spiralling lanterns his mates and loblolly boys stood like ghouls, their hands tucked in their clean aprons while they too waited.

Tuson entered his small sick-bay and stared unseeingly at the cots, at the cupboard which contained more rum and brandy. He found that he was clenching his fists, his mouth like parchment as he imagined what that first drink would be like.

He heard footsteps outside and saw Corporal Dobbs with his musket and fixed bayonet peering at him uncertainly. Dobbs had the additional duty of ship's corporal in which he assisted the master-at-arms. But now he was a proper Royal Marine again and was needed at his station on deck.

Tuson saw that Sir Humphrey Rivers was also standing by the door, his head bowed between the great deckhead beams.

Dobbs said uncomfortably, 'Couldn't very well put a gentleman like 'im in the cells, sir.'

Tuson nodded. In case the ship went down under them, he thought.

Dobbs continued, 'An' it didn't seem proper to leave 'im with the Froggies we picked up from the wreck.'

Tuson looked at Rivers. 'If you stay here, Sir Humphrey, it may not be pleasant either.'

Rivers looked at the swaying shadows, the sense of doom which seemed to lurk here.

'It will be better than being alone.' He nodded curtly. 'I appreciate it.'

His face filled with relief that he had rid himself of his burden, the corporal all but ran to the ladder.

Bottles and jars clinked on the shelves as a gun banged out from aft.

Tuson exclaimed, 'What are they doing?'

Rivers smiled coldly. 'Stern-chaser.'

Tuson massaged his fingers. 'You've not forgotten then?'

Rivers hung his richly embroidered coat on a hook. 'That's one thing you never forget.'

Deep in the ship's fat hull, in his own private store-room, Tom Ozzard, the vice-admiral's servant, folded his arms and rocked back and forth as if he was in pain.

By the light of a single lantern he could see all of Bolitho's possessions stacked around him. It seemed wrong to leave them in such careless disarray, Ozzard thought. The fine table and chairs, the splendid wine-cooler, the desk and the cot, like everything else above the orlop deck which had been removed and torn down when the ship had been cleared for action. Now on both gun-decks *Achates* lay open from bow to stern, the crews unimpeded, the way clear for the young powder-monkeys to run with fresh charges and shot.

Ozzard had heard the boats being swung out and lowered for towing astern. Once action was joined the boats would be cut free, to be recovered by the victor, whoever it was. But tiered boats on deck were an additional source of deadly, crippling splinters when an enemy's iron crashed inboard.

Ozzard looked at the bolted door and shivered. It was cold down here where he kept his wine, and in times like these took refuge.

Like Allday, he was privileged to come and go as he pleased, and was grateful for the profession Bolitho had given him. Now in his store, in the lowest portion of *Achates'* hull, he was afraid. But it did not trouble him. He had accepted it long ago.

When he had carried the fresh chicken to the cabin for Bolitho, he had found time to glance at the master's chart below the poop.

Ozzard held his arms across his narrow chest even more

tightly. Below where he sat was the keel, and beyond it there was nothing but a bottomless ocean.

He winced as another gun made the deck quiver. But it seemed far away and without danger. Later he might venture up on deck. There was another muffled bang and he decided to wait.

Isolated from the enclosed world between decks, Bolitho climbed to the poop and looked at the French seventy-four. She had spread more canvas, but although she had closed the distance between them she had not yet fired a shot. He estimated that she had changed tack slightly and was now steering along an almost parallel course. By contrast, the little frigate had run with the wind before coming about to take station on *Achates'* lee quarter.

He said, 'Open fire.' He heard his order being passed to the quarterdeck, felt the response as the helm went over and the ship came reluctantly as close to the wind as she could manage.

He watched as the frigate appeared to move over until she lay directly astern. Then, as the word reached him far below, old Crocker jerked his trigger-line and the starboard stern-chaser recoiled with a sharp bang. Bolitho did not blink, and thought he saw the dark blur of the ball as it reached the apex of its flight before it splashed down almost alongside, the tall waterspout falling and scattering in the wind.

Bolitho heard the marines at the netting whispering and probably making bets on the next shot.

Old Crocker was good all right. He had almost winged the frigate with his first ball.

Now he had the range, and the 'feel' of it, as every gun captain should. Furthermore, the *Diane's* captain would know it.

The frigate fired one of her bow-chasers, and its thin spout of water well astern of *Achates* brought a roar of derision from the marines.

Their lieutenant snapped, 'Sar'nt Saxton, you will oblige me by keeping those ruffians quiet and in good order!' But he was grinning as he spoke and the reprimand was more for Bolitho's benefit than anything.

Adam climbed to the poop with a telescope and looked astern as another gun fired from below the counter.

This time there was no splash to betray the fall of shot. Instead a great streamer of torn topsail broke free and curled from its yard like a pale banner.

Bolitho heard the muffled cheers from below. They had hit her. If one of Crocker's eighteen-pound balls struck the *Diane*'s slender hull it could be serious.

Adam exclaimed, 'Look, sir! *Argonaute*'s setting her main-course!'

The seventy-four seemed to puff herself up as with sail upon sail she leaned over to the wind, her lower gun-ports almost awash as she changed tack towards *Achates*.

Bolitho heard Keen shout, 'Let her fall off three points again, Mr Knocker! Steer nor'-east by north!'

Even as the hands hauled at the braces and Knocker stood over the binnacle like a watchful hawk, Crocker fired yet again, and this time one of the frigate's jib sails was cut away to join its ragged companion.

Quantock was yelling, 'Mr Mountsteven! Another pull at the weather-forebrace there! Now *belay*, dammit, sir!'

Men bustled about at the braces and halliards, while only the crews of the starboard guns, which pointed towards the enemy, remained at their stations.

Bolitho gripped the nettings as the deck tilted to the thrust of the canvas overhead.

The French captain would have to close the range whether he wanted to or not. Unless he ordered his frigate to stand away, in which case *Achates* would be able to meet his challenge gun to gun. Bolitho smiled. Well . . . almost.

One of the marines who was leaning against the hammocks, his musket already cradled against his cheek, saw Bolitho's smile and dared to say, 'Us'll teach them Frogs a lesson, sir!'

He seemed to realize he had spoken to a vice-admiral uninvited and lapsed into confused silence.

Bolitho glanced at him. He did not even know his name.

In a while they would be fighting for their very lives. The heaviest casualties were usually aft on the unprotected poop and quarterdeck. This marine might be one of them.

He said, 'I am relying on it.' He looked at their expectant faces, hating his own words. 'So give your best, lads.'

There was a jarring crash as Crocker laid and fired another gun. The frigate had changed tack very slightly, but it had not passed unnoticed by the grotesque gun captain. As her shape lengthened momentarily Crocker pulled his trigger-line and the ball smashed through the enemy's larboard gangway, hurling planks and splintered wood high into the air.

There were more cheers, and Bolitho held his breath as the frigate paid off down-wind, her torn canvas still whipping above the deck as she opened the range between them.

Then he ran down the poop ladder and strode to the rail above the gun-deck.

It would be very soon. He glanced quickly abeam and saw the seventy-four's bows edging into view, her canvas bulging to the wind as she changed tack still further towards the *Achates*.

'Stand by!'

The cheering ceased instantly and gun crews crouched beside their eighteen-pounders, staring through the ports.

'As you bear!'

The French ship had the wind-gauge, but so strong was the pressure in *Achates'* sails that her gun muzzles were elevated to maximum advantage by the slanting decks.

'*Fire!*'

Deck by deck, gun by gun, the carefully aimed broadside flashed along *Achates'* side from stern to forecastle. Some of the forward guns were traversed to full extent, their crews leaning on their handspikes until they too could train on the enemy.

Bolitho watched intently as the *Argonaute*'s topsails danced wildly, the wind ready and eager to explore the holes punched by the double-shotted guns.

Along and beyond her hull he saw the sea alive with flung spray as more balls slammed down with terrible impact.

It was impossible to determine if they had hit anything vital. But the range was still closing, the French captain just as aware as Keen of the danger of a lucky shot. One ship knocked out of the fight, another driven off by Crocker's two stern-chasers, the French captain would feel the humiliation too with his admiral breathing down his neck.

Bolitho saw the flashing line of bright tongues from the seventy-four's side, tensed for the sickening shriek of iron, the crash of shots slamming into timber. Instead he heard the insane whine of chain-shot and saw long streamers of broken rigging floating from the upper yards, the forward topgallant sail ripped apart like a handkerchief in the invisible onslaught.

'Ready!' Keen had his hand up high. *'Fire!'*

Again the guns recoiled madly on their tackles, their crews leaping forward to sponge out and ram in fresh charges while the muzzles were still spewing smoke.

'Ready!' Keen wiped his streaming face with his forearm. *'Fire!'*

The gunnery was superb. All the drills, the demanding discipline, were paying off now. Two broadsides to *Argonaute*'s one.

They were hitting her too. Her mizzen-topmast was dangling like a fallen bridge, and her sails were pock-marked by shot and flying splinters.

Bolitho held his breath again as the guns flashed along the enemy's side.

He felt the jarring thud of balls hitting the hull, and saw the fore-course punctured in several places at once. The wind did the rest, and soon the fore-course was little more than rags.

'Fire!'

The pace was slower, the response more irregular, as the gun captains jerked their lines and jumped clear as each great breech charged inboard again.

There was a great crack and then amidst a writhing tangle of stays and rigging *Achates'* main-topgallant mast thundered down. It ploughed into the larboard gangway like a battering ram, tearing aside the protective nets as if they were cobwebs before toppling overboard.

Rooke and his men were there in an instant, axes flashing as they cut the wreckage away. Two seamen were down too. Dead or knocked unconscious by falling rigging, Bolitho did not know.

The guns roared out once more, the din scraping at his mind, as fallen cordage and great strips of canvas fell over the sweating gun crews while they reloaded and then fired again.

Keen shouted, '*Argonaute*'s coming at us, sir!'

He looked wild-eyed, his hat knocked from his head in the turmoil which surged around him.

Bolitho wiped his eyes and looked at the enemy. The trick had worked. The *Argonaute* was charging down-wind with every available sail set, her forward guns firing haphazardly, some hitting, but others, because of the fine angle of approach, ripping through wave-crests far astern.

The little frigate had made no attempt to press home her attack, and was probably grateful to be a mere spectator. She was too far away now to be of any use. It was already too late for last-minute strategy.

Bolitho heard himself shout above the crash and recoil of the guns, 'It's *men* not ships, Val! They're what count in the end!'

Smoke belched over the gangway and a marine fell from the main-top, his scream lost in the bombard nent. One of the forward eighteen-pounders was on its side, two men down and bleeding badly beside it, another writhing and screaming, pinned to the deck by its overheated muzzle.

Men from the disengaged side ran to replace the dead and injured, others obeyed Quantock's speaking-trumpet and

hurried to splice hasty repairs and set the big main-course. It
was too close to the fighting, too great a risk if fire should
spread from sparks or a burning wad from a gun.

Bolitho gauged the distance. The French ship was a cable
away, her guns firing intermittently, but at this range she
was hitting *Achates* again and again.

Keen was right to set the bigger sails. If *Achates* lost
steerage-way now through lack of canvas, she would fall
down-wind and present her unprotected stern to the Frenchman's heavy guns and suffer the same fate as the frigate. If the
enemy got the chance to fire through *Achates* full length, both
decks would suffer crushing losses.

Bolitho raised his smarting eyes to the foremast and saw
his flag flying above the smoke and destruction. As the
French admiral would see it. The additional spur to drive him
on, to bring both ships together regardless of consequences.

'*Fire!*' Keen paused only until the guns roared out towards
the enemy. 'Mr Trevenen! Take charge there!'

Bolitho saw that Mountsteven was lying near one of his
guns. He had lost an arm, and part of his face had been
scorched like burned canvas.

The lower gun-deck was firing without respite, and
Bolitho could picture it as if he were there. It had once been
his station as a midshipman, a thousand years ago. The
red-painted sides to hide the blood of battle, the leaping,
grotesque shadows of the gun crews as they pranced and
struggled around their weapons, and all the while the low
confines of the deck filled with smoke, like a scene from
Dante's inferno.

A ball came through an open gun-port, and Bolitho could
follow its progress as men were hurled aside, some painted in
blood as one of their companions was almost cut in halves
before it eventually crashed into the opposite side. Men fell
and rolled in torment, and Bolitho saw Tyrrell striding
among the debris and patterns of blood, his wooden stump
adding to his fierce and wild appearance.

Another ball slammed through the quarterdeck nettings

and flung hammocks across the deck like torn dolls. Two helmsmen dropped, and one of the master's mates fell screaming, a foot-long wood splinter in his stomach like a barbed arrow.

Bolitho looked round frantically but saw Adam pulling himself to his feet. Through the smoke, his voice lost in noise and deafness of battle, he smiled before turning away to assist the after-guard.

'By God, sir, this is too damn hot for my taste!'

Bolitho looked at Allday. He was obviously in pain, but was gripping his cutlass with both hands like a broadsword.

Bolitho felt his hat plucked from his head and knew that they were close enough for the marksmen to test their skills.

'Walk about, Allday, or go below.' He tried to grin but his face felt stiff, like leather.

A midshipman darted forward and retrieved his hat. There was a neat hole just below the binding.

Bolitho made himself smile. 'Why, thank you, Mr — '

But the youth merely stared at him, the life dying in his eyes, like a candle being snuffed out. Then he fell, blood flooding from his mouth.

Bolitho replaced his hat and stared at the enemy. He had not even remembered the boy's name.

A great shadow swept across the deck, followed by a chorus of shouts and screams. The fore-topmast, complete with topgallant mast and spars, had been shot away as cleanly as a carrot. It thundered over the side, taking rigging, men and pieces of men in its wake.

He heard Allday gasp, 'Th' flag, sir! They've shot your flag away!'

Even in the midst of disaster and death Bolitho could feel his outrage and bewilderment.

Bolitho drew the old sword and carefully laid the scabbard on the deck without really knowing what he had done.

The enemy was almost alongside, the guns still firing, the air filled with flying, whining fragments.

So this was where it was to be. Destiny had always known. Men merely deluded themselves.

He saw some sailors below the quarterdeck cringing as more falling wreckage bounced on the nets or splashed into the sea alongside.

They had given everything. Far more than should be expected of them.

He flung his hat down on the nearest gun and yelled, 'Come on, my lads! One last broadside!'

A gold epaulette was cut from his shoulder by a musket ball and a marine scooped it up and hid it in his tunic.

Dazed, bloody and filthy with powder smoke, the seamen returned to their guns, their rammers moving like extensions of themselves, their eyes blind to everything but the bright tricolour above the smoke.

Bolitho shouted, 'One more broadside, then she'll be into us, Val!'

Then he realized that Keen was clutching his side and there was blood on his fingers and white breeches. He saw Bolitho's concern and shook his head.

Between his teeth he gasped, 'Not yet, the people must not see me fall!'

Quantock saw what had happened and waved his hat. '*Fire!*'

The guns roared out at point-blank range, the balls passing through a return of fire from the enemy. Splinters burst from the deck, men reeled about gasping, others yelled orders to those who had already fallen.

Quantock was aware mainly of a feeling of triumph. At the very moment when they were to engage at close quarters, when hard discipline and not softness would win through, he and not Keen had been the one to take command.

But something was wrong. He was slipping and then falling. But it was all right. Someone would help him. By the time he realized that the blood was his own, his eyes, like the midshipman who had retrieved Bolitho's hat, were dead.

18

How Sleep the Brave?

Here and there along both ships guns continued to fire right until the moment of collision. It was as if the men on the lower deck were out of control, or were so dazed by the continuous thunder of their guns they no longer associated with anything outside their private hell.

On the upper deck the air was filled with death as musket and pistol-fire was directed towards officers and seamen alike.

Bolitho watched the gap narrowing between the hulls, the trapped water leaping over the tumblehome and changing to steam on the blistered gun muzzles.

Shots hammered the deck or smacked into the hammock-nettings, while from the fighting tops a murderous hail of canister ripped above the smoke and painted the decks of friend and foe alike with glittering rivulets of blood.

Keen clung to the quarterdeck rail with one hand while he pressed the other to his side, so that his coat helped to slow the loss of blood from his wound. But his face was deathly pale, and he made no effort to move as musket balls ploughed into the deck by his feet or cracked among the men around him.

Adam drew his curved hanger and yelled, *'Here they come!'*

His eyes were very bright as the two hulls crashed together and more broken spars fell from aloft to hold them fast.

Allday thrust his shoulder against Bolitho, the cutlass weaving about as if to reach the enemy as he shouted, 'They'll make for you, sir!'

Indeed, some French boarders had already clambered

across from the *Argonaute*'s beak-head as it ground over the forecastle, the rigging and nets becoming further entwined as the sea lifted and rolled both ships together.

But a crackle of musket-fire brought some of them down before they could cut the nets, and several were run through with boarding pikes even as they tried to retreat.

Captain Dewar waved his sword. 'At 'em, Marines!'

They were his last words on earth as a ball took away his jaw and flung him down a poop ladder to the deck below. His lieutenant, Hawtayne, stared aghast at his superior, unable to accept that he was dead.

Then he yelled, 'Follow me!'

Bolitho watched the scarlet coats dashing into the smoke towards the bows, some falling, others firing their last shots before using their bayonets as more boarders dropped seemingly from the sky itself on to the decks.

It was too much and the enemy too many. Bolitho heard them cheering, the sound changing to screams and curses as another swivel cut through their ranks like a bloody scythe.

He saw Midshipman Evans cowering by the companion hatch.

'Get below! Tell them to *keep firing*! Tell them it's my order!'

It might set both ships ablaze but it was their only chance.

From the corner of his eye he saw more French seamen climbing their mizzen shrouds, the smoky sunlight glinting on steel as they waited for the sea and wind to push the two hulls into a closer embrace. Soon there would be more men to support them from the lower deck.

Bolitho winced as some of the *Achates*' twenty-four-pounders roared out against the Frenchman's side. Smoke, sparks and splinters flew above the gangway and several of the enemy boarders vanished to be trapped or ground between the ships.

There were Frenchmen running along the gangway, although he had not seen them fight their way aboard. One, a lieutenant, cut down a seaman as he tried to jump clear, and several shots cracked over the quarterdeck where Knocker and his men stood around the wheel like survivors on a raft.

The French officer saw Keen by the rail and lunged forward with his sword. Bolitho realized that Keen had his eyes tightly closed against the pain and stood no chance of saving himself.

Bolitho shouted, and when the lieutenant's eyes turned towards him he struck him across the neck with the old blade, and as he tumbled over, his scream choking on blood, Allday brought his cutlass down on his ribs like a woodsman with a rebellious tree.

Steel clashed on steel as *Achates'* seamen rallied on the quarterdeck, their eyes and minds empty of everything but the need to fight and not to fall under those stamping feet and cruel blades.

Bolitho saw Adam lock swords with another French lieutenant and wanted to reach him, to help in any way he could. But even in the noise and horror of the hand-to-hand fighting Bolitho was able to see his nephew's skill as a swordsman, the way he took the weight of a heavier opponent and used it against him. Then he began to advance, stamping down with his right foot as with each thrust and parry he forced his adversary back towards the forecastle.

Allday yelled, 'Watch out!'

Bolitho swung round and saw a petty officer aiming a pistol at him. A blade flashed past his eyes and the pistol dropped to the deck and exploded. The Frenchman's hand was still gripped around it.

With a cut across his forehead, a cutlass in one hand and a belaying-pin in the other, Tyrrell managed to gasp, 'Near thing!' Then like an unsteadying giant he forced his way amongst the struggling men, his weapons swinging and hacking while he bellowed encouragement to anyone who could still understand him.

On the lower gun-deck it was frightening because of the clatter and slap of feet overhead. It was as if a mob had gone completely mad and out of control.

Midshipman Evans groped through the smoke as he tried

to find his way back to the upper deck. He slipped on some blood and almost fell across the body of a dead gun captain, then as he regained his feet he saw figures clambering through an open port where a gun had recoiled and had been abandoned for lack of powder.

They were the enemy.

The shock held him motionless, unable to breathe, as he realized that the other ship was pressed tightly alongside.

He wanted to run, to hide from the fighting and terrible sights around him. But a wounded seaman staggered away from one of the guns, his fingers clutching a deep wound in his stomach, his eyes white and rolling with agony as he tried to escape.

Two French sailors saw him and charged beneath the deck beams. The seaman fell and tried to grasp Evans' foot with his fingers.

He gasped, 'Help me! Please, in the name o' God!'

Evans was only thirteen years old, but even in his pain and despair the seaman had recognized authority and perhaps safety in the blue coat and white breeches.

Evans dragged out his short midshipman's dirk and pointed it at the two Frenchmen.

They both slithered to a halt, their madness checked by the sight of their small opponent.

In the half-darkness old Crocker's white hair moved through the smoke like a patch of light.

He swung a rammer with both hands and knocked the men to their knees. Another seaman joined him, his cutlass just a blur as he finished it.

Crocker twisted his head to stare at the midshipman and then wheezed, 'Proper little fire-eater, ain't 'e?'

Evans stared up the ladder as someone clattered down towards him. His mind could not accept what had happened, other than that he was alive.

Adam Bolitho wiped his eyes as the smoke funnelled up around him. It was hard to breathe, let alone see what was happening.

'Where's the fourth lieutenant?'

He saw the long rammer in Crocker's hands, the reddened cutlass held by one of the seamen.

Lieutenant Hallowes lurched through the smoke, his hanger held at the ready.

'Who the hell wants me?' He saw Adam and grinned. 'Why, our dashing flag-lieutenant!'

Adam asked urgently, 'How are you managing?'

Hallowes waved his blade carelessly. 'I've got my people at the starboard ports, as you can see.' He gestured angrily. '*Simms!* Cut that Frog down!'

It was like a macabre dance. A French seaman dashed from the smoke, his hands over his head as if to protect himself. He must have flung himself bodily through a gun-port expecting to find the gun-deck filled with his companions. He dropped to his knees, his eyes very white in the smoky gloom.

A marine sentry from the main companion lunged forward with his bayonet, the force so great that he pinned the luckless Frenchman to the deck.

Adam tore his eyes away. 'I've an idea. We'll go aft, through the wardroom.' He wondered if Hallowes understood or cared. He looked half-mad. 'The *Argonaute* has a big stern gallery . . .'

Hallowes exclaimed, '*Board* her?' He looked up as a violent crash shook the deck timbers. 'How is it up there?'

Adam thought of the exposed quarterdeck and terrible splinters, the combined chorus of yells and screams as men fought each other to win mastery of the ship.

'Bad. But many of the French boarders came from below decks.'

He ducked as a ball slammed through a port and ricocheted from a gun on the larboard side.

He looked at Crocker. 'Could you blow down her mainmast?'

Crocker stared at him and then said hoarsely, 'Course, sir. I'm with you.' He rattled off several names and men ran from the guns to join him.

Hallowes glared at him, the wildness momentarily held at bay.

'Why? What's the point? We'll never get out alive.'

Adam tossed down his scabbard as he had seen Bolitho do and shrugged. How could he explain? Even if he wanted to. In his mind he saw Bolitho up there on the torn and splintered deck. He was the obvious target. Without him there would be no resistance now that Keen was wounded and Quantock killed. In seconds it would too late.

He said simply, 'I owe him everything. *Everything*, d'you understand?' He did not wait for an answer but shouted as he ran aft, 'Come on, boy, if you care to!'

Hallowes wiped his mouth with his hand and gave a wild laugh.

'Don't you *boy* me, Mister Bolitho!'

Then he was running after him, others snatching up loaded pistols to follow even though they knew not where.

Evans stared aft to the wardroom, his mind reeling. Then he saw an officer lying propped against one of the guards and knew it was Foord, the fifth lieutenant, who moments earlier had been trying to reassure him.

He knelt beside him and saw the blood which soaked the lieutenant's waistcoat and breeches. He was dying even as he watched, and did not even flinch as another ball slammed into the upper hull and made the ship tremble as if she had hit a reef.

Foord saw the young midshipman and attempted to speak.

Evans held his hand, not knowing what to say.

'Tell the captain . . . ' His eyes rolled up in agony. 'Tell him . . . '

Evans felt his hand stiffen and then go limp. He wondered vaguely why he was no longer afraid. With great care he prised the hanger from Foord's fingers. He could feel the lieutenant's empty stare on him as he stood up and walked deliberately aft towards the wardroom.

'Ready, lads?' Adam looked at their strained faces.

Crocker slung his leather bag over one shoulder and eyed

the Frenchman's ornate stern right alongside. The gallery was a few feet higher than the wardroom, but it would provide some cover when they attempted to board her.

Crocker nodded. 'Give the word.'

Adam pulled himself through the shattered stern windows and after a small hesitation leapt out on to the other ship's quarter. For a moment he thought he would lose his grip and fall into the sea. There were several corpses already bobbing between the two sterns. Unconcerned and untroubled by the savage battle overhead.

At any moment he expected a face to loom over the gilded rail, to feel the thrust of steel or the blast of a pistol.

He slipped his arm around a life-sized carved figure of a mermaid which adorned the end of the gallery. Her twin on the opposite side had been beheaded by a ball earlier in the battle.

Adam eased himself warily around the mermaid, very conscious of her unmoving stare, the touch of her gold breast under his fingers. All at once he wanted to laugh like Hallowes had done. The complete insanity of it all was beyond his grasp.

He looked again at the mermaid's placid features and thought suddenly of Robina. Just a dream. He ought to have realized it.

Hallowes shouted, 'Move yourself, *boy*, make way for a King's officer!'

They both laughed like madmen and then Adam was up and over the rail, his feet sliding in broken glass as he kicked open a window and vaulted into the big cabin beyond. As in *Achates*, the ship had been completely cleared for action. But the place seemed empty except for corpses and moaning wounded, while some other figures were leaning out through the ports to lock blades with the men on *Achates'* lower gun-deck.

A French petty officer, wounded in one arm, saw the figures burst through the smoke and opened his mouth to yell a warning.

Hallowes hacked him across the face with his hanger and ran on towards the great trunk of the ship's mainmast. It was huge, like a smooth pillar, and when Adam leaned on it to regain his breath he felt it trembling under all its weight of topmast, rigging and spars as if it were alive.

Crocker bent down without hesitation and with a gunner's mate made a quick lashing around the mast with bags of powder arranged at intervals like a necklace.

Figures swayed through the haze and a pistol ball smacked into one of the British seamen like a metal fist. He dropped without making a sound.

Crocker swivelled his good eye. 'Slow-match, matey!'

He pressed it to the short fuse and made to back away.

Hallowes aimed his pistol and fired into the nearest group of shadows. 'We'll hold 'em off! The buggers'll cut the fuse otherwise!'

Adam bounded forward to touch blades with a French officer. He felt the man's breath on his face as they reeled against one of the guns, the hatred giving way to fear as he pushed him clear with the hanger's stirrup-hilt and then cut him down with a blow across the shoulder.

Hallowes darted past him and hurled his empty pistol into a man's face, and when he staggered hacked him down with two quick slashes across arm and neck.

But more men were clambering down a ladder from the deck above, their legs pale against the trapped smoke and dark paintwork. One of Hallowes' seamen stabbed through the ladder with a pike and sent one of them screaming on top of his companions, but a pistol shot killed him before he could recover his balance.

Adam strained his eyes through the choking smoke. But he could see none of the others. Crocker had probably run aft before his charges exploded, and of Hallowes there was no sign.

Two French seamen loomed around an abandoned gun. One raised a pistol but Adam knocked it upwards so that the ball cracked into a deckhead beam. The second man hurled himself the last few feet and smashed Adam on to his back.

The lanyard around his wrist snapped and he heard his hanger fly clattering across the deck.

The seaman was big and extremely powerful. He held Adam's wrists, his tarred fingers like steel as he forced them out on to the planking, as if he were being crucified.

Adam could feel his knee smashing up between his legs to find his groin and cripple him before he could struggle free.

He tried again but it was hopeless, and knew that despite the battle which raged over both ships this man was enjoying the moment.

Adam heard himself cry out in agony as the man's knee jammed into his groin. He tried not to show his pain and despair, but lights flashed before his eyes as he hit him again.

A small shadow rose above the man's shoulders and then all the pain ceased as the French seaman rolled sideways on to the deck.

Midshipman Evans stared at the man with disbelief. Then, as Adam tried to get to his feet, he lowered the hanger with which he had hit his attacker and said urgently, 'This way, sir! I've found a place – '

The rest of his words were drowned by one terrible bang.

Adam got to his knees, the pain searing through his loins like a hot iron. He was blinded by smoke and flying dust and his ears had lost all sense of hearing.

He grasped the boy's shoulder and lurched through the choking fog, only partly aware of what was happening.

He felt Evans pull at his torn coat and wanted to protest as he lost his balance and fell headlong between two of the guns. Through his dazed and confused thoughts he knew he could see sunlight where there should be none.

Then as Evans crouched down beside him he saw a great jagged spar which had crashed through the deck above and then the planking within a yard of where he had been standing.

It was made worse by the complete silence. He saw Hallowes staggering through the dust and pausing to stare up at the seemingly endless length of mast and broken shrouds which poked through the hole like a battering-ram.

Hallowes saw him and yelled something, his face set in a crazy grin as he waved his blade at Crocker's handiwork.

Adam dragged himself to his feet and leaned on the midshipman's shoulder. His hearing was returning and he realized that the din, if possible, was worse than before.

Hallowes shouted, 'That'll give them something to ponder about!'

Now that he had completely given up the idea of staying alive he seemed beyond fear.

Evans thrust the fifth lieutenant's hanger into Adam's hand and they stared at each other like confused strangers.

Like his hearing, his memory came back with brutal urgency.

He heard himself say sharply, 'Come on then, let's be about it!'

Even that reminded him of his uncle so that he knew instantly what he must do.

Tyrrell yelled, 'Can't hold 'em back any longer!'

He brought his belaying-pin down on the head of a man trying to wriggle over the torn hammock-nettings and struck out at another with his cutlass.

Bolitho did not waste his breath to reply. His lungs were on fire and his sword-arm felt like lead as he drove off another boarder and saw him fall on to the mizzen-chains.

It was hopeless. Had been from the beginning. The whole of the upper gun-deck seemed full of the enemy, while *Achates'* men rallied again on poop and quarterdeck, their eyes blazing, their chests heaving from their efforts.

He saw Allday raise his cutlass as a French seaman clambered up through the quarterdeck rail, the terror on the man's face giving way to triumph as he realized that for some reason the English coxswain was unable to move.

Bolitho jumped over a wounded marine and drove his blade blindly beneath the rail. He felt the point jar into the man's shoulder-blade and then slide easily into his body before he fell screaming out of sight.

Bolitho thrust his arm around Allday and dragged him away from the rail.

'Easy, man!' He waited for Midshipman Ferrier to run to his aid as he added, 'You've done enough!'

Allday twisted his head to stare at him, his eyes blurred and wretched.

'It's my right to . . . '

A ball ripped through Bolitho's coat and he vaguely saw Langtry, the master-at-arms, cut down the marksman with a boarding axe.

They were all dying. And for what?

A new explosion made both ships roll and groan together, and for an instant Bolitho imagined that a magazine had caught fire, that both ships would be joined in one terrible pyre.

Swords and cutlasses hovered in mid air, marines paused in their desperate efforts to reload their muskets, as like a towering forest giant the Frenchman's mainmast began to topple. It seemed to take an eternity, so that even some of the wounded tried to prop themselves up to watch, or called to their friends to discover what was happening.

Bolitho let his arm fall to his side, the pain tearing at his muscles as if they were exposed.

Knocker yelled hoarsely, 'There it goes, by Jesus!'

Slowly, and then with greater haste, the mast began to drop. Topmast and topgallant, spars and loosely brailed canvas tore apart as shrouds and stays snapped like threads, unable to hold the tremendous weight or restrain its fall. The fighting-top, complete with swivel-guns, barricades and men, split in halves, hurling its occupants to the deck below, or carrying them down with the topmast as it crashed through timber, rigging and guns into the hull beneath.

Even in *Achates* Bolitho could feel the weight and power of the fallen mast, the way the deck beneath his feet tilted steeply to the new pressure.

A trumpet blared through the rising smoke and some of the boarders retreated into a larger group near the forecastle.

It was the usual sailor's instinct to save his own ship no matter what.

Bolitho cleared his raw throat and shouted, 'To me, *Achates*!'

It was their only chance, if a precious frail one.

But from forward came a sharp command and then a sparkling line of musket-fire. Bolitho stared, unable to believe it. It was like the moment at San Felipe when Dewar had chosen his moment on the track to the fortress. The neat lines of scarlet, the muskets ready and waiting. But now Dewar lay dead, his face shot away, his body trampled on a dozen times as they had fought back and forth across him. And the marines had not been waiting, gauging the moment. They had been in action since the first shots.

And yet they were doing it. He could see Hawtayne's hat above the smoke, hear his shrill voice as he shouted, 'Rear rank, advance! Present! *Fire!*'

The shots raked through the packed mass of French boarders.

There would be no time to reload.

Bolitho dashed down one of the quarterdeck ladders, the pain of his wound forgotten as he ran through the litter of bodies and fallen rigging, his eyes fixed on the enemy.

Hawtayne was calling, '*Advance!*' The bayonets glittered in the hazy light as the marines moved into the attack.

Bolitho saw a young officer running to meet his challenge. He was about the same age as Adam, with similar dark good looks. The steel clanged against steel and Bolitho was almost blinded by the realization that his nephew was very likely dead.

The young French officer lost his stance as Bolitho parried his blade away. Just for the merest split-second he saw the officer's eyes widen with understanding or acceptance. Then he was down. Bolitho pulled the sword free and felt his men surge past him, their voices strengthened by the sudden change of roles.

Lieutenant Scott waved his sword. '*Boarders away!*'

Cheering, cursing, and sometimes dying, a tide of seamen and marines fought their way across to the other ship.

Bolitho hacked another officer to one side but could barely raise his sword now. How long could they hold out?

He was on the gangway, carried part of the way along by his men as they rushed aft to seize the poop.

Small pictures flashed across Bolitho's mind. Adam's face when he had tried to tell him about the girl in Boston. Tyrrell's old pride returning as he had stepped aboard the ship for passage to a country he had never seen. Little Evans, watching the burning Spanish ship, or following him like a small shadow. And Allday, trying to protect him when his own terrible wound was tearing him apart. Pulling him down like a fallen oak.

Shouts and screams exploded across the broad quarterdeck and bodies were flung about in bloody bundles from a murderous blast of canister.

Bolitho wiped the sweat from his eyes with his forearm and stared up at the poop.

He must really be mad. But surely it was Adam and another lieutenant up there with some of *Achates'* men? The smoking swivel, depressed on to the mass of defending seamen and their officers, had had the same effect as the sight of the marines charging from the smoke with their levelled bayonets.

Lieutenant Scott forgot all his usual self-control and clapped Bolitho hard across the shoulder.

'By God, it's the flag-lieutenant, sir! The young devil's blown the heart out of 'em!'

He ran after his men but paused to look back at his vice-admiral. It was just a glance, but it spoke more than a thousand words.

The enemy still outnumbered *Achates'* men and at any moment a leader would emerge, one for them to follow, to renew the fight.

Bolitho looked at his gasping, gashed and bruised seamen, the way they leaned on their cutlasses and pikes. They could not take another battle.

Lieutenant Trevenen marched across the deck and touched his hat with the hilt of his sword.

Achates' junior lieutenant, who had been a hostage in Rivers' fortress.

Seconds ago he had been fighting with his men and working the guns in his division.

Now, filthy but bright-eyed, he was a boy again, and his eyes shone with emotion as he reported, 'They have hauled down their colours, sir.' He fell silent as the seamen and marines crowded closer to hear. Then he tried again, 'Mr Knocker has sent a messenger across . . . ' He looked down, the tears running unheeded on his grimy cheeks.

Bolitho said quietly, 'You've done *well*, Mr Trevenen. Please continue.'

The lieutenant looked at him. 'A ship has been sighted to the south'rd, sir. One of *our* seventy-fours!'

Bolitho moved through his men, hearing them cheering and slapping each other. It was as if it was all somewhere else and he was a mere spectator.

He found the French rear-admiral by the wheel. He had been slightly wounded in the arm and was supported by two of his officers.

They stood and faced each other.

Then Jobert said simply, 'I should have known when I saw it was *your* ship.' He tried to shrug but the pain made him wince. He added, 'You were to give me an island.' He struggled with his sword. 'Now I must give you this.'

Bolitho shook his head. 'No, *M'sieu*. You've earned the right to it.'

He turned and walked back towards the side, his ears ringing to the shouts and wild huzzas.

Hands reached out to assist him across to the *Achates'* torn and littered deck, and he saw Midshipman Ferrier and Rooke, the boatswain, watching him, grinning and waving their hats.

If only they would stop.

He glanced at the figures on the gun-deck, ones who

would never cheer now. *How sleep the brave?* And he thought of the others on the orlop who were paying the price of his victory.

He turned as he heard Allday's painful, dragging steps and saw that he was carrying Jobert's flag over his shoulder.

Bolitho gripped his arm. 'You old dog! Will you never do as I say?'

Allday shook his head, his breath wheezing. But he managed to grin as he replied, 'Doubt it, sir. Too long in th' tooth now.'

Bolitho walked blindly to the rail where Keen was sitting propped in a chipped and blood-stained chair while Tuson examined his wound.

Keen said huskily, 'We did it, sir. I'm told the ship which is heading this way is a seventy-four.' He tried to smile. 'You'll be able to shift your flag to her and be home long before us.'

Bolitho heard the cheering again and again. *Three to one.* Yes, they had won, and all England would soon know about it.

He said, 'No, Val. My flag stays here. We'll sail home together.' He smiled sadly. 'With *Old Katie*.'

Epilogue

Bolitho's home-coming was more than he had dared to hope for during the long months he had been away. In other ways it was sad, as he knew it would be. The farewells at Plymouth were as moving as the welcome when the scarred and battered *Achates* had dropped her anchor, her prize, the *Argonaute*, given immediately into the hands of the dockyard.

It must have been *Old Katie*'s finest hour, Bolitho thought, with her pumps going as they had every hour of the day since that terrible battle. Even her ill-matched jury-rig had somehow managed to look rakish with his flag fluttering at half its proper height. She had brought crowds to the Hoe which few could remember.

Adam had watched Bolitho's grave features as he had walked from beneath the splintered poop to say good-bye to those who had become so familiar to him since they had sailed from the Beaulieu River a year ago.

Scott and Trevenen, Hawtayne and young Ferrier. And Tuson, the surgeon, who had removed a metal splinter from Keen's side the size of a man's thumb. And little Evans, who in his own way had become a man.

Bolitho had been thinking of those he would not see again, who could not share in the home-coming.

The captured seventy-four would be under the British ensign in a matter of months, a very valuable addition to the depleted fleet. But *Achates* had taken the battle badly. It was unlikely she would ever feel the blue waters of the Caribbean again, and would probably end her days as a hulk.

It had been a slow and painful passage up the Channel, and they had sailed so near to the Cornish coast that Adam had shinned aloft to the mizzen cross-trees with a glass to see it for himself.

When he had returned to the deck he had said simply, 'I saw part of the house, Uncle.' It had seemed to bring to him then and there how near he had been to not seeing it again. 'There are crowds on the headland, all the way to St Anthony.'

So slow had been their progress in the warm spring airs that a carriage had been sent to Plymouth in time to meet him.

He was thankful Belinda had not come herself. He had made her promise because of Allday, and if she had seen the ship, listing and blackened, she would have been deeply distressed.

Keen had accompanied him in the barge for the last time. The crowds on the waterfront had cheered and thrown their hats in the air, and women had held up their babies to see Bolitho. The news of his victory had preceded him like a rainbow. He had noticed there were few young men in the crowds.

Once again England was at war with the old enemy, and the press-gangs would be quick to snatch any suitable hands left over by the recruiting parties.

He had also said good-bye to Tyrrell. That had been harder than he had expected. But Tyrrell's dogged independence forced them apart.

Tyrrell had grasped his hands in both of his own and had said, 'I'll be lookin' around for a while, Dick. Just to discover if I like what I see.'

Bolitho had persisted. 'Come to Falmouth soon. Don't forget us.'

Tyrrell had slung his bag over his shoulder and had said, 'I never forgot you, Dick. Nor will I. Ever.'

That had been a week ago. Now, as Bolitho stood by a window and looked out across the flowers and shady trees, he could still scarcely believe it.

Their first meeting had been one of joy and tears.

Belinda had pressed her face into his coat and had whispered, 'I made Ferguson take me to the headland. I saw you sail past. That poor little ship. I was so afraid, and yet *so proud*.' She had looked up at him, searching out the strain on his face. 'There were people everywhere. They began to cheer. You couldn't hear them of course, but they seemed to want you to know they were there.'

Bolitho saw Allday speaking with the groom, making the man laugh with one of his yarns. That was another memory fixed in his mind.

When Allday had walked from the coach, worried and trying not to drag his feet up the stone steps.

She had gone to him and had put her arms round his neck and had said quietly, 'Thank you for bringing my men home, Allday. I knew you would.'

She had given him life, as she had this old house, he thought. Her very presence here had made its mark.

How quickly the week had flashed past and yet they had not left the grounds. Her gentle understanding after what he had endured, her passion which she gave without restraint, had brought them closer than ever.

He thought too of his first meeting with their child. He smiled as he recalled the exact moment.

The way Belinda had laughed at him and had cried at the same time when she had said, 'She won't break, Richard! Pick her up!'

Elizabeth. A new person. Belinda had chosen the name herself, like she had managed everything else during his absence.

Nothing seemed to matter now beyond here and his family. Rivers had gone to London in the same coach as Jobert. The French admiral would be exchanged eventually, but Rivers' fate was less certain.

He looked from the window again but Allday had gone. It was hard to think there was a war again. What had happened to the peace?

The door opened and she entered carrying Elizabeth. Bolitho took her and carried her to the window while the child's hands tugged at his gilt buttons.

It was all perfect, and he felt he should be ashamed when so many had nothing, and so many had died.

Adam entered the room and looked at them. He belonged here. They had made it possible.

Allday hurried towards the outer doors and Bolitho heard him say to one of the maids, 'Quick, girl, here's a courier!'

Belinda's hands went to her breast. In a mere whisper she said, 'Oh no, not now, not so soon!'

Bolitho heard her despair and held the child more tightly to his body.

In this very room his father had once said to him, 'England needs all her sons now.' That had been another war, but the same was just as true today. It was here that his father had given him the old sword, and the last time he had seen him alive.

Adam strode from the room and returned a few minutes later with a heavy, sealed envelope.

He said, 'The courier's not from the Admiralty. He is from St James's in London.'

Belinda nodded without understanding. 'Please read it, Adam, I am too afraid . . . '

Adam opened the envelope and read it in silence.

Then he said, 'Thank God.'

Allday hovered by the door with Ferguson at his side as the young lieutenant handed the imposing letter to her. As he watched her surprise and happiness he said, 'Well, Allday, you must have influence in the right places. It's what you wanted.'

Allday stared as Belinda moved to the window and kissed her husband on the cheek, her arms round him and their child.

Adam smiled and said softly, 'I think my uncle is content with the reward he is holding!'

But Allday did not hear him, and his eyes were far-away as he said, '*Sir* Richard Bolitho.' He nodded firmly, the old gleam back in his eyes once more. 'Not before time, an' that's no error neither.'

Kent, Alexander
Success to the brave

DATE DUE

FEB. 3 1984	AG 9 '84	AG 16
FEB. 1 0 1984	OC 11 8	MY 30 06
FEB. 1 7 1984	OC 25 '8	JE 07 07
MAR. 6 1984	JA 28 '85	OC 11 07
MR 20 '84		FE 1 7 '11
	JE 30 '86	DE 0 1 '0
	NO 1 3 '86	NO 3 '87
	DEC 29 '95	
JE 8 '84	SE 5 '96	
JE 25 '84	FEB 23 '98	
JY 24 '84	MY 06 03	